ALSO BY JULIA KELLY

With My Lazy Eye

Julia Kelly was born in 1969, studied English, Sociology and Journalism in Dublin, and escaped to London for the mad, bad years of life. Her first novel, *With My Lazy Eye*, won her the Sunday Independent Best Irish Newcomer of the Year Award. She now lives in Bray, County Wicklow with her partner and their little girl.

The
Playground

JULIA KELLY

First published in Great Britain in 2014 by

Quercus Editions Ltd
55 Baker Street
7th Floor, South Block
London
W1U 8EW

Excerpt from 'The Child', a poem by Michael Roberts,
reprinted with kind permission of the Royal Literary Fund.
Every attempt has been made to attain licences to
reprint lyrics from the following songs:
'MacArthur Park' by Jimmy Webb and Richard Harris,
Universal Music Publishing Group;
'Bridge Over Troubled Water' by Paul Simon, Sony/ATV;
'The 59th Street Bridge Song (Feelin' Groovy)' by Paul Simon, Sony/ATV.
Any omissions should be notified to the publishers, who
would be happy to make amendments for future editions.

A CIP catalogue record for this book is available
from the British Library

TPB ISBN 978 1 84916 256 2
EBOOK ISBN 978 1 84916 780 2

10 9 8 7 6 5 4 3 2 1

Typeset by Jouve (UK), Milton Keynes

Printed and bound in Great Britain by
Clays Ltd, St Ives plc

For Ruby Mae and Lucia

How can I teach, how can I save,
This child whose features are my own,
Whose feet run down the ways where
I have walked?

Michael Roberts, *The Child*

Chapter One

If you'd been down on the seafront that Saturday, you may not have seen us. Everyone was out: the bony old man child in school shorts and brogues bouncing his rubber ball against the end wall of Martello Terrace, the power-walking, whippet-like woman with her whippet dog, the homeless man reclining on the low wall of the promenade – where toddlers like to take tentative steps – staring dead-eyed at the sea. Traveller boys in togs, gold chains and spiked, water-wet hair walked on their toes to the chipper, towels hooked round their necks like men, above jutting shoulder blades, neat whistles of spines, ahead of Italian tourists in scarves and quilted jackets, who didn't understand how the Irish called this summer. Old folk trundled along in mobility carts, overtaken by kids on rollerblades and scooters. The hulking, grizzle-bearded cyclist, too big for his boots and his bike, weaved through the throng, overseeing everything, like Poseidon on wheels. Billy Flynn was there that day too, before it all happened, balancing on his unicycle in an animated conversation with himself.

Everything was in motion: the sea, high, grey-green, crunching stones; the slap of the stays on yachts in the harbour; the rattle of cars on the big dipper; the slamming swing doors of the ghost train; the pink lights of the carousel flashing on and off as it rotated, horses gliding up and down in the air. A fat woman was hula-hooping on

I

the promenade on her own, smiling to herself as she gyrated her hips. On the Sky Master above her, a blur of hair and feet – laughing boys, screaming girls.

It was that time of the day – four o'clock – in a seaside town when things could get a little ugly. The litter bins were overflowing, the bars filling up. Clouds had been folding and expanding all day, and now they'd spread out in a vast grey fug and had taken the shine off everything – promenade, esplanade, harbour, beach – covering it all in the sort of dull light that incites arguments, forces the abandonment of plans.

By the train station a sombre swell of local community had come to a halt with their banners, neon bibs and megaphones. Children were hoisted onto shoulders, TV cameras positioned, local TDs handed microphones. Along the roadside, residents stood still in tribute and support.

'What do we want?' asked a lone, angry voice.

'A full-time fire service!' the crowd roared in reply.

'When do we want it?' she shouted again.

'Now!' they yelled in unison, their voices shaky with emotion about two voluntary firefighters who had lost their lives as they fought a blaze at a disused warehouse several weeks before.

'And in the words of our president, Mary McAleese, may we praise their heroism and selflessness and may we never forget the ultimate sacrifice these two men made to ensure the safety of others.'

We kept walking and I kept singing to stop me from thinking and to entertain my child.

My Aunt Jane she's awful smart,
She bakes wee rings in an apple tart

Past Marconi's, inhaling its sharp, vinegary reek, and on by the old hotel. All the windows in its sea-worn facade were black, aside from an open dormer at the top of the building from which a dull curtain billowed. No one had taken advantage of the special B&B rate of thirty-five Euro for the night. No one was serving in the empty bar. The dozen tables in the conservatory were draped with pink linen over white and laid with cup-saucer-spoon-sugar, but a handwritten sign Blu-tacked onto the adjacent window read: *Residents only. Absolutely no tea or coffee served.*

> *And when Hallowe'en comes around,*
> *Fornenst that tart I'm always found*

And on up the incline at the base of Bray Head, where the dog dirt gets under your feet. The missing woman was still missing, still smiling from torn and mildewed posters tethered to lampposts; moisture had penetrated their laminated covers, making her face appear gangrenous. The wheels of the buggy buckled on ridges of broken concrete. All terrains, the website said, that's the beauty of the Bugaboo. We almost broke up the night we tried to assemble it. The only instructions we could find online were in German and demonstrated by a smiling woman in slacks with slim, manicured hands. After three hours of effort, the damned thing still wouldn't recline.

I was pushing not a child, but a small plastic doll, like one of those unhinged American women who dress them up and talk to them, pretend that they're the real thing. My own real thing had stopped and was squatting on the ground twenty paces behind me, playing a private game with woodlice and stones, an impatient little hand shooting across her face as she concentrated, spreading snot from nose to hair.

We'd been moving at this stop-start speed for the past hour, aside from twice when she took a notion and set off, her little legs thumping downhill and away from me, still excited by this new skill and even more by the thrill of pursuit.

'Hold you,' she whined, arms outstretched, from where she stood, unwilling to walk any further. I lifted her and she settled into the baby-shaped space on my hip. 'Hood up,' she said, as we set off again, yanking it over my head. I imagined for a ridiculous moment that I looked exotic, Russian, as we walked along the cliff edge. She slapped her hands over my ears, sealing my face, insulating everything.

Now that she'd seen how cosy my head – the world – looked in its dark, fur-lined interior, she wanted to come in too. I told her it wouldn't work, that it was a physical impossibility, but it somehow did. Addie – Adelaide in trouble, Narky Nora, Bubbalicious, Little Miss Stink-a-lot – was always right about these things.

On up into the greyness we went, our cheeks pressed together in the hood of my parka like a two-headed Eskimo.

> *My Aunt Jane she has a bell on the door*
> *A white stone step and a clean swept floor*
> *Candy apples, hard green pears,*
> *Conversation lozenges*

Though we were moving away from everything, sounds travelled across the sea towards us: disembodied voices, the thump of internal music from the Martello, *Sweet Caroline*, children's screams. I told Addie I couldn't carry her much longer, that she was getting too heavy for me. 'Don't worry, Mummy,' she said, rubbing my back with her starfish hand.

This was where we came at the beginning – Joe noticing everything: the thousand different shades of green on the hills; the graffitied penis at the old widow's house which made him giggle; the litter and days so perfect that he couldn't handle the beauty of the light, the sea, the land – before hurrying, when the weather turned, as the weather always did, to the snug of the overly blue Harbour Bar at the other end of the bay where cats curled on sofas and students chewed on dope, snogging and nodding to second-rate imitation bands while waves beat against the land outside and swans gathered, disdainful but tolerating the oily filth of the harbour. I'd been happy, but frightened, not understanding any of it.

'Two, three, four,' Addie said, knowing that I'd gone; needing to bring me back. She was counting the chimes of a church bell ringing somewhere beyond us, taking big, deep breaths between numbers. 'Eleven, twenty-ten, seven.'

Above us masses of jagged grey stone bulged and jutted through a wire mesh, caged to prevent further rock falls. Below, the Wexford train clattered through Brunel's tunnel along the coast; beyond that fulmars fought for territory on white-flecked rocks. The sea was immense and seemed, as we got higher, to be disappearing into the curve of the earth.

The path we were on was now no longer a path, but a muddy track with pools of dirty water on either side of a tufty grass centre. It was the wrong time to be going uphill; walkers coming down, returning home, eyed us with curiosity; two sprite women, cropped hair, pink-cheeked, fleece sweaters tied round waists to conceal ample posteriors – stopped, hands on hips to watch us, in that frank, unapologetic way of the old.

'Mindless thugs.' One said to the other.

'Local lads no doubt.'

'Just think of all those poor animals. Nesting birds, little mice running from the flames.'

'Oh don't, Deirdre. And rabbits, young hares, desperate altogether.'

'You wouldn't want to bring that child any further.' One of them said to me.

'The gorse is on fire up there.' The other added.

I smelt it and heard it before I saw it. It was taking hold on the hills above us, crackling and sparking as it spread. Flames were rising, licking the air, carried along by the wind.

Now a heavy, general dullness took over, clouds of smoke combined with the darkening sky. And when the rain came it was sudden, violent, driving, monsoon-like in its intensity, soaking everything, making teenage girls squeal in their shorts and flat hair. Paper bags became hats, toddlers stomped in puddles, there was a rush for cars with wet picnic rugs, armfuls of kids and belongings. Awnings were lowered at the Beach House cafe, tables cleared in a hurry.

I grabbed my little girl and carried her to shelter under a struggling tree, squeezed in beside the two walkers we'd just met, and another mother whose baby looked so snug in her buggy – hat, blanket, waterproof cover – it made the older women's faces crinkle and turn to each other in silent approval. 'That's how it's done,' they seemed to be saying, 'that's how to look after a child.' In my panic and rush I'd abandoned our buggy – it was sodden, still out in the rain, Addie damp and red-nosed in my arms. As we waited we watched the muddy water cascading down gullies, forming vast puddles around the barriers by the beach, and inhaled, not just the smoke from the dying fire, but the stench of seaweed and other stuff thrown up at that end of the strand: rotting kelp, beer cans, plastic bottles, single shoes.

'Uh oh,' Addie said, studying my face, 'spot.' She pressed her finger against the tip of my nose, her tiny nail cutting into my skin. 'Kiss better?' she asked, holding my face steady, knowing what I needed, aligning our mouths and putting her lips on mine.

Crows crash-landed on the promenade for last pickings, a lone runner, florescent in Lycra, slapped his feet in a rhythm on the wet concrete and Billy Flynn was still there, circling around puddles in the rain, waving his arms in the air as he balanced, his face held up to the sky.

Chapter Two

I teased the key till it turned in the lock, shoved my shoulder against the front door and fell into the hall, stepping over pizza flyers scattered on the worn parquet floor. It seemed different to the first few times we'd returned home. We'd been here for almost a week; now there was a comforting smell of cooking, and a child's pink bicycle had been propped up against the gas meter.

'Hi, Joe,' I shouted, shunting the buggy over the mat. 'Hi, Daddy,' my little girl yelled, thundering ahead of me through the dark of the hall, no longer waiting as she used to, face lit up, to hear the sound of his voice travelling down from upstairs. I can't remember whose idea it was – Mum's, Bella's, mine? – but it was to give the impression, should anyone be watching from across the road or crouched between bushes in the front garden, that our home was full of happy, strong human beings. There's that weirdo again, the neighbours must have been thinking.

I dragged the buggy up the two flights of stairs to our flat, leaving a muddy trail along the carpet which was coarse, blue, worn in the centre of each step and frayed to a dirty beige outside our door, as if someone had been standing there for a very long time, waiting to get in.

'We didn't get a yo-yo, Alf, but we're going to get one yesterday. A green one. If I don't do whining and crying,' Addie said, wriggling out of her sodden coat. Alfie, a middle-aged lurcher with issues,

8

stretched and pit-patted over to us, sniffing around Addie for anything that may have missed her mouth. I should have brought him with us to the beach, but in the rush to get ready I couldn't find his collar or lead – now he'd be restless and energetic all evening.

We swarmed towards the kitchen, my little girl steadying herself by holding onto the banister until the dog had passed, catching me at the back of the knee as he liked to – ignorant bastard, Joe always said. When it was safe, she proceeded, step by step.

'OK, tea-time,' I said, slapping on lights, radio, kettle, illuminating and animating everything, like a surge of electricity after an outage. The kitchen was the worst thing about the new flat. It was narrow and dark with chipped Formica counters and a beige linoleum floor that curled up around the cooker (a stained and bockety two-ringed hob). I'd tied the curtain up over the small window at its far end, where a spider plant on its last legs balanced on the ledge.

There were too many teabags in the sink; congealing around the plughole, covered in old porridge. I took them in my hand – heavy, dripping – and flung them into the bin. Then I stood in front of the fridge, clueless. A thick layer of grime festered deep in the rubber lining that had lost its gumption. I picked at some grapes, popped one in my mouth, one in Addie's, closed the door again.

My child wanted to be chased. I chased her. I caught her. She giggled. 'Do it again.' I told her I couldn't, that I had to make tea. This made her cry and cling to my leg. Alfie took a wild swipe at her toy rat and charged off with it in his mouth. She screamed and broke free when I tried to towel dry her hair. I shouted at the dog, pulled Addie back towards me and sank to the floor in front of the cooker. I was aware of a dull irritation in my bladder; I'd needed a pee for hours, perhaps since this morning. I couldn't contemplate the two hours ahead.

On the radio, the six o'clock news was being read. Accident and Emergency was to go from Loughlinstown Hospital. Two hundred job losses had been announced at some pharmaceutical company. There was a warning of storm force gales from Malin Head to Mizen Head and on the Irish Sea.

'How about waffles and beans?' No reply. There was one squeaky floorboard by the cupboard beneath the toaster. 'Help me, help me,' it seemed to say in a tiny voice, every time I stood on it. I hitched myself onto the counter top and stretched up to the second shelf. I'd never had the patience for cooking; I was always too hungry to wait. Joe was the cook, reluctant but exceptional, as he liked to say himself, in the same way that he hated dancing but was a natural.

'My heart is starving for ice cream,' Addie said, practising her ballet positions in her gum boots, while I tried to figure out the electrical switch beside the kettle which appeared to be off in both positions.

They had a quiet ritual with ice cream, Addie and Joe. They'd share a mini Magnum every evening after tea – passing it back and forth to each other, both in silent ecstasy. On the beach she'd always ask for hers in a tub rather than a cone so she could hurry home before it melted to share it with her dad.

Alfie returned, still with the toy between his teeth, to make sure we'd noticed what he'd done. The under-unit light above the sink stammered, blinked, gave up. I waited a few moments and pulled out the bulb. Where the hell would I find another one? It was covered in a layer of that black sticky stuff that is always at the top of things, but I liked the atmosphere it gave the room; it made it more homely; suggested baking and warmth.

Addie had been quiet for a moment too long. Somehow in the thirty seconds it had taken to remove the broken light, she had become naked aside from her gum boots and was sitting on the floor examining her private parts.

In the bath I was more in control, at least in my position, by the taps, where beneath me, near the plug hole, I could feel the ragged edge where the paintwork had begun to peel. I had foam alphabet letters positioned on various parts of my chest, arms and legs and a blue plastic colander on my head. 'No, that's not the right game,' she said, cross with me for not understanding. She stood on my stomach, whipped the colander off, folded her arms in a grump. Her bottom was mottled red. I felt behind me for the cold tap and let it run. I sank lower, deeper in the water, letting my knees submerge.

On the bath's edge, I held her on my lap, wrapped in a towel. And there we stayed, for a perfect few moments, her heavy, hot, clean little body in my arms, her eyelashes wet, stuck together. I sang *Moon River* and she hummed along, watching my mouth, wanting to join in but not yet confident of the words.

I looked around me: the avocado-coloured sink, toilet and bidet were the sort that a house renovation show would have ripped out to give the room 'a more contemporary feel'. The toilet seat was loose and sticky to the touch. I had scrubbed at the brown rust stain along the back of the bowl to no avail. Tomorrow I'd bleach.

The water in the bathtub was sucked gurgling away. Addie stood between my feet on the thick pile mat, where they'd flattened and drenched the nap. 'Hold mine hand,' she said, moving carefully across the wet bathroom floor.

'Oh no, we forgot Ficus Jute!' Her tiny eyebrows arched in concern, her little palms upturned. Damn. Another job that would take too long. Addie liked to take life slowly; I needed to get through it fast. She climbed onto the wobbly white chair beside the sink, steadying herself before stretching over, a sponge in her hand, to wipe the bowl in which the plant was sitting. She used to follow Joe from room to room, taking turns with the spray bottle to water the plants, which he would finally turn on her and she'd run from him shrieking for me.

I filled a glass above her, poured it into the soil.

'No, you're doing it wrongly! I'm the peoples in charge,' she said, grabbing the glass from my hand.

'Dada said only dus a tiny bit,' she said, giving the leaves a quick rub and replacing the glass on the sink.

Back on the safety of the floor, she let go of my hand and charged away.

'Let's play hideseek,' she said, still wound up like a toy, shoving me behind the bedroom door where I'd hung Joe's old dressing gown, unsure of what else to do with it. She hid behind the curtains – pale-green heavy damask decorated with cream roses. We both counted to five and I pretended I couldn't find her coiled up like a fat sweet in the twisted fabric. She unwrapped herself. 'Here I am,' she shrieked with delight. 'Close your eyes,' she said then, and pottered about, moving teddies and dolls and balls. She forced me to lie on my back while she stacked toys on top of me, and put her sucky blanket, with its moist, vomitty smell over my face. I lay in a dull daze of submission. I heard her take a few steps back to get a good run up, then she hurled her compact little body on top of mine, using my face as a launch pad.

She wriggled and squirmed while I tried to get her into her pyjamas, then she trotted to the far end of the bed giggling, just out of reach. I grabbed her arm, feeling it loosen in its socket and dragged her across the bed towards me. She cried, of course, and I was a hopeless, cruel mother. I couldn't tolerate another minute of today.

On the bed we sat close together, her water-heavy curls wetting her pyjama top; the battle to dry it was one I was too tired to fight. We read an adventure of Rupert the Bear where he'd discovered secret stairs in a tree trunk that lead to a treetop nursery, where babies nestled in cradles.

'Why does that sentence have eyelashes?' she asked, halfway through.

'They're not eyelashes; they're called inverted commas,' I said, trying not to laugh – she hated it when I laughed at her.

'I'm not listening,' she said a little later, her cheeky face animated, her one dimple indented.

I sat on the floor outside the bedroom, my back against the wall, while her bunny rabbit mobile played the opening cords of *Swan Lake*. I put my head in my hands but tonight, for the first time in months, I didn't cry.

Chapter Three

Alfie was sick in the night. I'd heard him pit-patting up and down the landing, but it was too late, too early, to get up. I could smell it before I saw it: a green puddle of stomach bile near the front door. I carried a bucket and mop through the sitting room, in my grey dressing gown, which the task seemed to suit, cursing as I stepped on a creaky floorboard.

He was lying low, curled up in his bed, keeping a dark eye on me, seeming somewhat embarrassed by his effluence. I got to work, frowning as I slapped the mop into the vomit and circled it around. There was something solid in its congealing centre. Oh God. I flipped it over in my gloved hands, then lifted it, dry retching, in the air. There, covered in a greasy slime of seaweed, bits of a chewed plastic bottle and twigs, was Addie's left shoe – sunflowers on the toes – which I'd lost on the beach last Saturday. It was intact; he'd swallowed it whole. My mouth was curled down with self-pity, as if I were being watched, as if Joe could still see me.

He'd have remembered that today was bin day, but not which colour bin – refuse or recycling – and he wouldn't have been able to check the printout he'd Sellotaped to the cupboard above the Aga in the old house because he'd have lost his damned glasses again. So upstairs he'd go, cursing, leaving the kitchen door open, allowing the dog to stroll in and eat Addie's toast, while she rode her tricycle in circles and

I chased her with a spoon and that ad for Harvey Norman roared from the radio. Then he'd be back, still without his glasses, whacking his head on the edge of the opened cupboard door. So I'd stand on tippy-toes and read the printout for him. And out he'd go again, this time through the back door, leaving it open, letting the icy morning air rush in. 'Outside!' Addie would say, climbing off her bike and ripping off her bib to follow him. 'Finish your cereal first,' and that would start her crying but she'd take a break between whines to turn to Joe, who'd just come back in. 'We're having a fight, Dada,' she'd say straight-faced, composed, then turn back to me and continue whimpering.

Then they'd corner me by the kettle, Joe reaching over me to get something, Addie pulling out the cord of my dressing gown. And when I'd step back the dog would be there too, circling, pacing, thinking all this movement must mean a walk, smells, a piss and a shit at last.

Back upstairs to do teeth and as I'd wedge a toothbrush between my child's clamped lips, the barking would begin. Then shouts from all of us at the dog as he snarled at the letterbox, sounding vicious and a bit clichéd as he tried to bite off the postman's hand.

Downstairs again; Joe in front of us, walking with one stiff leg swinging out (These were quirks he'd brought with him from the North. Him and his friends used to mimic the physical impediments of the unfortunate souls – the big black foot, the bow-legged – of the town where he grew up). 'Just practising for old age,' he'd say, making all three of us laugh.

Then another search for car keys or wallet or phone and out with Addie, still in my dressing gown and socks over gravel and into the car and a face that looked fine indoors would be filthy in daylight, so back in to get wipes and out again and in the seconds I'd been gone she'd have put the keys in the ignition. She'd writhe and complain as I'd pull her away, astonished at her cleverness and my stupidity.

And into her seat where I'd fuss, pull, stretch, poke, tighten and secure until my child was at last ready, fed, washed, safe and someone else's responsibility for the next three hours. I'd kiss her, tell her I loved her, that she was my best friend and slam the car door. We'd give each other little waves through the window while the dog dug out some vile fleshy thing in a bag in the bushes or headed up the road to shove his snout in strangers' bums.

Then I'd direct Joe out the gate, half looking for the dog, and just when it was clear, there the dog would be, beside the back wheels, and I'd shout and bang on the boot to warn him and he'd swear and jam on the brakes and we'd all shout at Alfie again and then Joe would curse like someone with Tourette's, this time at the bastards who wouldn't wait for him to reverse. 'Fucking cunt, shite hawk,' I would read his lips say. And I'd whine through the glass, 'Jesus, Joe, watch your language.' And he'd mouth something back, something indecipherable, and then they'd be going, almost gone, and in I'd run, calling Alfie behind me. And I'd close the front door but I wouldn't relax, knowing Joe would be back through it at least once, for some forgotten thing.

'Go away,' Bossyboots shouted as I approached her bed, but I could see her small smile. She pulled her sucky blanket over her mouth. 'Numnumnum,' she whispered in her quiet rhythmic ritual, tiny inflections of teeth, lips, tongue. She rolled away from me, onto her side. 'I wanted to dream about jellyfish but you kept getting into my dream.' She was always grumpy in the mornings. I wanted to curl up beside her, keep the curtains drawn, listen to the wind funnelling down the chimney and watch shadows, lines of sunlight, move across the ceiling, until it was evening again.

We were having the usual wrestle with getting dressed, though I was saner, more robust at the beginning of the day, when the doorbell rang, as promised, at precisely nine o'clock. My mother was obsessive, almost competitive, about punctuality. 'Coming,' I shouted, as I went downstairs still in my dressing gown with my naked three-year-old in my arms and the fear, always that fear, of missing my footing, of falling, of letting her go.

Mum was talking to me from the other side of the door – she knew I couldn't possibly hear her but she didn't do silence. Neither did I – I chatted futilely back. I put Addie down to undo the double lock and remove the safety chain, and glanced at the closed door of the ground-floor flat, hoping our new neighbours wouldn't meet us this way.

She was standing on the doorstep with the postman. Somehow in those few seconds they had formed a sort of alliance and she was addressing her conversation at him rather than me. She was always polite to strangers; the sort of person who would apologise when someone else stood on her foot. I once heard her thank the speaking clock. And she loved men. She used to trap Joe with her eyes and hold him like a spider with its prey while she spoke to him about Robert the Bruce or Protestants or about Addie, or even about me, though I would be right there beside them.

She blustered in, all business.

'Still not dressed? Gosh, I've been up for hours; been to Mass, read the papers, had a swim in the Forty Foot.'

'Mum, that's dangerous. It could stop your heart.'

'Nonsense. It's wonderful,' she said, rubbing the knuckles of one hand against the palm of the other, eyeing the postman who was still standing at the doorstep with a registered letter for me to sign.

I could see her exhale as she lowered herself into the Irish Sea, stunned by its coldness but determined not to let it show. 'This is heavenly,' she'd say, when she was able to move her mouth again, making small, swift breaststrokes that somehow propelled her forward. And then, with a proficient flip, she'd be on her back, eying her bobbing toes, her bathing cap of white roses high on her head and everything still, aside from her hands gently weaving water.

The postman said something I missed. Off he went and back up the stairs we went, Estée Lauder's Knowing filtering through my nostrils. It was the scent Mum had settled on after years of experiments. 'Well, it just seems to suit me,' she said.

'So how are you settling in, pet?' she asked, looking around her, silently evaluating for herself. The sitting room, which had appeared vast and bright in its emptiness on the day we moved in, now seemed small and grubby with our few ill-fitting possessions apologetically positioned about the place. The sofa which had settled so well in Sandycove, looked sunken and scruffy beneath the bay window.

'OK. I'm just tired,' I said, sighing, feeling sorry for myself and feeling my bottom lip tremble – Mum's presence was always unburdening. We moved into the kitchen. I rooted through a box labelled 'miscellaneous' for a second tea cup. 'And I need to get this place clean.' I felt like the addled woman in an advert before Mr Muscle appears to sort out everything. 'Well, yes, you could really do with more storage,' she said, meaning that the flat was a mess.

Though we didn't meet eyes – we knew each other too well for that sort of intimacy – I could see from them that she was also tired; they were pink-rimmed and small from insomnia, but now she forced them wide to talk to her little grandchild, bending to her level with questions and exclamations. 'And where are your clothes, cheeky monkey? You can't feed the swans with no clothes on.'

Addie giggled, grabbed Alfie's lead, ran out of the kitchen, both of us smiling at her perfect, peach-downy little bum. Then she was straight back in with a brilliant idea. 'You be the doggie, Mummy, all right?' This was another of her favourite games, me on all fours being a dog, while she 'walked' me on a lead. Alfie was never considered for this sort of task – she didn't consider him a dog at all.

When she'd tired of this game and everything seemed organised, we sat down at the kitchen table, my mother still making tiny adjustments to the position of things: her placemat, saucer, spoon. Although she was always moving, patting, prodding, organising and straightening, rooting and fixing, her presence made us calm and within minutes of her arrival, my little girl was content on her knee, the dog asleep at her feet.

She looped her bag over the side of the chair and immediately un-looped it again, remembering the gift she had for me. She often brought back loose, brightly coloured garments from her travels that she genuinely expected me to wear. Her latest trip had been to Peru – a trek across the Andes to Machu Picchu with a nomadic assortment of widows, gay men and always the one unfathomable (no one was sure why she was there), all partaking in a frantic ticking off of antiquities and places and events that they felt were essential to a life fully lived. I braced myself. Today's gift was altogether more practical: a hand blender – one that she didn't use any more – 'great for soups,' she said, as she looked for somewhere to put it, knowing that I'd never even attempted soup before but that now as a single mother of a small child I would jolly well have to learn.

'Milk?' she asked, sitting again, sounding a little weary, the carton hovering over my cup. Something about this question had always irritated her. A tedious thing that had to be got through, an interruption. Or perhaps it was because it was something she should remember (does my daughter take milk in her tea?) but couldn't seem to. And then another small irritation as she poured, her hand trembling as she tilted the carton. 'Say when, will you? Say when.'

'Anything interesting?' she asked, watching my fingers as they sifted through the post, ripping open each envelope. When I didn't reply she lifted her feet off the ground and began to do small scissoring exercises. 'I had my dancing last night. I'm pretty stiff this morning, I can tell you.' I could see her in the evenings as she waited for the milk in the saucepan to warm, practising what she'd learnt at ballroom dancing that week with her invisible partner, slippered feet skimming across the kitchen floor.

'You should come along one evening, it's terrific fun.'

'You know I hate dancing. I'm far too self-conscious.'

She threw her eyes to the ceiling, bored by my vanity and lack of daring. Then her expression softened and became wistful. I could tell she was remembering her own agility at my age, seeing herself once again waltzing across a room with grace.

'So, anything from Joe?'

'No, Mum, I think I might have mentioned if I'd heard from him,' I said, sounding repulsive. 'Sorry, I'm just so stressed.'

'Well of course you are, pet. I mean what mother of a toddler isn't? And you've just moved house, for goodness' sake. I think you're coping admirably.'

'I'm not really, Mum, it's all going round and round in my head and I'm still not sleeping,' I said, feeling my throat constrict.

'Well, what about a nice hot bath in the evenings?'

A nice hot bath. My family's solution to everything. An eye mask, thirty drops of Valerian washed down with Chamomile tea, soaking my pillow with lavender oil and an emergency pink Xanax at two-thirty in the morning hadn't made the slightest difference, so I was pretty damn certain a bubble bath wasn't going to get me through.

'And I'm lonely.'

'I know you are, sweetheart. I remember those first few months without your dad. I'm afraid you are just going to have to get on with it.' And her expression then was exactly as it had been at my father's funeral – eyes lowered, stoical, serene.

His death, twenty years earlier, had given her a new lease of life. He used to drive her demented. She'd lock herself in her room in the evenings when he came home from the bank, with her *Readers Digest*, the Teasmade and a view of the ocean which she loved, unable to hear his rants about the meat not being hung for long enough or there being too much coal on the fire, because she'd put her ear plugs in. When he died, she found some letters inside socks that confirmed what she had always suspected: he'd had a 'fancy woman' in London for years.

'I'm worried that he doesn't have a forwarding address for us – whatever about me, I really thought he'd make some effort to keep in touch with Addie.'

'Oh, Eve, we've been through this.'

'And I don't know if we'll be happy here – no one's the slightest bit friendly. I'm starting to think we shouldn't have moved.'

This annoyed her, as I knew it would. She wanted to see me sorted. She liked things to be black and white. 'For heaven's sake! It's a bit late for second thoughts now.'

I crumpled. She moved her chair closer to mine, put her arm around my shoulder and said more softly, 'Please don't get upset.'

This only encouraged tears. 'I honestly, honestly think you've done the right thing. Honestly, love. You could never have afforded that big house on your own. I'm sure you'll make friends here – what are the people like downstairs?'

'Don't know, haven't met them yet.'

'Why don't you pop down? Introduce yourself. You might find you have all sorts of things in common.' She rubbed her hands together at the prospect of this burgeoning friendship.

'OK, I will. Later.'

'Good girl. And I do think it would be very sensible to get a lodger.' My sister, Bella, had come up with this suggestion. 'Though be sure to tell your landlord first.'

'Maybe. But I'm just not like you, Mum. I'm not as social or as tolerant. And, anyway, I've sort of gone off the idea. I don't know. I'm worried about Addie. First Joe, now this. And then a complete stranger moving in. It's too much change for her.'

Mum held me. How often had she held me like this over the years? Rocking me as I shed snotty, mascara-stained, bitten-nail tears about having no friends, or no boyfriends or failing exams or being broke or fat.

'Addie is doing wonderfully. You mustn't worry about her so much. She'll be fine. Honestly,' she said, stroking my hair and kissing me on the ear.

'But how will he know how to contact Addie?'

'You told that neighbour of yours, didn't you? Annette, Andrea—'

'Anna.' She always got this wrong. She seemed to have refused to memorise her name purely because she wasn't keen on her, always found her a little aloof.

'You gave Anna your forwarding address, didn't you? If he wants to find you, he will.'

'He didn't even like Anna and he's not that resourceful – I need to think of something else.'

'He's an adult, for Pete's sake. It's jolly well up to him.' And tender again, 'You'll be OK, sweetheart. I promise.' This was the rhythm of our relationship.

She had gone from saying 'Joe is marvellous, and really quite charming when you get to know him,' to her friends to 'He just abandoned them. I can't understand how he could walk out on his family like that.' She felt personally abandoned too because they had been quite close – Joe would often do little jobs for her, cut the grass, hang paintings in her home. She thought he was just in 'poor form' when he left, suggested that I give him some space.

'You'll just have to accept that he's not coming back,' she said, stroking my arm as she delivered the blow. She'd become blunter as she'd got older.

'I *have* accepted he's not coming back. It's just—'

'Who's not coming back?' Addie said, eying me with concern.

'Me, if you don't get your clothes on this minute!' Mum was up, animated, taking her grandchild by the hand. 'Now, I want to see your new room!'

'Go on, show Granny your special magic curtains.'

'Come on, Granny! And do you know what . . .' I heard her voice trail away, then her little footsteps charging back.

She gave me a toothy smile – the forced sort she uses when having her photo taken – handed me her sucky blanket for comfort, hugged my leg, kissed my knee.

'Be happy, Mama.'

'Omnia transeunt.'

They were back from their tour of Addie's room.

'I'm sorry?' Addie was on my knee now, wriggling as I tried to put on her socks.

'Ah, pet, you've heard that expression, haven't you? Didn't you learn it at school? Omnia transeunt,' she said it again, liking how the words sounded on her lips. 'This too shall pass.'

'I know. I'll be – we'll be – fine but it's just the practical things. I think the immersion heater's broken for starters. I can't get any hot water this morning.'

'You've probably just tripped a switch.'

With that, she was up a ladder on the landing, peering into the fuse box. I watched her flesh-coloured tights straighten and gather around her ankles as she stretched and lowered herself.

'But you're fine,' she said, face a little flushed as she landed on solid ground again, problem solved.

'I mean, you've got your monies sorted?' she asked, on our way back to the kitchen.

'Yes and no.'

'How much do you need?' she asked, exhaling as she sat back down, her voice a little weary.

'Oh, Mum, I absolutely hate this.'

'I know you do. Go on, how much?' She flattened the ancient, curled-up cheque book and held her pen poised above the amount field, no longer bothering to fill in the little stub opposite as she used to do so meticulously, before my endless requests for help. Her eyes went vacant, dazed-like as she filled it in and signed her name.

'Will that do you?' she asked, handing it to me. I thanked her, hugged her and slipped the cheque into the back pocket of my jeans.

Difficult stuff out of the way, we both scurried in the other direction.

'Are you ready to feed those swans?' Mum said, smiling again, turning to face her granddaughter.

'No. I want to stay with Mama.'

'No meaning yes?' I said, sweeping her up round the belly and putting her, protesting, into her coat, hat, buggy.

'Listen, thanks a million, Mum. You look lovely, by the way. That colour really suits you.' I was doing what she did, that subtle but frantic scrabbling back when I'd offended or been short with her or when I just felt guilty.

'Good colour, isn't it?'

'Lovely. Where's it from?'

'It's an odd label, something like "prison" or "empathy" or . . .' She stretched her arm over her shoulder and tried to fish for the tag. She turned her back to me, gathered her hair, held it in her hands and stood still. I separated some strands caught up in her necklace and felt for the label, fighting sadness as I imagined her standing just like this while my father, or some boyfriend before, closed the clasp on a piece of jewellery or fastened a zip on an evening dress. Now she had to struggle with the wretched, fiddly things herself. I turned the label in my fingers: 'Therapy,' I said, knowing I could never say that I didn't intend buying one, that I was just admiring it to be nice to make up for not being nice moments earlier and that I was surely too young to be wearing the same clothes as my mother. But this had happened several times lately – older women giving me fashion tips. Somehow I had caught up with her and her friends. For so much of my life they had been old while we were young but we'd begun to seek each other out and now when both generations were together it wasn't the awkward or bored imbalance it used to be. I would find myself listening, nodding, interested and impatient to get my point across.

My mother put her hand round my neck, drew me close to her, kissed me on the forehead.

I watched them leave from the sitting room window: my child cocooned in her granny's care; Mum puffing her cheeks out, singing off-key, eyes to the ground, trusting neither the uneven pavement nor her own increasingly unreliable feet.

I opened the window and climbed out onto the balcony. I was still excited by the novelty of having one. When we first moved in I'd spent a good deal of time ducking and bending as I clambered in and out of it, organising things. I'd put the potted Windmill fern I'd brought with me from the old house in a corner to hide an ugly and hazardous cracked Doric pillar. This was the third flat we'd looked at. The first, a basement two-bed below a doctor's surgery, had no garden and felt subterranean. In the second – a chintzy new development with candy-striped wallpaper, free gifts of honey and waving, life-sized teddy bears – Addie had used the facilities, yet to be plumbed, sullying the aroma of fresh hydrangeas in the hall and colouring everyone's first impressions of the place. We'd got out of there quick.

I looked around me in the cool morning air. Beyond where I stood, the chestnut and elm trees in the park were house-high and glorious in the early morning light. The one good thing about the flat was that it overlooked this little park, which had a playground at its centre and was hedged on all sides behind high Victorian railings. I would take Addie to visit it in the morning. From where I stood, I could see there was a swing and a slide. An old woman walked and smoked along the curled path with her even older dog; a man kicked a ball to a little boy.

The traffic on the road that separated the house from the park was another worry. Sporadic but fast, it swept around a blind corner. I could see a child charging across, not looking, excited by the sight of a friend. And then the memory of the solitary plimsoll, left on the roundabout after the accident, belonging to the little boy I used to play Cowboys and Indians with. Lesley French, almost six.

I liked the idea of living beside a home for the elderly. I imagined happy little trips in to visit them with still warm homemade buns and small gifts at Christmas and Easter, but the skip in the front drive was ugly: overfull with the flotsam and jetsam of the dying and the dead – old armchairs, soiled cushions, surgical gloves and incontinence pads and needles that surely brought sniffing dogs and snippy complaints from the neighbours who did not wish to be reminded, as they walked along Altona Avenue, that the sea was not all that lay ahead of them.

Chapter Four

From a distance and from the waist up, Bray appeared to be a pretty seaside town: the humpback bridge over the pewter water of the Dargle; the clusters of red brick houses rising up into the green; tall chimneys and village spires; the domed church at the hill top and the breast of the sugarloaf with its perfect nipple visible through mist beyond. It was only at street level that things got ugly.

Most of the shops on the high street had yet to open, or had shut down for good, padlocked behind graffitied shutters, except for Shoe Zone which had wearily begun trading – Scholl sandals for nothing in a wire basket by the door.

There were a few early risers on the street, most of them aimless, just standing and watching. A pink-track-suited woman, 'Babe' emblazoned across her bum, pushed a buggy full of groceries towards the golden arches of McDonalds, which glowed from the Tudor beams of the once-magnificent town hall. An old woman with nicotine hair, a red raincoat and rash-red face, and arms over-stretched from a lifetime of carrying heavy bags, hacked her way along the road ahead of me, head lolling to the side. She stopped for a cigarette outside the chemist on the corner. 'Blahhh!' she shouted as I passed, making me jump, her gaping rubber lips exposing the rottenness of her gums. If the old men weren't limping, they were dripping from the nose, blue-faced and defeated on a long uphill walk.

It was cold that morning; the sky cinderblock grey and threatening. I was glad of it. Recently the sunshine had been rubbing it in, making me feel that everyone else was happy which made me all more miserable.

On the pavement outside the church, where people were gathered waiting for a hearse, pigeons picked over vomit the colour of Pepto-Bismol. I bent my head and braced myself for insults or wolf whistles as I walked by a group of teenage boys squatting on a wall outside the train station, all spunk and angst, their faces pale and papuliferous from a strict diet of chips and burgers. Nothing happened. They were silent. There was nothing to say. I had reached an age where I'd become invisible to a large section of the male population. They simply didn't see me any more. In fact, a weird, more worrying thing had begun happening. Elderly men had started staring at me. Not just saying hello to the nice young girl as we passed on the street, but stopping and turning and giving me the eye, as if there might be a chance.

I had period pain. I missed Joe. I didn't want to live in Bray. The town had always seemed out of focus and out of fashion to us; in a time warp of its own, a bit like an episode of *Coronation Street*. It was too far from the city, we had said in the days when we had money, too far from friends, a bit parochial, a little bit rough.

I caught my reflection in the window of Fab Framing. Here was me being snobby about the locals but actually I fitted right in, in my too-high heels, too-short leather jacket and skinny jeans, too tight on solid thighs. I'd tied my hair up – Joe always loved me with it tied up, until I told him that women only did that when it needed a good wash.

'Why are you looking at me?' I'd snap when I felt him watching.

'Because you're so beautiful.'

'Why are you being nice?' I'd ask if he put a blanket around me in the evenings or brought me up a hot drink.

'Because I love you more than life itself.'

I nodded while a man, who was clearly not from Bray, possibly Spanish, gave me a long and complex set of directions to the supermarket, which I knew I was never going to follow. I was hopeless with directions, always drifting off after the first left, and his voice was being drowned out by a torrent of incomprehensible gibberish coming from the loudspeaker of a car with a Sinn Fein banner on its roof. I thanked him and decided to go downhill in search of sponges and bleach.

Outside the supermarket, which I somehow stumbled upon, there was a tangle of wriggling limbs between cars and a woman's backside in the air. A child – too old to be naked from the waist down – was being held under the arms, encouraged to have a pee or worse. By the door where baskets were stacked in a careless heap, a sign, scrawled in Biro and Sellotaped to the inside of the window, read: 'No Messers' as if Bray had more than enough of them.

I found a tub of lethal-looking bleach and some sponges in a dark corner of the shop where boxes and delivery trolleys had been abandoned, and smiled at the thought of Joe and the phobia he'd had about them. He couldn't even be in the same room as a sponge – I suggested that he must have had a bad experience with one once, though I couldn't imagine what this bad experience would have been.

The girl at the till was worrying a nail that she'd bitten down to bleeding skin, and our transaction, me handing her money, her packing my bag and giving me change, was completed without her looking up or saying anything. I felt even lonelier when I heard, as I walked away, her greet the woman who'd been queuing behind me. 'How are you, Mrs O'Malley? How's Sean getting on in the States?'

It will take you a year. Give it a year, everyone said. A year would sort everything out.

Out again in the open air, I crossed the road and strode back up the hill towards home. The sinister, Pied Piper melody of an ice cream van clashed with the sound of an Irish reel coming from the scout hall. I peered in through the window: leaping shadows of little Irish dancing girls reflected in stained glass, backs and arms stiff and rod-straight, circling, following the barked orders of their teacher. I watched as they thumped their soft-shoed feet on plywood; one over-zealous young dancer high-kicked across the floor at such speed that she almost collided with a stout, ginger-haired girl jigging and reeling over to her glass of orange. She took a few gulps and a mouthful of Tayto, then skipped back into the fold, ringlets bouncing, teeth munching. It would be ballet for Addie. No ringlets, red knees or fake tan.

At the level crossing by the train station, an election poster had blown off its pole; the hopeful candidate grinned from where he was lying, in pinstriped suit and red tie, in the middle of the road. When the green man appeared, how people approached this obstacle seemed to depend on their political preference: some veered off course to walk around it; others marched straight over it, leaving muddy footprints on the candidate's poised, neat-haired face.

Back in the flat I was a whirlwind of domestic activity. I scrubbed every corner of the kitchen, even the oven, leaving great brown streaks up my arms. I pulled out and washed all the shelves of the fridge, ran a J-cloth along the cruddy rubber. I mopped and cleaned the old lino floor. I hoovered up enough of Alfie's fur to make a sweater. I pulled out a tangle of the last tenant's black hair that had been clogging up the plughole in the shower and used an old toothbrush to clean the grouting between the tiles. Then I wiped down the mildewed bathroom cabinet, and began to sort through the plastic bag into which I'd intended, when packing up the old house, to put only viable medicines that were of use and still in date. But I'd got bored five minutes into this job, had given up and shelved everything in: an ancient jar of Vicks VapoRub, gouged to its midnight blue base, some indigestion tablets, a packet of Beano plasters, one sachet of Alka-Seltzer, the stub from a Van Morrison concert, a Boots voucher expiring in November 2002, a little Playmobil man, two of Joe's rusty Gillette razors.

I dragged the first bin bag of clothes into the bedroom and emptied them out on the unmade bed. It was ridiculous how many bras I didn't own. Other women had pretty lace ones, expensive ones they would only ever hand wash, ones given to them by a boyfriend in fabrics that caressed the skin, that made them feel wonderful; I had just two: both ancient, black, gel-filled.

I folded Addie's baby clothes and put them into the bottom drawer of the cupboard, hoping to use them again one day but not now sure how that would ever come about. I stuffed the shelves above with my own bally sweaters, unmatched slippers, things I would never wear again but was not quite able to throw out.

He could never throw anything away. Even when he left, he left everything behind. Whenever we'd have clear-outs, he'd get distracted by some old jacket or hat he used to wear and he'd put them on and adopt poses like those men in Damart catalogues and I would giggle but at the same time whine at him to hurry up. Now his empty suits hung in the wardrobe like ghosts in a queue.

The American one, black with a purplish sheen to it, still had a stain on the lapel from the night of that disastrous dinner party. It had been conceived, and guests invited, six months before it took place. The host was his boss at Browne & Davison. Joe had gone to the Dockers with one of his clients that day and after too many Jack Daniels, had ridden home on his motorbike to freshen up. He already had a hangover at five in the afternoon.

Small boys in white shirts and grey flannel trousers, hair brushed and shining, opened the door to us and collected our coats. The house was merry and filling up with lots of faces that Joe should have known but couldn't put names to. I smiled beside him feeling childishly shy and unsure of what to do with my hands. He was still a little unsteady from the whiskey but thought another drink would perk him up. And as he went to have a glass of wine, his boss said I have your favourite tipple here and produced a bottle of Patrón Tequila.

At the dinner table, Joe sat doing his best, beside a big Beryl-Reid-type woman who asked for a taste of his tequila. I had been seated opposite him, beside a funny little man with a moustache who was fascinated by the forthcoming election and wanted to talk of nothing else, gesticulating wildly with his thin, womanly hands when he spoke about what needed to be done to save the country. I was still in that phase of besottedness where talking to anyone aside from Joe, or talking about anything other than Joe, was a little tedious. Bella said that I was too into him; that it just wasn't normal or healthy.

So I wasn't listening to the little man beside me that evening, I was watching Joe as he poured the Beryl-Reid-type woman a glass of tequila. She took a gulp, then Joe got up and stood behind her. 'You do it like this,' he said. He put his hands on either side of her head, pulled it back and rocked it from side to side like a cocktail shaker.

Inspired by her enthusiasm, he forced this trick on other guests: the ladies seemed to quite enjoy it; their partners glowered at him. I squirmed in my seat. Then out came the white wine, red wine, cigarettes. And after a short respite on the journey over, Joe plunged back into drunkenness.

I suggested that he take some air. He went out to the back garden and I forgot about him for a little while, becoming great friends with an accountant and part-time fortune teller. She said that I was going to have three babies and that we'd live in a house with high ceilings by the sea. I spotted him once through the bathroom window. He was slumped on a child's swing in the sleet but I didn't dare gesture, I was quite happy for him to be there, away from potential trouble. I hadn't seen when, seconds later, he'd fallen backwards off it, banged his head, tried to stand up and had fallen again, this time into the flowerbed. Or the moment when his boss's wife, Brenda, had come out to try and help him up and he had told her to fuck off. It was the drunkest he had ever imagined or been.

When he fell back in through the sliding doors, wet, bleeding, covered in coal, having mistaken the bunker for the back door, people were already leaving. The woman who'd sat beside him at dinner was being helped into her coat by her husband. Joe made a lunge at her, to say goodbye and sorry and they'd both toppled over. Joe fell on top of her; she kicked and struggled beneath him like a capsized beetle. Her furious husband lifted him off her and onto his tiptoes. I pleaded with him to go home.

I apologised to everyone and put him in a taxi, begging him not to throw up. He held his hand over his mouth, got sick into his shirt. Then he told me he thought he was dying, said he wanted to be dropped off at the hospital.

When we got home I told him to stay outside while I went to get the garden hose. It was four in the morning, freezing cold. I returned to find him naked, waiting to be hosed down. I got him inside with great effort and up the stairs into the shower. Then he refused to get out.

So I left him there. I locked the door because I didn't want him in the bedroom. I heard him groaning, rolling about all night. In the morning he had carpet burns on his elbows and backside. He couldn't do anything for the next two days. He just stared at the TV, understanding nothing.

I double checked that the front door was locked (it was), that the iron was unplugged (it was) and that Addie was still breathing (she was) and climbed into bed.

The silence was ringing in my ears like tinnitus. Then I heard something. I hadn't got used to the sounds of this house. I slid out of bed and locked the bedroom door. This caused Addie to sit up in her sleep; she felt for her sucky blanket, found it, turned the other way and lay down again. I slipped back in under my duvet and tried to soothe myself with the statistic I'd read that houses with dogs are rarely targeted by thieves. I counted backwards from a hundred in sevens. Just knowing I had to stay still made me desperate to move. I wanted to cough and to turn onto my other side – into the recovery position – but resisted in case the rustle of sheets would wake her.

In my half-sleep I was a child again, back on the wooden changing bench of our local pool, whimpering as Mum pulled a brush through my hair; the girl sitting beside me had a verruca on the underside of her foot that she was examining with great concentration; the large woman opposite us was towelling herself, one leg propped on the bench, a talc-y imprint of her foot on the tiles, too many wobbly bits on view. 'No running. No diving. No jumping. No petting' the laminated poster above the pool had read. I'd obeyed the first three, and the fourth, though I wasn't sure what it meant. An older boy had told me that the shallow end was where the deep end was, just for a joke, and I had sat on the edge and slipped in and down and underwater for too long, limbs flailing, my screams unheard and unseen.

'Let's dance, Mama,' Addie was standing up in her bed opposite me.

'Shush.' I whispered, inwardly cursing.

'How about you be a crocodile?'

'Back to sleep now, sweetie.'

'It's too boring! How about *Where's Wally?* That's a good idea.'

'That's a very bad idea.'

'Is it morning time?'

'No, it's the absolute middle of the night.'

'But my tummy says it needs a cartoon.'

I glanced at the clock; ten past three. I got up, sat on the edge of her bed and sang 'Mocking Bird' over and over. Then I rubbed my thumb along her forehead the way she liked me to. I listened to her breathing become deeper, crawled back into my own bed and lay utterly still in the darkness, fighting the urge to scratch an itch on my leg.

'Wakey wakey!'

'Damn! Addie, I mean it. Mama is sleepy.'

'Wake up, Daddy,' Addie would say, giggling, whenever Joe played dead. And the longer he stayed there, tongue lolling, still, the more she would giggle. 'Daddy, Daddy, wake up,' her voice getting thin and sharp with expectation because she knew what was coming.

All at once he'd pop his eyes open, sit up, grab her, pull her into his chest, hug her and tickle her and she would roll around screaming with delighted protest while he'd blow hot raspberries on her soft, warm coiled-up little neck.

As a boy he used to play dead to scare his parents when they went out for an evening. He'd lie just inside the front door in a sort of broken position with ketchup on his head and face for ages until they got home, whereupon his mother, a busy, no-nonsense Women's Institute woman, would step over him, saying 'Oh, don't be so silly, Joseph. For goodness' sake, get up.'

'*Mum*my*!*'

I was now in a sleep-deprived rage. I was talking in warnings and capital letters. I got up and searched for Calpol in the boxes still to be unpacked in the kitchen and bathroom, not the manufacturer's intention but it generally made her drowsy. It turned up in an old wine box marked 'Xmas'. I was only halfway there. I held the bottle under the bedside light to read the dosage, my fingers sticking to its tacky sides.

'Some delicious pink medicine,' said Ratty – she only obeyed orders when they came from her toys. She whipped her head away just as the spoon reached her mouth, spilling Calpol all over her pyjamas.

'Christ!' I was lashing out, brittle. I lifted her out to be changed, then settled her back into bed.

'*Mum*my, m*um*my, m*um*my.' She was upright again.

Jesus, that sound. That word.

I got out of bed, stood over her, grabbed her round the waist, forced her little body backwards and held her legs in a lock. She kicked herself free, turned onto her knees and stood straight back up.

I shoved her down again on the mattress, this time with such force that she was stunned for a second – we both were – then she howled in disgust and protest.

'I'm going to tell my Dada that you hurted me!'

'I didn't mean to hurt you. Mama's just very, very tired and you are doing very bad misbehaving.'

'I want my Dada,' she howled again and again. I held her until her breathing softened.

'What's Dada's favourite colour?'

'Silver, I think.'

'I'm going to make Dada a card with silver sparkles and jewels for his birthday. Is that a good idea?'

'That's a great idea. Now let's get you back to bed.'

'But I want to sleep in your bed.'

'Absolutely not.'

'Absolutely yes,' she said, stumbling a little over the word.

She won. She always did. I lifted her into my bed. She wanted to share my pillow. Then she wanted to hold my hand. She moved and wriggled beside me – at one point I was lying horizontally across the bottom of the mattress and she was vertically above me – until her movement slowed and I could hear her working her sucky blanket. Then she was still.

'Mummy?' she whispered, smiling, curled up beside me.

'What is it?'

She moved her face closer to mine on the pillow, asked me to lift my head. She slipped her arm under my neck and hugged me.

'My eyelashes sound quite sandy when I do this,' she said, opening and closing her lids against the pillowcase.

'That's just what they sound like. Quiet now.'

'Mama, I love your boobies,' she said in the darkness.

'Thank you.'

'I love your nose,' she said, touching it.

'Thanks, sweetheart. Now, off to sleep.'

'And I love your ears. I love your muscles. And I love – what are those things?'

'Eyebrows.'

'I love your eyebrows.'

Chapter Five

When we arrived at the park that first time, there was no one else there. We had observed it through the railings as we walked around to the gates, Addie on one side of me, tugging at my hand, jumping up and down in anticipation, Alfie on the other, pulling on his lead, panting, wanting to be free. I released him and he bounded ahead of us, round the corner, in through the gates and straight for the bushes, where he found an empty cider bottle and settled under a tree to chew on it.

Addie and I made our way around the small winding path that skirted the playground, until she could no longer resist. She let go of my hand and ran towards the swings, slowed as she approached them, then turned and waited for me.

'Can I be the leader?' she said, getting ready for a race.

'See? This is the face I need if I'm going to win.' She scrunched up her nose, bared her teeth, made her hands claw-like and took off.

'Be careful!'

'I will, Mama. I'll be very, very, up to the top careful.'

'I winned!' she said, making the see-saw the finish line.

What had seemed quite idyllic from the distance of the sitting room window was, I could now see, very shabby: the rope bridge leading to the slide was missing several logs; the picnic table was broken and etched with kids names and Tippex-ed hearts and all around the boundary to the play area, there were dusty bald patches where the grass had given up.

Unwatched, we played hopscotch; my little girl shadowing me, shrieking as she stomped along the numbered squares, champagne-coloured curls bouncing, chubby arms in the air. Then we moved in a rush from the roundabout to the see-saw to the slide, shouting and singing as we went. I heard myself use that verbal tic of parenthood – 'Now' – in a satisfied way, as I settled her into each new thing.

I held her around the waist, slotted her solid little legs into the bucket swing, bending her knees – my knees – into place. I gave her a push, then swung on the grown-up swing beside her, so that we were moving in unison, singing to ourselves as we glided off the earth and into the air, holding our heads back to stare at the upside-down world.

'Push me. Push me,' she demanded, swapping to the big swing. 'Higher,' she shouted and 'Again.' We were having a great time until I pushed her too strongly by mistake. She slid off the seat and fell forwards onto the hard muddy ground underneath. I held her, told her I was silly and sorry and waited through the long inhale that comes before tears. A small piece of skin had come away from her knee. 'You're very cheeky,' she said, between sobs.

'She OK?'

I turned to see a boy emerge from the slanted roof at the top of the slide: he looked about sixteen, dark hair over his eyes, a Bauhaus T-shirt, black jeans, Converse high tops. His movement seemed to trigger more general activity and now behind him there was a further languorous sense of stirring; glimpses of feet, heads, backsides.

There were at least eight of them: a group of teenage Goths with tattoos and piercings, purple lipstick, black, kohl-rimmed eyes. A large, ginger-haired boy in a leather car coat jumped down from the slide, wiped dust off the legs of his jeans; a sullen girl in a deodorant-stained chiffon dress clambered over the rope bridge, her friend followed behind her in sleepy resignation, a carton of hair dye in her hands, black paste still in her hair and stained around her forehead.

'Can we play?' The same dark-haired boy asked politely.

'Of course. Do what you have to do.' I said, attempting to sound edgy.

He smiled at us and began swinging on the monkey bars, his T-shirt riding up, revealing an adult line of hair from his belly button down. A blonde girl chewed on her lip and tugged her T-shirt over her bum as she passed us and went over to him. I breathed in the hormonal reek of her early adolescence. He swung his legs forward and gripped her round the waist, then they both fell to the ground, laughing. 'Get off me, Dylan. I mean it!' she said as he writhed around on top of her. I felt a jolt of jealousy watching them: their young bodies; the drama of all they had ahead of them; the darkest, loneliest lows of course but also the extreme emotional highs.

'I want to go home,' Addie said, still whimpering in my arms after her fall. I was feeling a little intimidated too but I didn't want it to show, so we lingered for a few moments, her neck craned with a child's curiosity as a group of them stood on the net swing together and began setting it in motion.

'Your dog stole my drink.' This came from a tall, Nordic-looking man who was standing outside the park railings near the climbing frame. I'd seen him pass our gate before. 'Oh, God, I'm sorry. Drop, Alfie! Drop.' I said, yanking the bottle from his clamped teeth. The man watched us for a moment, laughed and walked away.

'What's her doing?' Addie asked on our way out, pointing at a boy lying prone on the grass by the bushes, his head bent low – he seemed the same sort of age as the others but wasn't part of their gang. He looked like he was searching for something, or maybe he was unwell. We walked towards him; he didn't seem to notice us, or if he did, he didn't turn around. We moved a little closer. He was holding a magnifying glass in one hand, a jam jar in the other, burning the wings of a trapped butterfly through the rays of the early morning sun. I pulled Addie away. 'Stop that, it's cruel.' He turned around. He had a pale, flabby face, red rings circling his eyes.

'Ah, bugger off, barge-arse!' he said, grabbing the jar and moving on.

With a lump in my throat, we left the park and walked towards home past the high hedges and electric gates of the villa-style houses opposite the entrance, Addie behind me, side-stepping along the railings. Most had been given modern extensions and facades, bay trees on either side of their freshly-painted front doors, fat polished people carriers in the driveways. On the other, dark side of the park, were several grand Victorian homes that looked as grey and as worn-out as their owners, who I'd seen tread daily to Mass, the library, the butcher's; old-fashioned things like fuchsia and nettles still thrived in their front gardens, Virgin Marys and Children of Prague stood forever over fanlights. At the new house on the corner, a modern, energy-efficient replica of the old red bricks, coils of turf had been stacked into a pyramid, waiting to be rolled out to make an instant lawn. My landlord, Nathan Lyons, also owned this site. There was no sign of him today or of any work being done. Beside a stationary JCB, there was a carton of milk, a bag of sugar, and what looked like an old pair of boxer shorts – the usual debris of builders.

Addie offered me her hand as we approached the road back to our flat. I took her small, warm fingers in mine and when it was safe, we crossed together, me and my perfect companion, her little head turning as we walked, eyebrows arched, watching everything.

Why hadn't I investigated the playground before agreeing to rent the flat? When we bought the house in Sandycove, we had driven round the area at different times of day to see if there were other children living there and to see if there was somewhere our imaginary child could safely play. Why was I so untogether now that we were on our own?

On the gravel of our front drive, a young girl, the owner of the Barbie bike we'd seen in the hall, was being attended to by her mother, who was squatting, strapping a pink helmet under her chin, unaware that she was exposing her sensible knickers to her new neighbours. The girl scowled at Addie and inched backwards, still straddling the crossbar.

'Stay still,' her mother said, looking around at the same moment, then getting to her feet. We exchanged compliments, ages, names, though I didn't quite catch hers. She repeated it but I still didn't get it. I knew I couldn't ask her a third time.

'You're the new people upstairs, right? You settling in OK?' Her accent was Eastern European, her hair crew-cut. There were several angry-looking spots between her eyebrows.

'Well, we didn't have a great night last night. I'm sorry if we kept you awake? But we'll get used to it. It's all a bit strange for her.' She looked down at my child, who was eyeing the girl on the bike with shy intensity.

'Hello, cutie pie,' the woman said, squatting again, pinching Addie's cheeks.

'Oh, your mummy hasn't dressed you right, has she?' she said then, in a sing-songy voice. 'You need another top on top of that top. A proper waterproof one – look, see, like Charlotte's.'

I tried to defend my sartorial choices, too stunned by her criticism to come up with an appropriate retort. I wanted to tell her to fuck off.

'God, you might be right,' I said laughing but feeling a tightness in my throat, resenting her and her freckle-faced little brat hermetically sealed in her helmet, all smug on her horrible bike. I wanted to tell her that my child was safe and happy and loved, which of course I didn't, and that at three and a half years old she had yet to need an antibiotic, which I didn't say either.

'So, tell me, Eve,' she moved close up to me, frowning, 'did those leetal shitheads chase you out? They did, didn't they? Those leetal pigs.'

Chapter Six

There was nothing on. From where I was lying, I could see right under the television set. A layer of soft grey dust was punctuated with small missing things and tufts of dog hair, like little balls of not coping. Joe loved dusting. I didn't, don't.

I slid my hand in and pulled out a flimsy brown thing, now covered on one side by fluff. Ratty. Addie had been crying about Ratty for the past week – a cheap cuddly toy Joe had picked up for her from Ikea, that she now wouldn't sleep without. 'I need Ratty,' she'd plead from her bed when I'd turned out the lights. And each night I'd tell her that I'd look for it. 'How about Dada's car?' she'd shout after me as I closed her door, believing that I was really going to search for it rather than pour myself a large glass of red wine and collapse in front of *Coronation Street*.

But one night she was so insistent, so distraught that I did go outside and across the gravel to Joe's old car: the hearse, my mother called it, a black, low-slung Volvo estate, hunkered down in car parks, sidling along laneways, it always seemed perfect for an affair. He hadn't even taken his car. His beloved Volvo. 'You'll need it more than me, for all your socialising,' he said the day he left. It always irritated him that I was gone so often, so busy on play-dates and meeting friends.

I'd turned on the overhead light, stretched and felt under the seats, around the oily runners and rivets. Then I'd lain still for a moment, crouched on the floor behind the driver's seat. This was how I liked to travel as a child, curled up in my own dark and private universe, aware of, but not listening to, my parents chatter, the shipping news on the radio, watching the upside-down world of electricity poles that we passed on interminable journeys from the West, licking the leather seat, the road bumping below me, being safely returned home.

I stayed in the shower till the water ran cold, then stood on the weighing scales and immediately stepped off. I bent down, reset the dial to five pounds below zero then stood on it again, this time with one foot only, leaning on the sink and the toilet top until the reading said what I wanted. I didn't understand how I could be almost half a stone heavier than I'd been when we lived in Sandycove. Surely after all my suffering I deserved at least to be slim?

I wiped condensation from the mirror above the sink and examined myself. There was a sleep crease running vertically down my left cheek. I put my hands on either side of my face and stretched the skin taut towards my hairline, then let it sag again. There were mornings in the mirror – with my glasses on in particular – when frowning back at me was not Eve at all, but an Irene; an older, jowly version of myself, with insipid grey eyes and librarian hair. At almost forty, my face looked acceptable in fewer and fewer mirrors, always appearing puffier and paler than the last time I checked. One of these days I'd look at my reflection and it will have just collapsed. I sucked in my cheeks and my stomach, yanked my sweater over my bum, bared my gums, stood back to study myself sidelong, groaned with disapproval and turned to go, pulling the door behind me, the vortex created by the open window causing it to slam. I peeped into the bedroom to check on Addie. She was still enjoying her lie-in, face down, backside in the air.

I felt a small rush of excitement when my phone rang, always expecting Joe, even though it was me who was ringing it from the landline because I couldn't remember where I'd left it the night before. What was happening to me? I had become the sort of person whose phone only rang when they'd rung it themselves. Still, some introverted part of me was enjoying this shadowy existence – seldom leaving the house, ordering my groceries online and getting them delivered and, even on the odd occasion that we did venture out, we moved through the streets of Bray invisibly, recognised by nobody; at home we lived behind blinds and walked in socks on wooden floors.

Emma O'Byrne wanted to be friends on Facebook. Emma O'Byrne. Emma O'Byrne. And then there she was, sitting beside me in sixth class with her lisp and Swiss-roll rubber – it looked and smelt like a real Swiss roll – which I coveted and later ate. Her profile photo was Kermit the Frog. I accepted her friendship, though we were never especially keen on each other; it wasn't just the rubber, I also lost her hockey stick by accident. I had a snoop around her photos: three children in a swimming pool on holidays somewhere. All red-heads. A poorly taken shot of her husband holding a prize-winning fish. And Emma herself, all her childish features now huddled into the middle of her round face, in between two other beaming girls, concealer caked around crow's feet, so close to each other and to the camera you could almost hear the giddiness of their girls' night out.

Joe hated me being on Facebook. He just didn't get it. 'Why would you tell the world what you had for dinner? That your child has diarrhoea?' That's another thing I should have done. I should have switched it off in the evenings and talked to him the way we used to. 'Who are you on to?' he would always say. Now I could surf with happy abandon.

I Googled 'sudden, sharp, shooting pain in head', put three new tops in my shopping basket at Zara Kids but stopped short of buying them when I saw the total add up. I believed for a while after Addie's birth that maternity had made me less materialistic because I had lost all interest in buying clothes for myself, but all I had done was to transfer this materialism to my daughter; I bought endless outfits I couldn't afford for her instead. I logged out and logged onto Rollercoaster.ie:

Hi all, just wondering if you have any good ideas for entertaining DD between the hours of five and seven? All suggestions welcome. Am on steep learning curve! XX

Responses pinged into my mailbox, lots of helpful suggestions, some with bullet points, others with no new ideas but lots of empathy and sympathy. And then one from the Pink Panther:

What sort of mother are you that you need to ask strangers how to entertain your child?

I formulated all kinds of vitriolic responses in my head, all sorts of justifications, fuelled by a flood of supportive reactions:

Don't mind her.

What a bitch!

She obviously doesn't have kids.

The Pink Panther strikes again.

I logged out, got up, clicked on the kettle.

How much time and energy did I waste every day boiling and re-boiling the kettle? I did it without thinking, finding comfort in the hissing sound of its building. I liked that it was something with a very definite start and finish. And that for those few moments of the day nothing else was expected of me. I could just exist. It was always in this position that I fell into a sort of mesmerised daze, capable of hearing and responding to things around me but unwilling to click out of it, enjoying its soporific nothingness. Virginia Creeper curled round the edges of the kitchen window, its virescent leaves wet after rainfall. It was eating into the brickwork and overtaking everything. A gate was banging against the fence of the Cherry Glade next door. There was the sound of a spade being dug into the earth, the screech of children in a playground somewhere nearby, the Tannoy and rumble from the train station.

On the road below me, the morning commute of oddness had begun. I didn't know where they came from or where they were going, but they were a group of individuals who passed by under our kitchen window at this time every day: the sad, solemn man, his head permanently tilted towards his shoulder, who always stopped to check the sole of his shoes for dog dirt just outside our gate. He must have stood on some once, months or years before, and had been checking his shoes ever since. The one who strode along in his military-style cap and jacket, thumbs hooked round his rucksack, as if he were setting off for Camp Bastion to sort things out. A Roy Orbison lookalike in studs and leather – a brush of greased black hair, just when you thought you'd seen the last of Brylcreem. The middle-aged woman with the tartan trolley. She looked livid as usual, hating life, hating human beings. 'Go back to England, you stupid cunt,' she shouted at me the other morning when I caught her furious eye on the high street. Their trousers were always just that bit too short, their caps pulled too far down, there was a wildness or blankness in their eyes. Something was somehow just wrong.

Beyond them, in the park, the Nordic-looking man I'd seen on that first visit to the playground – the one who said Alfie had stolen his drink – settled down on his bench, as he did every day, with his rucksack and bottle of something.

'Jesus Christ, Alfie, don't do that. You'll give me cardiac arrest.' The postman had fled with his hand intact, leaving a chewed flier for *Soon Fatt* take-away on the hall floor and a final demand from Airtricity. I ushered the dog back to his bed where I found what was left of my glasses. 'See this? No,' I said in the deep, growly voice the dog behaviourist had taught me. 'What pleasure could you possibly get from chewing glass?' Then I sat at the kitchen table feeling homesick, waiting for Addie to call me.

'We'd like to make an offer,' Joe said to the pretty estate agent as she stood with her clipboard, neat trouser suit and clenched buttocks at the doorstep of our house, our first home.

'It really is a trophy home. The aspect, the original features. Stunning!' she said, casting her eyes towards the cornicing, 'And the garden is to die for.' It was the first day of viewings and seven or eight other families had stomped up and down the stairs, inspecting things, taking rough measurements, making plans, but we knew it was ours from the offset and the presence of these strangers in our home was making us tense. Even so, we did what they did, looked under things, turned taps, knocked on walls, switched switches, stared out the windows. And then we did something that no one else did – went in at ten thousand over the asking price – neither of us had any experience of these things and though I panicked later when our offer was accepted, it was a perfect home: a Victorian house with high ceilings near the sea, with three bedrooms and a secluded, walled garden. The attractiveness of the estate agent, all wet-lipped and shiny-haired, made it seem more perfect still. I saw us sitting by the fire in the cream, lamp-lit sitting room. The tiny third bedroom would become the nursery, which I would decorate with cloud wallpaper like the little boy's room in *Kramer vs. Kramer*, a jellyfish growth chart on the wall by the door – or maybe not – wooden bookshelves at toddler height, wicker baskets full of toys. And I'd paint the floorboards white.

'That's what swans do,' Joe said. 'They build their nests, line them with their own down and grasses and anything soft, so the eggs won't break or get crushed. They get everything ready and then they have their babies.'

'Did you know that a swan can also break your arm?' He thought this was ridiculous.

We began trying about a year in. Our new home was still not organised, the spare room was full of boxes yet to be emptied, but all our friends said it was the perfect house for a family. Joe's best friend said he felt a bit of sick rise in his throat when he came through the front door because it was so great: the garden with its tree house waiting to be discovered, the rope ladder, the old wooden-seated swing, and the yellow gate, under an arch of white clematis, that led down to the sea. 'Wonderful for children,' his wife said, peering out the kitchen window, a child at her breast. And so idle discussions about baby names began in the ad breaks between *Coronation Street*.

After a few months of happy and energetic effort, I knew we must have been doing something wrong. I poured through books about fertility and began to monitor my monthly cycle. I kept a thermometer on the bedside table and took my temperature every morning, him in bed beside me, snorting at my eccentricity. We started timing 'intimacy' (Dr Percy's word for the act) around my most fertile days of the month.

I explored bits of my body I'd never thought about or visited before. My cervix, was it low and hard? Or high and soft? And could I describe my cervical mucus as having the consistency of egg white? After 'intimacy' I held my legs in the air and kept them there for as long as tolerable, and slept through the night with a pillow under my bum, fighting the pressure in my bladder till the following morning. Joe watched, waited, suffered, drew back.

Another few months passed and still there was no baby, nothing to get excited about. I started to worry, went back to Dr Percy who told me to stop worrying, start exercising and give up alcohol and caffeine. I teased Joe about his swimmers being lazy; we laughed as we imagined them with snorkels, treading water or floating on their backs, taking it easy. Then I stopped laughing and started to look for answers elsewhere; I went online and tried all the things that had worked for other women. Doggedly I followed each of them. They didn't work. We got a dog.

I started eating almonds though I'd never liked them, and bought ice creams – excellent for female fertility according to the books – from Teddy's after work each evening. Joe would cycle along Sandycove seafront to meet me on the days he worked from home; eating ice cream is something you really can't do on your own.

I became fascinated and resentful of other women who seemed to possess an ability that I appeared not to have, like Anna who lived next door, the one Mum wasn't sure about, an introverted woman who I never got to know, who always seemed to be obscured by an open boot, or half inside her car sorting out her babies. Their cries used to travel down the chimney in the night, along the wall that the two houses shared, taunting me, infiltrating my dreams.

While we were in this nothing time, I sometimes caught glimpses of her from the window of the utility room – we had a house with a separate utility room for goodness sake, we were clearly ready for kids. I'd watch her and her husband and their rowdy get-togethers in the back garden with their friends and their children, their endless laughter heightening my loneliness, my exclusion from an exclusive family club: her husband, Lee, in knee-length shorts, muscular, sun-tanned legs and feet in ugly Crocs, stretching and scratching the hair above his belly, pulling on a polo shirt that he'd pull off just as easily to fuck his wife, to make more babies, when he was drunk and all the guests had gone home.

I carried pineapples, like tufty-haired cartoon characters, back from the local Spar and ate them each evening, but only around weeks three and four, as instructed, and took a tablespoon of cough mixture daily to make things more sticky downstairs. And I prayed and prayed and prayed to Saint Martha around the second half of each month and dropped in to light a candle for my baby whenever I passed a church.

We visited Dr Percy together. She told me I talked too fast, that I needed to calm down, that it often took couples a year. Joe started to get a bit bored of it all, became sort of Buddhist. 'Maybe you just can't have kids,' he said, one evening, and I lay in the shadowy dark of our bedroom stunned and sobbing, staring at the height chart of the previous owner's children, etched into the door frame. This was unthinkable. I was good with kids. I could do a Donald Duck impression.

Joe began to resent organised sex. And I resented him when he couldn't or wouldn't perform on the *most* important night of the month. Then I caught him looking at porn. It was late; I'd been on my way to the loo when I saw a sliver of light beneath the door of his office. I opened it to find him in a panic, thumping Ctrl Alt Delete and Escape. On his screen were a dozen frozen images of 'mature women' in compromising positions. 'I don't know how any of it got there,' he said. The mature women part was what worried me most.

I took up yoga to help me relax, acupuncture to sort out any blockages – my chi was all wrong according to my therapist. I bought and boiled foul-smelling herbal concoctions. I exercised, but only at the right time of the month (the first half) and not the wrong sort (running, horse riding) and always gentle, not too much. I bought more books, endless books, relaxation tapes, meditation CDs and month after month after month I purchased pregnancy tests, convinced that my early symptoms – stuffy nose, sore boobs, frequent urination, stomach pains, blurry vision, increased appetite, slight nausea, tiredness – were real rather than imagined. And each time I got a negative, I got more bewildered, angrier, more determined.

It had been over a year of trying and babies now filled my every waking thought. I leafed through magazines with a pair of scissors and cut out anything baby related. I created baby collages, pinned them to a cork board and kept it hidden in the wardrobe in our room. I thought only positive baby thoughts; I saw mothers and babies and buggies and swollen bellies everywhere. The mums so smug in their happiness, so damned lucky. How come they could do something I couldn't? Look at their faces, my sister used to say, trying to make me feel better. Do they really look so happy? Are they not exhausted and stressed? But all I could see were perfect babies, big fertile bodies, huge motherly breasts. I held my friends' newborns, breathed in their delicious new smell. We returned to Dr Percy. She looked a little more concerned this time and agreed to send us for tests.

Six months later, tired, broke, no longer excited, we embarked on our first round of IVF. Around about the same time, Joe was made

Creative Director at Browne & Davison. Now I was going it alone and I was out of bounds. I was bloated, crotchety, hormonal, my thighs covered in square patches where the progesterone was entering my body; the skin underneath pink and sore and itchy as anything. I set alarms that woke me too late at night and too early in the morning, to remind me to take drugs that made me flatulent and swollen and grumpy. There were no bottles of wine together, no runs with the dog. I was on my own with my private obsession. Just me and my maybe baby.

I went to bed early after each attempt and tried to picture a busy little embryo burrowing into fleshy darkness. Why couldn't I stretch my head inward, disappear under my polo neck and travel internally down through my throat and on past rubbery tubes and wires and workings of purple, black, rich red, to have a look, one huge upside-down animated eye staring at the fleshy, pulsating womb and see what was in there, if anything, and what it was doing?

I Googled success stories and waited and waited and purchased endless pregnancy tests. And when the day came I held the little white stick up to the light with shaking hands and turned it and squinted at it and saw – there it was! Was it? Maybe – the faintest of faint pink lines? I checked it and checked it again. With glasses, without, threw it in the bin only to retrieve it ten minutes later, to study it and study it further. And on it would go for hours, all day. Because I must have been. I had all the signs, the drugs mimicking pregnancy symptoms, convincing me that this time, at long last, it had worked. But always my time of the month arrived, as violent and bloody as negative can be, a shouting scream of NEGATIVE, NOT A CHANCE, NO BABY, NO HOPE. I wasn't just a little bit not pregnant but absolutely un-pregnant, no baby whatsoever.

Fresh, streaming, bright-red blood stained the hard, shining white ceramic and crisp layers of toilet tissue.

Joe would open a bottle of wine; I'd peel the patches off my thighs, their black sticky outlines, so difficult to remove, reminding me of my failure for days after. I'd tell my friends and feel their disappointment, their overly long hugs. 'I'm so sorry it didn't work for you. I can only imagine how you feel,' they'd say as they fed coins into a parking meter and waited for the little ticket to print out.

But they didn't know that I'd already moved on. They were still getting over Plan A, whereas I had galloped on to Plan B. A new cycle. A fresh start. Hands over my ears and humming to block out their concern and questions and to fight the gnawing feeling that nothing would ever grow. That at not quite thirty-eight years of age, I was barren, acarpous.

I'm doing it again, grinding my teeth. Working away on that enamel.

Chapter Seven

'You have passed,' the instructor, a very kind man from Germany, told me on the day of my third driving test.

I beamed at him, disbelieving.

'Not,' he said then.

'I have passed not?'

'Yes. I'm sorry. You have passed not.'

It was the single sentence he had to get right in his day.

'She failed,' I heard Mum say as I sat in her kitchen, quiet that evening. She had stumbled on the stairs on her way to answer the front door, such was her speed, her need, to impart the news to Bella before anyone else. She was girlishly competitive about these things too, always first in line. Like a child, she was energised by drama of any sort.

After three failed tests (everyone promised I'd pass in an automatic) and five instructors, I had accepted that driving wasn't for me. I would travel by train, I would walk, cycle, keep trim, become happy with my quirk, happy to be in the passenger seat, reading magazines, my socked feet pressed up against the windscreen, happy to be chauffeured about by Joe for the rest of my days. Then Joe was gone, but his car was still there, moss growing along the rubber sills of the windows. And I was living in Bray, miles from anywhere.

Little Miss Muffet liked to keep a keen eye on my driving, her head craned forward from where she sat in her throne behind me. Her complaints were varied and continuous: 'Too fast, Mama!'; 'Slow down,'; 'Too bumpy over the bumps.' 'That's better,' she sometimes said, settling back into her seat, turning her face and thoughts to the window.

That afternoon we were on our way over to my mother's for tea. 'Thank you,' Addie whispered, imitating me, holding up her hand as I gestured to a driver who'd let me go ahead of him as I turned onto Bray High Street. It was just after that, that I clunked into the pot hole. The full force of it hit the front left wheel, but we seemed to be still moving and the tyre felt OK and I was now too terrified to stop. I'd been jumpy already, driving Joe's hearse on my own without a licence, and every time I set out I was convinced that I was going to kill us or someone else.

We took the back road through Shankill and Killiney to avoid other traffic and the possibility of being stopped by the police. Before we'd reached Dalkey, Addie had begun whining behind me, having dropped my phone during an overly vigorous game of Candy Crush Saga.

'Look at the sea!' I said, trying to distract her. It was the single thing I'd learnt about being a mother – distraction works. 'And look at the island. Would you like to take a boat over to that island one day? We could bring a picnic.'

'Is that Dada's island?'

'No, what do you mean, darling?'

'You said Dada was on an island.'

I'd told her he was on another island, England, in the early days, when I thought he'd just needed to clear his head, when I thought he was still coming home.

'Oh, no, he's not there, sweetheart,' I said smiling, but feeling it physically.

'It's not funny. I want to see Dada.'

'We can't, darling. He's not there.'

'Let's visit Daddy! Mama, no, this way! You're going the wrong way.'

'No more shouting or Mama will have a crash.'

'Daddy!' she began to cry.

'I'm getting cross, Addie.'

'Well, I'm one hundred crosser than you!'

'I'm warning you—'

I pulled over, found a new game, handed her back my phone and though she was still whimpering, she soon became absorbed by its little beeps and chirps. I put my foot on the accelerator; I couldn't wait to be with my family – I needed them to sort everything out.

'Hail Mary, full of grace, please find me a parking space,' I said, entering a car park that was about three miles from my mother's house but large and quiet and therefore appealing.

I lifted Addie up to let her press the doorbell. She held her little finger on it. It made its flat drone, like the wrong answer on a quiz show. And then we waited. She turned her face to mine. I rang it again and listened for the sound of footfalls on the stairs, the out-of-tune hum and the indecipherable greetings and apologies that always followed. Nothing. Puzzled by our inaction, Addie shrugged her shoulders, turned her little palms upwards. I bent to peer in through the letter box: fresh lilies on the polished hall table, a brown bag of something waiting to be collected on the chair beside it, a jacket hung across its back, beneath it, a pair of Mum's tiny, powder blue tennis shoes. An umbrella was still propped over the top of the old, no longer working, grandfather clock to protect it from the leak that had developed in the pipes above. It seemed too still, as if it knew it was being watched. I pressed the bell for a third time and felt that slow heavy dread in my stomach.

I pulled my phone from my back pocket, dialled her number, heard the click of the answering machine. I turned towards the street. Across the road a suntanned man in unseasonal shorts was lifting a lawn mower from the boot of his car, his Sunday going on just as before. He looked up, gave me a half-wave.

'Are you looking for Dot?' he shouted over, setting down the machine. He strode across the road towards us, glancing into the distance and then down at his own feet to avoid the embarrassment of having to keep meeting my eye.

'She was expecting us at five. She's not answering. I've rung the bell three times. It's just so unlike her,' I said, sighing to dissuade tears.

'Maybe she's just popped down to the shops. Wait there and I'll have a look round the back.' I nodded, thanked him and he set off down the gravel path of the adjoining house in a half-run that made me more, not less, concerned.

So this was how it was going to happen. This was when – a bright Sunday in September. The thing I had feared and dreaded for years, ever since my father had died and even more since Joe, which I had played out in a dozen different scenarios, was now taking place and I needed to be brave. In my mind I was making phone calls, at the funeral already, trying to come to terms with my mother being gone. Her tiny tennis shoes no longer of use.

We'd been on a ship together in a dream I'd had a few nights before. Her face was sketchy, unsmiling, distant, her eyes sort of scratchy and vague. I'd shown her my cabin at bedtime and she'd pointed to where she would be sleeping – in an enormous shiny white coffin. I'd begged her not to get in. I needed her not to be dead because, then, who would look after me?

Sean – I remembered him now from my mother's drinks party last Christmas – was striding back towards me, shouting, 'It's fine. She's fine. Her bathroom window's open. Elaine said it was closed five minutes ago.' I didn't see how this was proof of anything but we crunched back up the gravel path together. I gave the bell another long ring, Sean rapped on the knocker. Seconds later my mother was standing before us, a garden spade in her hand, bringing with her that particular, comforting but impossible-to-define, smell of home.

She'd been putting cuttings on the compost heap and hadn't heard the bell. 'And you're not normally that punctual,' she said, pulling me towards her and kissing me on the head, apologising and blaming me at the same time. She thanked and excused Sean, both of them amused by my neurosis.

The kitchen floor was slippery with grease. The two chickens in the oven needed to come out. Still suffused with the relief of her being not dead, I watched Mum work around us, confident but rather irritable. She was trying to locate the oven glove the cleaner had tidied away, settled for a T-towel, put the peas on to boil, then lifted the heavy, ancient oven dish containing the chickens – 'Ay yi yi' – from the top to the bottom oven shelf. 'I really don't need little people under my feet right now,' she said, encouraging Addie out of the way.

Bella arrived just after us, with a litre bottle of 7UP, 'the worst PMT' and without her husband Sean who'd stayed at home to watch the match. She warmed her backside against the Dimplex heater in the kitchen, which wasn't in fact on. Her two children, Emma and Jack, were slumped in the sitting room, legs lolling over sofa arms, eating tortilla chips, bored, whiffy-socked, half-watching *The Simpsons*.

Older than me, more practical, more sensible, more dependable, and more like my mother in every way, Bella was Mum's perfect company and comfort. They moved about the kitchen in sync as they spoke – Bella in her Sunday best: navy hoodie and tracksuit bottoms, hair scooped back into a bun; Mum more formal in cashmere, pearls and tapered slacks – knowing what to do, how to do it and when, whereas I just got in the way. I was an irritant, a tsetse fly, as Joe used to say.

The table which Mum had set minutes earlier was already in a state of disarray; a brush matted with brown hair and a copy of *I Can Make You Thin* had somehow made their way on to it, and Addie was rearranging the table settings, moving along the bench on her knees, putting one fork at a time in her mouth as part of her quiet game of make-believe. Mum tried to clear some space for the roast potatoes and broccoli. Rosacea had flared up in a butterfly pattern around her nose as it did when she'd been rushing. 'Gosh, it's like an oven in here,' she said, when I complained of feeling cold, using the back of her hand to brush a stray hair from her eye. She always suggested Sunday dinner but you could tell that she had begun to find it too much work. She'd have been far happier snoozing in front of *Midsomer Murders*.

I tried to divert Addie by making rather unconvincing noises of pretend interest when she handed me several small dull objects to admire. I wondered if there could have been someone somewhere in the world sitting, as I was then, holding an acorn, a small plastic fish and a toy shark. When you spend a lot of time on your own and in your own head, you contemplate such things.

Emma joined us in the kitchen. She slid along the bench seat, punching her chewed, half-varnished nails on the keyboard of her iPad, her pale face concealed by her unwashed hair. She kicked her legs against the table leg in a zombie daze, but a slight grin was detectable on her face as she knew she had our attention. She wanted to look miserable. She hated being thirteen. She wanted her parents to be divorced. She dreamt of being an orphan.

Bella disappeared with a plate of chicken for Jack who was still watching TV.

'Did you hear that Wendy O'Brien had a baby boy?' Mum asked, picking at some broccoli.

'*Mum*. Yes. I was the one who told you,' I said, then tried to soften my tone by smiling. I was irritated by other people's good fortune when I was having such a miserable time and further irritated by my mother reminding me of their happiness.

'Oh, yes. Well it's great news, isn't it? Though I'm not at all sure about the name.'

'Hector.' We said in unison to Bella, returning now with Jack who had his hand between his legs, but insisted he didn't need a pee.

'Such a strange choice. Hector. Sounds like a bad cough.'

'Do a down dog,' I said, cajoling my child who, bored of eating, had slipped down from the table. Of course she refused, only assuming the position, shooting her little bum in the air, when we'd all given up looking at her. Then she cried because no one was watching.

There had been a time, pre-children, when family dinners were for adult conversation and politics and great howls of laughter, but now they were always halting and disjointed and no one was ever sitting at the same time.

Mum was trying to tell us about the itinerary for her next trip, a five-night break in Paris with a few girlfriends to see a special exhibition at the Louvre. Her children and grandchildren were continually interrupting her, not listening and even leaving the room as she read, but she was used to this sort of distraction and it never deterred her. 'So then on the Friday evening we're going to a restaurant in the Latin Quarter that I've never heard of, oddly enough.' This *was* rather odd for someone so ridiculously well travelled.

'What's it called?' Bella asked; she'd stayed in that area before.

'TBC,' Mum said, showing us where it was printed on her itinerary.

'Restaurant TBC – Mum, that means to be confirmed.' We all giggled about this, even Mum, while shaking her head and benating herself for making such a silly mistake.

'I've been so bad this week,' Bella said, picking a walnut from the top of the coffee cake, popping it into her mouth, clearly suffering a combination of Sunday evening melancholy and postprandial guilt.

'Me too. You know I've put on half a stone since Joe left.' Both Bella and my mother regarded me as slim and were therefore affronted whenever I mentioned weight or diets in front of them.

'Never mind. Tomorrow's another day,' Mum said, drumming the flesh on her thighs with her hands then flinging her head back, shaking her hair behind her.

She was up again and looking for teacups in the cupboard when I started feeling sorry for myself. I knew that she was deliberately making as much noise as possible because she was irritated by the sound of my voice and was attempting to drown me out. Bella's expression was compassionate but she had one sneaky eye on her iPhone. Actually I didn't blame either of them. By now I was boring myself.

This was the time of the evening when Bella and Mum would take out their diaries and begin discussing childcare arrangements for the coming week.

What had always, for me, been a tedious half hour of checking and scribbling in and crossing out, now had an added dimension. Mum's travel plans had become ever more frequent and adventurous, making us feel rudderless without her and a tiny bit resentful, never acknowledging that as two hefty middle-aged women, we should be quite capable of looking after ourselves. And sensing how bereft we still felt whenever she was gone, she couldn't help feeling guilty and neglectful though it didn't dampen her excitement about her next trip. So, on they both went, chewing pens, flicking through pages writings things in, crossing things out.

'Leave that. Honestly, pet,' Mum said as I loaded the dishwasher, trudging from table to sink, to bin, scraping leftovers, earning silent brownie points over my sister because for once I was helping and she wasn't.

'You know what you should do?' Bella was advising me as she struggled into her coat and tried to motivate her kids into action.

'I know what you're going to say – get a lodger and get rid of the dog.'

'No, actually I was going to say join a toddler group in your area.' I pulled a face. The thought filled me with dread – it was dull enough talking about kids with my own friends – how much duller with people I didn't even know. 'Or go to a cafe in the mornings.'

'Yes,' Mum said. 'That's a great idea. Get Addie to take a nap in her buggy, get a coffee, a quiet corner, a book.' They had clearly been discussing my situation, were concerned about my growing reclusiveness, but they weren't letting on.

I tried to visualise this suggestion. What sort of cafe did they mean? I felt tense at the thought of self-service, of waiting in a queue, under pressure to order using the correct terminology (tall for small, light for less coffee) then to find a table that was clean and well away from the toilets and other human beings, somewhere I wouldn't be knocked into or pushed against, and what book to read? Or maybe a magazine?

'Come on, guys. We have to go.' Since having children, Bella always had to go. I had a fierce longing to stay where we were, to stay part of that tight family unit. The light, the warmth, the scent of the house, the same smell I grew up with, the dread of the drive home. Mum gave me a box of chocolate hearts as she led us to the door – they'd been given to her as a gift from an old lady she drove to and from bingo. 'No, no, you take them. I don't want them,' she said, ushering everyone out.

'Change is possible.' The ticket machine said.

I carried Addie in my arms through the empty car park, footsteps echoing, imagining that at any moment someone could come up behind us and do something dreadful. Maybe I wasn't even on the right row. The thought that we might be there for hours made me panic. I felt for my phone in my pocket. Took it out.

'There it is, Mama!'

'Such a clever girl,' I said, breaking into a run, Addie bouncing in my arms, when I saw the clampers beside my car.

'Hello! Here I am. Sorry. I'm just leaving.'

'You won't be going anywhere, love,' said a bald man, kicking his foot against the flat front left wheel.

'I don't believe it.'

He despatched another, quieter, foreign, man to a garage to blow up my spare tyre, while he set to work on removing the burst one.

I stood by, making inane comments and asking silly questions, hoping to appear completely inept so that they would continue helping me. Men loved to be needed. I should have needed Joe more.

When the tyre had been replaced, I thanked them, told them I was poor, bit my lip and dug my hand into my pocket. 'All I have are these chocolate hearts,' I said, flirting. They didn't want them. The bald guy said he didn't like chocolate, the foreign man said nothing, just smiled and waved his hand as he walked away.

On the road home, I fought the feeling that the replaced tyre was not secure and would, at any moment, roll out in front of me. It frightened me that my child, asleep behind me, trusted me so entirely. Driving at night was like driving in a dream, the endless flashing lights like a giant pinball machine. I sat right forward in my seat. I couldn't see anything with clarity. I felt reckless, imagining that I was leaving small, nocturnal animals – foxes, badgers, cats – dead in my wake. Whenever I'd overtake anyone, I'd glance in the overhead mirror to check that pedestrians were still standing, that cyclists were still on their bikes, dogs still breathing.

Halfway through Shankill, I felt a horrible whooshing sensation in my head and my heart and breath seemed suddenly very faint and far away. I knew the signs – I was having a panic attack. Eat a cold apple, I'd read somewhere. I had no apples, cold or otherwise, there was nowhere to pull in and I was too frightened to stop so I sang 'The Sun'll Come Out Tomorrow' as cheerfully as I could to distract myself and to stop the panic from developing. Somehow it seemed to work.

As I turned off Bray High Street, the broad blue Aircoach careered around the corner, forcing me into the very same pothole that I'd hit on the way out. 'Oh no, Mummy. I'm scared,' Addie said, jolted awake by the impact. The replacement tyre burst. I could feel the ragged rubber, the hard metal beneath as I tried to find somewhere to pull in. I reversed into a space outside the launderette, damaging the burst tyre further as I tried to ease back into it. I called my Mum for help, tears coming, as they always did, as soon as I heard her voice.

We sat in the darkness together while we waited for the recovery van, singing *Ten Little Indians* and eating the chocolate hearts.

I switched on the radio. The eight o'clock news.

A four-year-old child had been abducted in England by a man driving a jeep. I shivered at the thought of the anguish of the mother, at the terror and loneliness of the little child.

'Never, ever get into a car with a stranger, OK? Are you listening? Even if they offer you sweets or toys.'

'OK, Mama.'

She was silent for a moment, considering this.

'Well, I might just see what they'd got.'

A sudden loud knock on the window made me jump. Even with her bicycle helmet on, I recognised her – eyebrows fierce, angular, lips pursed – it was the woman who lived in the flat downstairs. 'Oh, hi,' I said, unheard through the glass, then I smiled, rolled it down. 'You can't park there!' she spat in at us. 'Can't you not see the yellow lines?' I had to change my expression mid-sentence. She was waving her hands around, looking furious.

'Sorry, I'm sorry,' I said, trembling. I didn't know if she recognised me and I was too embarrassed to say anything. I turned on the engine, watched her cycle away through the rear-view mirror, all lit up in her reflective gear, her sensible arm out to indicate as she turned the corner and disappeared. As soon as she was out of sight, I turned the engine off again and we sang Old McDonald till we ran out of animals. 'Stupid cow!'

'Come on,' Addie whined as we waited. 'This is too boring.'

'It's just crazy!' she said, a minute later, burying her head to disguise her smile at her use of a new phrase. 'It's a disaster!'

Where was she getting these words?

The recovery van was cartoon-like in its size and seriousness. 'Nee-naw, nee naw,' Addie shrieked, turning around and standing up on the front seat watching as it reversed towards us, lights flashing, lowering its long lip.

I lifted Addie up into the van with the strange man, then hoisted myself up into the cab like a cowgirl or biker, holding onto the black bar. The driver, in fluorescent dungarees and jacket, was dark, greasy, silent and seemed suited to the nightshift. There was something unidentifiable in white cellophane by my feet. I fought the awful fleeting thought that this might lead to our doom, held Addie tight around the waist as we set off. She was silent; transfixed by the strangeness of the situation. I kissed her curls and blew on her neck the way she liked me to – it sent her into a small trance of pleasure. 'Again,' she whispered, her hot little fingers closing around mine. 'Look, Mama, the moon's following us. It really is.'

When we pulled into the front drive, a woman I'd never seen before was standing, arms folded, on the doorstep. 'Oh, God, no. Not a canvasser. I'm not in the mood for this.'

'Looks like a Green,' the recovery man said. I took in her grey, centre-parted hair, the cloth bag slung over her shoulder, the walking boots. I was irked by her folded arms. She looked impatient.

'Hello, I'm Joy,' she said, walking towards us, one of her hips a little stiff, her hand outstretched. 'I saw your advert for a roommate? Looks like a bad time.'

There was a flurry of negotiations and slips of paper.

'No. No. It's fine. Come in. God, the place is a bit of state. I wasn't expecting a response so soon,' I said, yanking the key from the door. 'Stupid thing always sticks.' I was apologising, talking too much with panicky thoughts of unflushed toilets and dirty dishes in the sink, of bad smells, of being exposed.

Chapter Eight

Alfie sniffed out the stranger, circled her, slotted his nose in her crotch.

'You lead the way, good dog,' the woman – I'd immediately forgotten her name – said, sounding at home already. He pit-patted down the hall ahead of us, methane gas seeping from his rear end. Her accent sounded American; her windcheater and walking boots seemed to confirm it. She looked older than I had imagined a potential flatmate, perhaps in her late-fifties. And what a strange time to call around, eight o'clock on a Sunday evening. What was she doing in Dublin? I guessed at her profession – photographer, writer, artist – and pulled the bathroom door shut as we passed, not confident that it was quite ready for inspection.

I led her to the second bedroom, the room I was hoping to sublet. I still had to sort all of this out with the landlord, but I would, in the next few days. It looked grotty now, seen through another's eye. It was small and appeared even smaller with the floor to ceiling, vinyl fitted wardrobes – you had to inch around the base of the bed to get in or out of the room – and with it being still full of boxes to be sorted, towers of paperbacks that I had some idea of organising into theme or author order.

'Small is good,' she said, enunciating each word as she looked around. 'Oh, my, just look at all those candles. How wonderful.' She had her hands on her hips and was gazing at the top row of the book shelf, where I, having no other use for them, had lined up the dozen scented candles Joe had been given as a thank-you from his last client.

She unhooked her shoulder bag and flopped down on the bed, which Addie was bouncing on, excited to have a visitor in the house and at being up so late. She exhaled, grinned, looked around.

'I like it here, it's homely. Isn't it, little lady?' she said, turning to take Addie in. 'Oh, my, aren't you a pretty one? Such a face. And look at the Celtic ring in those eyes.'

This made Addie shy; she buried her head in her shoulder then sought out my arms. 'It still needs a lot of sorting, we've really just moved in.' I said, lifting my little girl and encouraging everyone out of the room. 'Let me show you the sitting room. We've got a great balcony.'

Before I could explain or apologise about the lack of furniture in the room, the emptiness of which made our voices reverberate around the white-washed walls, she said, 'There is such a sense of peace in here. A real feeling of calm.'

We climbed out onto the balcony, all three of us, followed by the dog. She seemed even more excited by 'the scent of the sea', 'the gorgeous trees' around the square, by 'the wonderful Victorian houses' and by the playground. 'Oh, it's all so Dickensian. I can just picture being here in winter, with the fire going,' she said looking in towards the room and then back out across the square, 'and little kids making snow angels in the park.'

I didn't mention the Goths, how rundown the playground was close-up or that it was now, according to the woman downstairs – Irenka, I'd just remembered – besieged with rats. What was wrong with me that I kept forgetting people's names? Irenka was blaming our landlord's building work for having disturbed them from their underground nests. Addie and I hadn't been there in weeks.

Over tea in the kitchen, the woman – Joy Steinberg – told me about herself. She was Californian, born in Santa Barbara, and she worked as a visual artist – I'd guessed right twice. She took a spiral-bound notebook from her cloth bag and I flicked through it, bracing myself. Her passion appeared to be female pudenda like the erotic flower paintings of Georgia O'Keefe. I was in dodgy territory. I tried to recall Art Appreciation from fourth year in school.

'Em, so would you work mainly with acrylics?' Why oh why would I ask a question like that?

'No, watercolours generally. That's why I want to be in Bray, I want to focus on landscape work for a while. I have a little studio back in Santa Barbara which I show at yearly. Though I do some portraits too.'

'Oh, really. And, um, would portraits tend to be the head only or the whole body?'

'Well, they can be both, I guess.'

I reminded myself of something Joe used to say: always take a thought once round your head before expressing it. I stayed quiet and let her talk while I took her in. She had the look of a native Indian; there was a blankness to her face that was hard to read, her small brown eyes were shallow set and crinkled with age around the edges. She seemed a little intense, she would say something then stare at me as she waited for its import to sink in, holding my gaze for so long that I had to look away, or down, fiddle with my fingers. But then her face would broaden into a smile and within fifteen minutes of being in our home, Addie was sitting on her lap, playing with her Wampum beads.

I'd placed the ad online, on impulse one evening when Addie had

fallen asleep early and I'd been feeling lonely and worried and broke.
And though she had turned up without contacting me first, I had a
good feeling about Joy: she seemed to like children and dogs (I
imagined walks and art classes) and she was single so I wouldn't have
to put up with canoodling on the couch and, best of all, she would be
out all day at a studio she'd rented in Bray.

Joy moved into our flat the very next night, too late for the pasta I'd
prepared – not great to begin with, it was stodgy and cold by the
time she arrived, with endless bags and questions and confusion
about parking. She was too alive, too awake, so ebullient about
everything that it was hard, a physical strain, to raise my voice to
meet her level, but my whispering seemed to calm her; suggested
imminent bed and sleep.

I lay in the dark of my bedroom that night, unable to sleep,
needing the loo but too nervous to venture to the toilet for fear of
those awkward nocturnal encounters that come with bathrooms and
new flatmates. The bathroom, which was between both our
bedrooms, had a frosted glass panel in the door, which showed if it
was occupied at night and made going to the toilet both visible and
audible.

I could hear shuffling and squelching sounds coming from her
room. What was she doing in there? Obscure Kundalini yoga poses?
Nailing small mammals to the floor? I rummaged about in the bedside
drawer for the small see-through bag Dr Percy had given me, 'to be
used only for emergencies'. I popped a pink pill from its plastic
capsule and bit it in half between my teeth. I swallowed it with some
water, put the remaining half back into the plastic bag and into the
drawer, turned the lock, turned my pillow, sank my head on the
delicious cool of the underside, settled, sat up again to check on

Addie, and sank back wondering whether I'd made another big mistake.

There. I felt it again, that shooting pain in my chest, near my heart, ouch! It was worse when I breathed in. What the hell was wrong with me? I tried deep breathing to slow down my heart rate, had a go at the Valsalva manoeuvre – pinching the end of my nose and blowing out, letting my ears pop.

Addie had been watching me as I'd got her into her pyjamas that night.

'Mama?'

'What is it, cheeky monkey?'

'You need to fix yourself up.'

'What do you mean?'

'That's why because you're broken.'

Chapter Nine

The rain was still coming down, sliding off the slates, leaving them black and forming watery tassels from the parapet to the gutter. I could hear it as it gurgled and twisted down into the drains. Since the floods six months earlier that had left two people dead and cars floating head high in basements, heavy rain was no longer something to moan about in Ireland, it presented a real danger. Bella's neighbours had had to swim out of their house to safety. Their sloping garden backed onto the River Poddle and a graveyard beyond and the floodwater had rushed in and crashed through their kitchen window.

Joe had left the house in gum boots and what he called his 'leesure pants' (adopting American accent) during the subsequent clean-up. He'd offered to help his ex-girlfriend try to salvage some of her belongings from her flooded basement in the city centre. They'd gone in with torches, waded through mud, picked over old photo albums of their lives together, ruined furniture from the flat they had once shared. He was gone too long; it had made me vulnerable – for the first time since Addie was born I was focusing my attention on him. He had enjoyed reassuring me when he got back, wet-eyed and dirty that night. And I had seen him again as I had when we first met. After his bath, we had sex for the first time in weeks.

Outside the wind was picking up. The plastic windmill Addie had stuck in the dead hydrangea pot on the balcony whirled around in pretty multicoloured spirals, faster than either of us could blow it. It was four-thirty; almost evening; it had been dark since we'd got up.

How I loved days like these. Days when things were cancelled, when fires were lit and shutters closed, when no one was doing anything, when the weather forced us all indoors, providing us with permission to sulk, to not get dressed, to watch *Lady and the Tramp* under a blanket at four in the afternoon if we wanted to.

I squeezed Addie's soft thigh, trying to get her attention.

'Do you think there could be a little mouse in a little boat sailing down the river outside our house?' No response.

'Maybe he's in a little matchbox boat,' I carried on, warming to my story.

'Using teeny tiny matchsticks as oars,' she said, humouring me. She fell back into her television trance and worked on her sucky blanket. There was a whistling sound to her breathing, I'd noticed it a few times lately. Her blanket was so snotty and ragged it looked like something from the Famine – I'd have to sneak it from her one of these days and wash it, get rid of all those germs. I tried to slide it away from her, still wanting to play, but she yanked it back with an irritated little sound and inched away from me. I played instead with her pigtails. Joy had done them for her. There was always something different about her when she'd spent time with Joy; a plait in her hair, her clips adjusted, her scarf rearranged around her neck. Subtle improvements, subtle little criticisms. Once, without saying a word, she took Addie from me, wiped her chocolatey mouth and did up the toggles on her duffle coat.

It felt like a small, silent victory to have the flat and the television to ourselves. When Joy was about, it was either not switched on at all or there as background colour and noise which we talked over and

I was still shy enough around her to feel that I had to comment on everything that we watched.

I looked around me for diversion; I stretched over Addie to grab the *Vanity Fair* from the coffee table, reminding myself to cancel my subscription ASAP. Joy's reading glasses, folded on top of its glossy cover featuring a naked Kate Winslet (also sprawled on a sofa but looking somewhat more seductive) slid off and onto the floor.

Her possessions were everywhere: her walking jacket wedged between the banisters; an alien sheepskin slipper in Alfie's mouth; a brush in the hall, tangled with dead grey hair; her facecloth draped over the bathroom sink.

Addie and I had snuck into the kitchen for breakfast that morning. 'Let's whisper,' I'd said and she'd walked on tippy-toes beside me along the corridor. I was very much hoping to have our cereal in peace. But she was with us moments later, embracing us and lingering by the toaster to give my back a prolonged rub, telling me, as she caressed my ribcage, that she'd heard me snoring in the night, that I had kept her awake. I imagined her hand ceasing its circular motion, sliding up to my neck and tightening around it.

Joe would have hated all of this. His throat used to constrict when he was forced to eat in front of anyone who wasn't family. Once, badly hungover, he had gagged over his breakfast when Mum was telling him a story about some cousins of hers who had bought a house on a hill and had moved further up the hill, then further up the hill again. He'd had to escape to the back garden to regurgitate.

Joy had gone into the Royal College of Surgeons that afternoon to sketch dead foetuses in jars. Maybe this was where I'd gone wrong. Never in my life would I have chosen to spend a Saturday in the city sketching dead foetuses in jars when I could have been buying jeans at Topshop. 'Perhaps I can return with a more soothed spirit and proceed,' she'd said as she'd left.

But life in general was much better with Joy. She put out the bins every Tuesday, Joe's old job, and took Alfie for long walks on the beach and up to the top of Bray Head – he'd return so exhausted and happy that he was a dead dog for the rest of the day. She filled the fridge with healthy, organic food. She baked pies. She lit scented candles in the evenings. 'Shut *up!*' she said one day in disbelief, when I told her the washing machine was broken. She took her domestic duties seriously. She gave me shoulder massages, did arts and crafts with Addie and took her to the beach to collect shells and stones. She was calm. She was even-tempered. She was a homemaker. She was so much easier than Joe.

'We needed some rain and now the spirit needs a little shelter,' Joy said as she towel-dried her hair in the sitting room that evening, having returned from her afternoon of sketching dead babies.

'Now this is the sort of cupboard you'd expect to find a skeleton in,' she said, referring to the Indian cabinet in the corner of the room, though she had surely noticed it before. She leapt two feet in the air when she opened it to find a human skull leering back at her.

It had been given to Joe by a friend who was moving to Australia and didn't want to chance taking it through Customs. Joe was fascinated by the sensation of holding the head of someone who had passed away – someone he never knew and never would. There was a power to it he said; the inner sanctum of someone's existence. He suspected keeping someone else's skull was illegal, which made him even more delighted to have it.

'I can tell you miss your dear husband terribly. Would you like to share what happened?' I didn't think real-life people said things like this, but this was how Joy spoke. She was curled beside me on the sofa now, her kind, small eyes regarding me with intensity. She had made us a snack of hummus on gluten-free crackers which I wasn't looking forward to. I'd watched as she'd licked her thumb liberally after coating each one. She gave her fingers one final sticky lick and rested her hand on my knee.

'You know I was once married to a wonderful man. Our wedding was so unique. Akihiko danced down the aisle towards me, naked aside from a fig leaf. Don't you think that's amazing? We're still very close. He helps to run the gallery I show in. I still love him and I still get sentimental,' – she said, emphasising each syllable as if it were a word she didn't often use – 'when I think of our past together.' I tried to listen to this with a straight face, wondering what on earth I was going to say in response. 'You said Joe was in advertising?'

'Yes. He was a creative at Browne & Davison. He was good at his job but bored. He said he found the superficiality of what it was about a little soul-destroying. What he really wanted to do was make films – he'd made a few short ones and was working on scripts for some feature-length ones. Then his advertising work dried up and he couldn't get funding from anyone for his ideas.'

'Oh, don't I just know all about it? It's so tough for us creative souls.'

'Well, he wasn't being one bit creative in the weeks before he left. He was just hanging around the house playing computer games, searching for lost glasses, chopping wood. And then he got his mushroom idea. He started growing mushrooms everywhere, in every cupboard I opened, on every shelf. He said it was a business that could really take off, he just needed a year to get it started.'

'Oh, my! How enterprising of him. What kind of mushrooms were they?' Joy loved the sound of this. Perhaps I should have shown a little more enthusiasm for the venture.

'I don't know – shiitake, I think. Anyway, he was upset that I didn't believe in his mushrooms and I got fed up finding them everywhere. They were rooting all over the place, swollen, useless fungi.'

'He was just trying to find his way out of the recession. I admire him for that. It is a tough puzzle indeed that we face in these times.'

Joy had a way of making me tell her too much; I found myself revealing things that I hadn't even been honest about to myself. Our intimacy was making me uncomfortable, as if we'd shown each other our private parts. I didn't want to think about private parts, but trying not to think about them made me think about them more. I thought for a moment that she was going to kiss me.

I tried to explain what had gone wrong between us. I told her how our evenings had once been about books and art, wine and long beach walks, and always home in time for *Coronation Street*. And then when Addie arrived how all my emotional energy was used up by my curly-topped, cherry-lipped, glassy-eyed, rubber-thighed little leech; I became a shrivelled old carcass, a muslin cloth between my boobs where my cleavage used to be, and Joe a stranger I'd sometimes pass in the night on my way downstairs for bottles.

I told her how I used to get irritated with him in the evenings when all I wanted to do was relax. He had a habit of bringing up some topic of conversation, often a continuation of one we'd had maybe three or four weeks earlier. 'So what did your Mum do?' 'Do about what?' 'Did she buy that table at the auction?' he'd ask, when I was just about to discover who the murderer was. 'You'll think I'm mad but isn't he quite like your sister Bella?' he'd say about some middle-aged black man he'd see on TV. 'No, I mean how? In what way?' I'd ask, intensely irritated. He'd happily talk through an entire thriller and stay quiet for the adverts, never the other way around. He was silent at breakfast, or at restaurants or at parties or on long car journeys but talkative when Addie wanted my attention or last thing at night, in bed, where he liked to read whole passages of his book aloud.

We'd had a fight on the day he left. I hadn't said anything about him putting Addie's clothes on over her pyjamas, but I couldn't stop myself when he gave her the saliva-stained cup with the cruddy black grime at its base – the one which held our toothbrushes – to rinse out her perfect pink bud mouth.

He'd flung the cup across the room. Then he'd called us cunts. Five minutes later he'd climbed down the stairs on all fours because he wanted to see what it felt like to be Alfie. I thought that meant that everything was OK.

'And you have no clue where he's gone?'

'England, I've heard.'

'And what about Addie?'

'Nothing.'

'Really? But what do you tell her when she asks for her Daddy?

'I tell her how many other people love her.'

'Oh, my. You poor, poor dear.' She leant forward and gave me a hug, flattening herself against me, her wiry grey hair tickling my chin.

'You know what you need?'

'A good shag,' I waited for her to say.

'Faith, trust and a sense of humour.' She held me and I sobbed in her arms, cameras panned away and above us and out through the skylight window, sad music played, credits rolled.

Chapter Ten

I walked over to the sitting room window in a somnambulant daze. Why did Joy keep leaving the windows open? I liked them shut. I kept the blinds down; she pulled them up. It was cold and foggy and not yet light: the great chestnut tree opposite us was still in shadow, street lamps still shone. A shift worker, head down, rucksack on, walked along the empty street below, echoing; a Filipino nurse from the Cherry Glade dragged a wheelie bin across the gravel next door.

Joy was up and out and in the playground already, setting up for the first day of her boot camp. The idea had come from a woman she'd met at a one-day yoga workshop called 'Winds of Change'. She'd returned home breathless and buoyant declaring that it had been an 'awesome' day. God, how I hated that word.

She was kneeling on the grass near the gardener's shed unpacking Swiss balls and resistance bands from a box. Juliette Larson was on her way round the corner, in a pink Juicy Couture tracksuit, all wiggly bum and jiggly breasts, her yoga mat rolled up under her arm, looking somewhat tentative about the whole idea and the location. Solly from the drug dealer's house on the corner was carrying dumbbells back and forth on the grass; Irenka was doing hamstring stretches by the cherry tree. Soon Joy had them all lined up on the grass in front of her, demanding sit-ups, push-ups, jumping jacks, five laps around the path. Outside the park, watching them, holding the railings while balancing on his unicycle was Billy Flynn, the boy I'd seen burning the butterfly, resident bastard, ne'er do well.

It hadn't been difficult to enlist the locals. In the month that we'd been living together, Joy had got to know everyone, the way Americans do. Juliette, a big-eyed, blonde and giggly teenager, who lived next door to us with her father, Mr Larson; Dylan Freeney, who Juliette had begun seeing, without Mr Larson's permission. He was the boy we'd met that first day in the playground – chatty, confident, handsome. 'Such a sweet child,' Joy said about him, everyone did. Solly, full-time dope-head, part-time sculptor, who was squatting in the derelict house on the corner – overtaken by weeds, concealed by leylandii – full of ideas that would never be realised; he was a dreamer, not a doer. Joy had also signed up with a local volunteering group and the first job she'd been given was to help residents of the Cherry Glade to cross the road to the park, whether they wanted to or not. And she'd discovered a much handier shop two streets away, outside which a homeless man stood silent, head bowed, all day. She'd begun taking sandwiches and snacks down to him.

'We are privileged and we are blessed,' she said to me the other evening, placing a single stone from Bray beach on her bedside table. She had just returned from an afternoon of painting on the promenade and declared herself to be 'filled with art and with the sound of water and boats'.

From the safety of his position at the other side of the railings, Billy began shouting military commands at Irenka who was attempting star jumps, all stiff and out of time. 'Up two three four, round the park and ask for more. Up two three four. Up your arse, you little whore.'

Irenka curled her lip at him, tugged her knickers out of her bum, told him to get a life. I thought his dad would thump him when he came up and stood behind him; instead he put his hand on Billy's shoulder and encouraged him away. I hadn't met his father yet but I'd seen him in the playground, chatting to the local teenagers – he seemed to have a way with them, they listened when he spoke.

'Dus kicking down the cobblestones, looking for fun and feeling groooovy . . .'

Addie was behind me in the kitchen, standing on a chair by the sink, refilling the dog's bowl. He slid off the sofa, stretched, paws extended on the carpet, walked a few paces, stopped for a frenetic bit of scratching and wandered over to us.

I helped Addie off the chair and offered to carry the bowl but she wanted to do it by herself. 'I'm the persons in charge of Alfie, bemember you promised?' I didn't but I probably had, I promised her a thousand things daily.

The glint of the metal made it difficult to judge water depth and as soon as she started to move she knew she had filled it too high. She held it with both hands and carried it with the careful concentration of a child, the short distance from the sink to the sitting room floor.

She dropped the dish down on the carpet, causing a slurp of water to rise over its lip. It splashed against her hand and soaked the layers of newspaper beneath.

'Help, Mama!'

'What do you say?'

'Joy says I actually don't need to say please. That's why because it's not rude.'

'It is terribly rude!'

'And Joy says I don't need to say thank you or hello to each others if I don't want to as well.'

Things between Joy and I had begun to get a bit bumpy. The other day when Addie said she said needed a pee, Joy took her – didn't ask me or anything, she just took her by the hand and led her away. 'If it's yellow, let it mellow.' I heard her say as they re-emerged. 'But Mama says that's disgusting,' 'Oh, baloney!' Alfie pit-patted in after them and had a lovely long drink from the bowl. Later that same day she told me off for shouting at Alfie, who'd just eaten the family-size bar of Green & Black's chocolate I'd been looking forward to having with my cup of tea. 'I assume you'd never shout at your child that way,' she'd said, as she strung monkey nuts onto a thread for Addie to hang from the balcony to encourage birds – 'or maybe even squirrels from the park,' she'd added, getting the child excited.

One Monday I was under my bed, searching for my missing ring – a ten-euro one bought by Joe from a stall in Mexico five years earlier. And what did I find? A pair of Joy's Camper walking shoes. What were Joy's shoes doing deep under my bed? And yesterday she ordered a book on Amazon called *Do I have a Daddy?* for me to give to Addie when the time was right.

But the biggest problem we had was around food. After a few uneasy weeks of parallel cooking or looking after ourselves, we had come to an agreement about meals. Joy would cook every other night: healthy vegetarian dinners such as 'Joy's lentil surprise' which bubbled with unidentifiable things and made everyone flatulent for the evening and on through the night. Cheese is bad for children, Joy said. As is milk in porridge. And yogurts – 'You know you should really wean her off them. And I wouldn't give her tap water, if she were my child. There's too much fluoride in it, in this country.' A little later while they were doing yoga together on the floor, she rubbed the BCG scar on Addie's arm and said, 'In America, they don't leave marks.'

And yet here I was, two-faced as anything, lying on the sofa trying not to giggle as Joy sat over me, still flushed from the success and exertion of her boot camp, performing what she called the Bowen manoeuvre, to help me relax. 'It's a simple yet incredibly powerful technique that helps relieve all kinds of pain,' she said, as she prodded different parts of my back with her fingers and thumbs.

After the first set of moves, she strode out of the room, slamming the door behind her. She was gone a long time; I started to wonder if she was coming back. Ten minutes later, she was thundering towards me. I felt another nudge of her finger on my ribs and off she went again. And so on it went, for at least forty minutes.

'Oh, my, but you're uptight!'

'Am I? Maybe I am. My neck feels a little stiff.'

'You're tight all over, dear heart.'

'Addie had me up early, I probably just need some sleep.'

'What you need is to get outdoors. Breathe in that glorious sea air! Loosen up. Relax. Join my boot camp.'

I nodded and tried to reply though my mouth was sunken into the velvet seat.

'Oh, it's splendid out there today. It's like fall in Vermont. The chestnut trees are turning gold and red gold and just look at that deep, deep-blue sky – it's almost too much.'

I attempted to sit up to see for myself, but her hand was firm on my back so I mumbled consentingly from where I was lying.

'You know there are some awesome women in this community,' Joy said, as she pressed her finger into my skin. 'You should really take the time to get to know them. Irenka was just talking about having a meeting to clean up the playground for the kids, why don't you join her? Ask her about it? Look.' This time she let me move. I sat up. We both stared out the window.

'She's still over there, why don't you go on over and talk to her?'

I considered this the next time she left the room. The day was beautiful and I needed a reason to escape from my therapist. The next thing she had planned was a sinus drainage massage.

'Trust me. I am part of your path,' she said, hugging me like a proud parent as I put on my coat.

I waved at Irenka through the railings but she didn't see me. I quickened my pace to be sure I would catch her while she was still there – she was not the sort to linger, she moved swiftly from one task to the next. As I came in through the gate, she set off in the opposite direction. I passed a group of teenagers in a dark huddle around the picnic bench, lank-haired, hunched shoulders, rolling up cigarettes, and followed her, embarrassed, as she pursued a small boy on a bike.

'You've dropped something, young man!' she shouted, catching up with him, eyebrows fierce.

The boy stared at her, then at the ground. He checked his pockets for his pellet gun and pocket money, then looked back at her, confused.

She took the Kit Kat wrapper from behind her back and held it up in front of him.

'Is these not yours, eh?'

He shrugged, held out his hand.

'In the bin, please.'

'Erm, sorry, Irenka?' I said, a little out of breath having followed her all this way.

'See? Look at this, Eve,' she said. We watched the boy drop his bike, schlep off to the bin with his sweet wrapper, lift its wooden lid and toss it in. 'I get very happy when I see that. And what about you? You missed the boot camp, you lazy girl!'

I made the usual excuses about Alfie, bad knees, Addie.

'Oh, and what are the swings for? Can't she not play while you work out? Come on, Eve, you could do with some!' She gave my backside a sudden, sharp, quite painful slap. Then she hooked her arm around my shoulder to embrace me. 'I'm joking with you!' I smiled, reddened, got myself free.

'I just wanted to say that I might join you tonight, if that's OK? Joy said you were having a drink to discuss the problems with the playground?'

She clapped her hands. 'Excellent! For our ladies' night out! Oh, it will be fun! And not all work, eh?' She dug her elbow into my ribs.

'Sumita, you know Sumita?' she said, counting on her fingers, 'She will be joining us.' I had seen Sumita before, a small, round Indian woman who came to the playground every afternoon, always dressed for the cold in woollen hats and scarves and oversized coats, and always with a blanket, a rucksack of food and flask of coffee. She'd settle on the grass till closing time, trying to exhaust her hyperactive child, smiling and chatting to everyone.

'And Sophie said she'll be there,' she said pointing at her house, my favourite on the square, a lovely villa-style home with pillars, raked gravel and a duck egg front door. Sophie was the beautiful mum – shiny-haired, glossy-lipped, long-limbed – I'd watched with envy from the sitting room window, arriving and leaving with two blonde children and endless shopping bags. 'And Belinda,' this time Irenka gestured with her hands over her stomach to show that she was a large woman. 'Billy the Bastard's mum, you know her? Works in the library, she's a nice lady. Don't know how she manages with that boy.' Then she listed off a dozen other local women I didn't know who had all promised to be there.

I got out of the bath that evening. Joy's dressing gown was hanging over the frosted door. Something like knickers or tights were stuffed in its pocket. Something too intimate; it made me hold my breath. God, I was silly about this stuff. She was right, I needed to relax. I did two hundred squats in front of the mirror. Joe always smiled at this, looking like a skinny sailor as he bobbed up and down, mimicking me. And my Facercise exercises, my futile battle with age. Then I changed into my Spanx, put on my face and my dress, and tottered into the sitting room.

Joy was on the floor with Addie, both of them were leaning back against the sofa, Joy with her long, bony, high-arched feet crossed on top of the coffee table, Addie's tiny ones crossed identically beside hers. Joy was folding white printer paper to demonstrate how to make an Origami swan. Her student was wide-eyed, riveted.

'Oh, my dear! But don't you look pretty?' she said, admiring me as I clip-clopped self-consciously into the room, fiddling with my hair and tugging at my too-tight dress.

'Don't worry, Mama.' Addie was up, art abandoned, and straight over. 'I'll hold your hand so you don't fall off your high shoes.'

I lifted her into my arms and carried her over to the fireplace where we looked in the mirror together. 'When I'm a big lady and you're small can I have that sparkly dress?'

'OK, sweetie, now don't pull at it.'

'And can I stay up early to watch a cartoon?' I nodded, touched the tip of her nose with my finger.

'Thank you, Mama,' she said, delighted with herself. 'You can borrow one of my broken pencils if you like?'

Seeing me pull on my leather jacket, Alfie perked up, skittered after me, scratching the wooden floor. His nails had scraped into the wood everywhere, leaving indelible crisscross patterns. Nathan wouldn't be happy. I told him 'No' and he lowered his head, took a few steps backward – the poor old mutt was used to this sort of rejection. I pulled the front door behind me.

The Hibernia Inn was a large pub near the train station, at the quiet end of Bray, a five-minute walk from the flat. I'd never been inside, but from the outside it looked quite imposing and grand. I passed much livelier pubs as I walked along the seafront towards it and although it seemed pretty unexciting when I arrived, I was happy to see there was somewhere to sit and it wasn't too noisy. I was becoming middle-aged before my very eyes.

There were two men up on bar stools, silent, just watching a match. I ordered a gin and Slimline tonic. The barmaid wasn't Irish and didn't understand; I repeated what I wanted more slowly. One of the men leant over to murmur something in the other man's ear, probably something about my accent or my get-up. This time the barmaid nodded, told me to take a seat.

I sat down, stood up again to take off my coat, changed my mind, put it on again, checked my nose in the mirror of my compact, checked my nails, my phone. The waitress arrived with my gin but no tonic. 'Is OK?' she asked when I looked puzzled. 'You say slim lime right? I cut as slim as I could.' I thanked her and giggled to myself, sucking on the remarkably slim, alcohol-filled lime while I waited for the others.

Seconds later, Irenka stormed in, out of breath, in a Tidy Towns T-shirt, fleece jacket and jeans, a large plastic folder in one hand, a Tesco reusable bag the other.

'Funky,' she said, examining me. 'Leather is very much in at the moment, but aren't you a leetal bit glamorous for a meeting, no?'

Mortified, I asked her what she was having. 'A hot tea for me,' she said, rubbing her hands together. 'A bit of a coldish wind out there.'

Gradually the other women arrived. I'd got it wrong. They all wanted tea, aside from Belinda Flynn, who, spurred on by me, ordered a vodka and Coke and a packet of crisps. She ripped the packet open and put it in the centre of the table to make it communal, leaning forward every so often to take one with a very dainty pinch, holding her hand over her mouth as she munched, then rubbing her fingers together to get rid of the crumbs, but you just knew that if she'd been by herself she'd have held the bag in her hand, shovelled them in and run her crispy fingers down the legs of her jeans or along the velveteen pile of the seat.

Sophie cancelled at the last moment with a text because her husband was working late. Sumita was the last to arrive, with quiet apologies and explanations. 'Rashi won't let me leave. She wants all the time to be with me. Never with her daddy, only me.'

Although visibly disappointed with the poor turn-out, unable to fathom the apathy of her neighbours and now with far too much paraphernalia for the motley crew assembled, Irenka began the meeting with gusto. She sat forward in her seat as she handed out the agenda, literally spitting with enthusiasm as she talked about the playground and what needed to be done. She held the floor while we sat quietly and listened. We were trying not to find the whole thing farcical and we were all a little nervous of her. Her laugh was an unpredictable, noisy cackle that went on for far too long and made the rest of us uncomfortable, forcing us to giggle along with her but without the sentiment. And she flipped from this to furious without any warning.

'They are animals! Leetal pigs. Did you know a young girl told me to fuck off to my face when I asked her to sit at the picnic bench in the correct way, you know, without her shitty shoes where people have to sit.' She continued to exclaim and complain and clearly wanted us to join in.

An hour and a half later, she was only on point three of her agenda. Belinda and I were on our third drink and beyond bored. Even Sumita, ever the diplomat, had a vacant look in her eyes as Irenka showed her pictures she'd taken with her iPhone of graffiti and rubbish and possible perpetrators.

'So how are you settling in?' Belinda whispered. 'I've seen you out with your little girl. You're gorgeous together, the two of you, so you are.'

I smiled and thanked her. I could see how the meeting, the evening itself, was awkward for her as a mother, wanting to help make the playground safe and clean but knowing that her own child was its biggest problem. No doubt she wanted to protect him, defend him, or both.

'Listen, I just wanted to say about my son, about Billy. I know he's given you a bit a trouble,' she said, as if she knew just what I'd been thinking.

I reassured her, but the last time we'd been in the park together, he'd been bad. He'd been running around behind Addie, holding onto the hood of her coat. And Belinda had come up to me and told me to keep a closer eye on *my* child. The cheek of her.

'Look, I'm not saying he's perfect. I know he has a few odd quirks, but he's not a bad lad. His dad moved out a while back and he's after taking it very hard.'

I told her I understood, terrified that I might have all of this ahead of me with Addie.

'At least he still sees his dad, I saw them together earlier, they look like they get along.'

'He hasn't seen his dad in months. Ah no, Jesus! That's Frank you're thinking of.' Irenka looked up from her phone and scowled at us – we were supposed to be considering the next item on the agenda.

'We'll be with you in two minutes, ladies – we're just getting some drinks in,' Belinda said, nudging me out of my seat and urging me up to the bar.

'He's a youth worker – Mimi's boyfriend, Dylan's dad,' she said, scrambling onto a bar stool. 'Me and Frank, can you imagine! For Christ's sake, he's only a child.'

He did look quite young, now that I considered him, with his side-parted hair, bomber jacket, always moving around Bray on his bike.

'God, you must hate being shadowed around the place by someone like that?' I asked, signalling to the barmaid for another round.

'Sure it was me who asked Mimi to ask him, but he already knew all about Billy from the kids at the community centre. I spent five hours with that lad in A&E the other week, after one of his stunts, and it was really quite enjoyable, things were that bad at home. I was able to read a magazine without worrying about what he was up to or where he was. Frank seems to be getting him back on track, he's got him back at school for one thing. So, how are you settling in, then?' she asked me again, seeming keen to move on now that she'd got Billy out of the way.

'It's taking a while to get used to and we don't really know anyone, but we'll be OK. And the sea is magical for Addie,' I said, hearing my mother's voice in my head.

'I don't know if you're looking for work but there's a job going at the library – part-time maternity leave cover, if that's of any interest to you?' Joy must have put her up to this. Is this why she had encouraged me to join them in the first place?

As I paid for our drinks, I tried to visualise myself working in a library; it was quite a comforting prospect. Of all the half-careers I'd had before Addie, my years of freelance proofreading and editing, even though I was pretty hopeless at both, had been quite lucrative and would look relevant on my CV. Addie would be starting school in September so I'd have a few hours free every morning. She'd got a place in a lovely little Church of Ireland school after a year of sending cards to the principal and a shotgun baptism. She had been so outrageously rude to the reverend the first time he met her, I was worried he might refuse to welcome her into his church. She kept shouting two words – 'ice cream!' – over and over, while he tried to talk to her in a very gentle voice about God and I gripped her ever tighter around the waist. Afterwards Joe said he'd felt like shouting 'ice cream' too.

'Let me know if you're interested and I'll put in a word for you,' Belinda said, sliding off the bar stool.

Back in our seats, Irenka asked Belinda to look at the photos she'd taken of the graffiti – watching her reaction to see if she recognised the handwriting. 'Pure poison,' she said as Belinda poured Coke into her glass. 'I hope you don't let Billy drink that crap.'

Sumita shoved herself and her belongings up the bench beside me.

'I'm sorry, I forget your name? And your child. What is it?'

'Eve and Addie, Adelaide.'

'I've seen you in the playground. I live at Frank's.'

'Now I'm confused. You're Mimi?'

'No, not like that! I'm Sumita,' she said, getting giddy. 'We only rent rooms from Frank and Mimi – my husband, daughter and me.'

She told me she and her child shared a bed and that her husband slept in the other room because he liked to watch football and needed sleep because of his job.

'My child very bad sleeping. She is all the time kicking, kicking and sometimes wetting too. Does she sleep, your little girl?'

'Yes. She's pretty good, though she likes to get up around five.'

'And now, no sleep for me anyway because I have a very big problem. A very big decision to make.'

Sumita explained that she'd been offered a childminding job for ten Euro an hour but that she would have to take two buses to reach it as she didn't drive. If she took this job for a year she might have enough, along with her husband's savings from his job at Aldi, to put a deposit on a house.

'My big problem is my employer won't let me have Rashi with me. If I send her back to India for a year to my family, I could take the job. But now the lady says she will pay only nine Euro an hour as I would need no more if I don't have my child to feed.'

I wasn't sure why she was telling me all of this but I wanted to try and help.

'Why don't I ask some of my friends if they need a childminder? You can't work for a woman like that.'

'And what do you think of these, Eve?' Irenka interrupted, putting her phone away. She handed me some bright-yellow stencils inscribed with the words 'Pick it up!' above a little illustration of a dog. She'd made them herself and intended to put them along the path in the playground. I felt they had been designed and printed just for Alfie.

'Now, ladies, a little bit of fun,' she said, having tossed some stencils to each of us, as though she were dealing cards. 'I cannot claim this idea as my own – the wonderful Frank suggested it, but I can't wait to know what you think.' She sat forward to hold our attention and explained Wednesday evening games.

'So this is how it will work. Each Wednesday evening from five to eight o'clock we will organise games for the kids – rounders, red rover, chasing – and we will provide refreshments for them afterwards such as sausages, orange squash, those sorts of things.'

We listened and nodded, made encouraging sounds.

'Each week we would take turns to supervise,' she said through narrowed eyes as if she could already see a few of us skulking off and her being left to run the damn thing on her own.

And then, with all the formal business over, all the items ticked off her agenda, Irenka rummaged in her reusable bag.

'Listen, ladies, I have gone earrings mad! This pair is very delicate and dainty.' She passed several samples of her homemade jewellery around the table and we all murmured encouragingly. She was the ultimate multi-tasker – the sort of woman who would do her pelvic floor exercises while peeling potatoes and talking on the phone. Clench. Release. Clench. Release. She was making all of us weary.

'Since spikes are very much in fashion I used them in this pair of earrings, one must fall in love with them, or not,' she said, eyeing each of us in turn, as if we dared not to. 'And look at these. Red is in. Every shop I look into is displaying red dresses.' Belinda purchased a pair of glass pearls and dangled them from her ears playfully. I pretended to be searching for money in my jacket and bag, Sumita said maybe next time.

At the end of the evening I left Irenka and the other women – they headed down to the promenade to stick Tidy Towns posters to lampposts. I was all ready to make excuses as to why I couldn't come with them when I realised that I hadn't been invited to that part of the evening.

I took off my high heels and thumped along Station Road in my tights, walking in the centre so that no one could leap out of the bushes and grab me, not that anyone was inclined to. It was really quite freeing. I was humming 'Hakuna Matata' from *The Lion King*.

A black cat passed me, but he was going the wrong way. What did that mean, if anything? I saluted him, then blessed myself. I was definitely tipsy.

There were lights on in my landlord's new house and a pile of timber stacked up in the front garden. It made me think of Joe. He'd carry great hulks of wood home after his walks with Alfie. He'd dry them out on the radiators and around the Aga and they'd smoulder in our fire in Sandycove for months after.

Just as I looked in the window, Nathan happened to be looking out, his face lit up by a bar of fluorescent light above him. I waved and walked on a few feet, feeling horribly self-conscious, then I stopped, put my high heels back on – excruciating – turned around and hobbled to the front door. There was no bell yet so I knocked.

'Off out or coming home?' he asked, resting his elbow against the door frame, airing a large sweat patch around his armpit.

'I was just at some boring old residents meeting down on the beach, I'm heading home now.'

'You're looking good,' he said to my cleavage. I'd folded my arms in awkwardness but also to accentuate what was left of it.

'Thanks,' I said, ears burning, giving it the quickest of glances too. 'So how come you're still here? It seems a bit late for a builder?' That was none of my business. I needed to calm down.

'Ah, I'm on my way now, was just checking that no water's getting in and that my subbie did what he was meant to.' He explained what a subbie was when I looked confused.

'I often call in late at night when they're all gone to check everything, then I'll ring them first thing to give out.' I'd never seen him this close up. He had ridges, like parenthesis, on either side of his mouth; they made me think of a ventriloquist's dummy. His face was broad, but not too broad, and craggy with deep furrows and lines. He was also ridiculously tall and broad, like a real life Action Man. I only came about as far as his belly button. And he smelt delicious.

'So, what can I do for you?' he asked, taking a packet of cigarettes and a lighter from his shirt pocket. He pulled one out, cupped his hands to light it, squinted up at me.

'Well, two things really. Did my last rent cheque bounce by any chance? I mean there's no problem paying or anything. It's more of a cash flow thing.'

'Well if it did, I didn't notice. Don't worry about it, OK?' One down, excellent.

'And, well, I've been meaning to tell you. God, I really hope you won't be annoyed about this but I've taken on a lodger. Is that OK?'

'Thought I'd seen a strange woman coming and going, right enough.'

'She's a bit of a hippy but a very clean and tidy one. She's American, loves the flat and keeps it beautifully, and—'

'Relax. It's not a problem, OK?' he said, leaning over and giving my arm a quick rub. He seemed so laidback, so agreeable, so unlike Joe. 'God, the poor woman sleeping on that old mattress though. I'll try and sort something more comfortable.'

'Well that would be brilliant, but she hasn't complained. She's glass half full about most things.'

'No problem at all, leave it with me.'

I was smiling too much. How many bets I'd find a nice black thing at the top of my front tooth when I got home. I wished I wasn't looking so tired, I felt cross-eyed, grotty. I knew I was talking too fast. I could smell cigarettes on his breath. Whatever mood I was in that night I found it sensual, rather than disgusting.

'You can have some of them if you want?' he said, seeing me look at the timber. 'They're no good to me. I'll drop some round during the week.'

'Really? That would be brilliant! Thank you,' I said and went over on my heel like a fat slag as I walked down the gravel path.

The sitting room was empty, the fire guard in place, the embers dying in the grate, Joy's patchouli oil lingering in the air. Alfie looked up, ears alert, his tail bashing against the side of the armchair, but he was too comfortable to move. I sat on the sofa and felt that disconcerting feeling you get when you sit on a seat still warm from someone else's bottom. I got up again, dragged Alfie's collar over his head, listened to the silence and went to check on my daughter.

I tried to open the bedroom door but something was impeding my entrance. I pushed against it and peered round the frame, praying the noise hadn't disturbed her. 'Shush,' I heard a cross voice say.

There, lit up by the night light, sitting forward on the nursing chair – the one that my mother gave me when I was first breast-feeding – frowning with concentration in her horn-rimmed glasses was Joy.

'Isn't she a serious beauty?' she whispered, not looking up at me. 'You almost woke her, oh but she's a tired little angel. Still in dreamland,' she said, smudging pencil marks with her thumb, eyebrows arched with intent.

'Don't let me disturb you,' I wanted to say back, but I was too stunned. She was sketching my child as she slept.

'She's a bit wheezy, isn't she? Listen,' she said then, holding her hand in the air to command silence. 'Maybe you should try a few drops of Olbas Oil in a bowl? I have some in my fanny pack, if you want to go get it?'

'All right,' I said, wincing at the expression.

'How do you think it's coming on?' she asked, following me out to the landing and holding it under the light. It was irritatingly detailed and accurate – she must have spent several nights watching my child as she slept. 'I'm so happy you like it. It's a gift for you, dear heart.'

Chapter Eleven

Ruth was standing so close to me by the wash handbasin, I could hear little stomach pips and churns. I knew what she was waiting for, but I kept my head down and held my hands under the running water for far longer than I needed to. I didn't want to do this today. I didn't want to stand cheek by cheek so that she could compare our two faces in their reflection to see whose foundation was more dewy, whose jawline firmer, who had fewer wrinkles on their forehead.

I rooted through my grubby bag, holding it close to me, trying to conceal its torn, make-up-stained lining. I pulled out a half-eaten lollipop, coated with hair and fluff, a chewed nail-whitening pencil and some baby wipes, located my lipstick, smeared it on, applied some concealer under my eyes, fiddled with my hair, smiled, frowned, gave up.

'So you don't like my new top then?' Ruth asked, turning away from the mirror to face me, straightening her taupe-coloured, Margaret Thatcher style blouse over her stomach. She was the sort of person who wore strange and unflattering clothes which told you she was at the cutting edge of fashion.

'I do. Why would you say that? I was just going to ask you where you got it,' I said, irritated with myself for sounding a little scared.

'Nah, it's OK. You didn't mention it. I probably can't get away with it any more,' she said, studying herself again in the mirror, this time adopting her special mirror face.

'Don't be silly, you're waif-like.' I said, thinking that she'd put on a few pounds round her middle since the last time I'd seen her.

We left the Ladies and made our way to the bar while we waited for our table.

This dinner – no kids, just the two of us, at an expensive city centre Italian – had been anticipated and talked about for so long it couldn't hope to live up to expectations. All our breathless plans for summer: the picnics; the barbeques; the few days away; the tennis lessons; camping with the kids, had somehow never materialised and this evening was the first time we had seen each other in over three months.

Our conversations were always so frenetic and relentless that we would afterwards joke about being dizzy and hoarse. Tonight, we were out of kilter. Ruth had been expecting me to be as lost and miserable as I'd been for the last seven months so that she could spend the evening continuing to cheer me up and go to bed feeling happily reassured about her own intact relationship and life. But I was in irritatingly buoyant humour and this made our friendship less straightforward. The ticket collector at Tara Street station said I was the best-looking girl he'd seen all day and that that was saying something because he'd been on his shift since seven a.m. And I'd got the part-time job in the library. I was also quite excited about the Wednesday evening games – the inaugural one was the following night. We were finally starting to settle into our new neighbourhood.

As we were led to our table we went through the usual two second rigmarole of offering and declining the more comfortable, better-vantage-point-for-people-watching bench seat by the wall, though we both knew that it would, in the end, be Ruth's backside lowering itself onto its cool, expanding leather, reaffirming the status quo of our relationship.

Despite her fragile state, Ruth was looking well. Sexy, in a tired way: her eyes were hooded and had the look of last night's make-up; her mouth seemed swollen from lipstick and drink and her voice, already husky, sounded deeper than ever, her laugh a little dirty. She'd scooped her hair into a messy up-do and she was wearing a colourful, tribal-style necklace I hadn't seen before and liked, but the waitress had already asked her about her earrings and I didn't want to compliment her further – why on earth not? What was wrong with me? With us?

Our conversation had got off to a bad start; I'd given her the news that a mutual friend of ours had decided to get a puppy. This was irritating to Ruth on two counts, one, that I'd been in contact with Caroline, who was in fact *her* friend, and two, that yet another of her friends was getting a dog.

We both put our heads down and read the menus in silence, aside from the occasional 'mm' sound, playing with our hair the way women do.

'I mean, I just think it's ridiculous,' Ruth said after ordering seafood linguini, sinking her teeth into some buttered brown bread. 'I'm the biggest dog lover of all of you, even bigger than you to be honest, but all of you have dogs and I don't.'

'Ridiculous. I think it's really for Jules.'

'Jules?' Ruth said, irked further by this intimate abbreviation of *her* friend's little boy.

'I mean Julian,' I said, my voice sounding a little high in my throat. 'It's just easier for Addie to say. Caroline says he's been asking and asking.'

Ruth was shifting in her seat and not enjoying herself. 'Aren't you going to have any bread?' she asked, passing me the basket when she noticed I hadn't taken some. Translated, this meant don't tell me you're on a diet again and I really think you have some sort of eating disorder.

'So, what was I saying?' Both of us did this more often since kids, lost our train of thought several times in an evening. Some of these thoughts came back after prompting or remembering, others were recalled only on the journey home, some were unuttered, lost forever in the mush of our middle-aged minds.

It was raining that night and a leak had developed in the ceiling just above where Ruth was sitting; drops began hitting her cheek. We both stood and lifted the table along a few inches; Ruth moved her bag to the other side of her, but still the drips came, now splashing onto the red leatherette seat. The waitress was concerned and apologetic but explained that the restaurant was fully booked that evening and there were no other tables available.

'So, any news?' We both knew what she was referring to.

'Nothing. Not a word.'

'God,' she said, but I knew she wasn't one bit surprised. She'd known Joe was gone for good before me, everyone had really. For a long time I hadn't realised that it hadn't worked out between us, I thought he was a little down, that he just needed a break from us, or rather a break from me, from my bossiness and whining. I'd waited two days for him to arrive back, pour himself a large whiskey and say sorry for calling us cunts. When this didn't happen I'd spent three weeks phoning everyone: his family, his friends, his old agency. And then he'd phoned me one day and agreed to meet up – in the car park of Killiney Hill – but he'd been like a stranger, utterly detached, staring ahead at the woods. He'd had a gift for Addie; a little book on wild birds still with its price on it. 'She doesn't need me,' he'd said.

'She only ever wants you, to help her with her clothes, to change channels on TV.' He said he was of no more use to her, that he wasn't cut out for parenthood and that he was of no more use to me. I hated when he spoke this way – that was a big part of the problem, all his navel-gazing and self-pity and yet I knew what he was saying was true. And that was pretty much that. I knew once he'd made up his mind about something there was no way to persuade him otherwise.

'Bastard,' Ruth said.

'I know,' I agreed.

'Unbelievable.'

'So, anyway.'

'So.'

'So. How's Addie?'

'Great. Adorable.'

'How are your two?'

'Fine. Sasha's amazing. I'm not boasting or anything,' Ruth said. I braced myself, looked down at my dinner, 'but I started toilet training her three days ago and she hasn't had one single accident. Not one. Isn't that incredible?'

'That *is* incredible. But would it be something to do with leaving it quite late?' I asked. Sasha had just celebrated her third birthday.

'And Steve is in love with Ruby. I mean, he's actually in love with her. The other day he spent four hours doing a diorama with her. I know, I didn't know what a diorama was either,' she said, seeing me look confused, 'but he did this brilliant ocean scene with octopuses, sharks, seaweed, all suspended from the top of an old shoe box. It was amazing. He is so brilliant with her. You should see them together.'

It felt somewhat disloyal to be so unreservedly complimentary about her partner, not just because I didn't have one anymore, but even before Joe left we would only say positive things about our other halves to compensate for having just been cruel about them.

I sometimes made up faults or exaggerated my irritation with Joe just to make Ruth feel better about some shortcoming of Steve's. And if I went too far in agreeing with her that it really was appalling to switch off your phone when your wife was trying to contact you because you were in the pub and wanted to stay there for the evening, she would start defending him and I would back down. It was a tricky balance but a rhythm we both understood.

'They are amazing though, aren't they? You won't believe what Addie said the other night.' She interrupted my flow by running her finger across her top teeth to indicate that there was lipstick on mine. 'I was reading her a bedtime story when she took the book and said she wanted to read to me instead. And this is how she started: "Once upon a time there was a little story that lived in a book."'

'Wow. That's so cute,' Ruth said, but her eyes were glazing over; she dug a spoon deep into the sugar bowl.

She also didn't believe me. Addie was often so quiet in her girls' company. Sometimes she said nothing at all, just ran after them and copied them in awe.

So I didn't tell her my bigger boast about Addie being able to stand on one leg for fifteen seconds without holding onto furniture. She was bored of listening to me go on about my child, when she knew her children were so much better. And she knew she couldn't push any further about Joe. Her own relationship was steady and loyal and I envied it. 'We're really growing into each other, like a comfortable pair of slippers,' she'd said of him last time we met.

She was great after Joe left. Practical, on my side. Helping me move things, enduring long evenings of tears and analysis over one, sometimes two, bottles of red wine. There had been no pity, no fawning, no slipping of particular books about break-ups, no emphasis on the 'are' in 'how *are* you?' And that was a relief compared to most other women who would tilt their heads to the side when they saw me and say things like, 'You're still one of us you know, don't worry, we still love you.'

'You know, he really shat on you from a great height,' she said, blinking her eyes rapidly, waiting for me to open up. I'd heard her say this before. She seemed to think it was a good expression, but to me it sounded repulsive. I know she thought there was someone else – I'm sure everyone did – but it wasn't what I wanted to think about or hear. So back to the kids I went.

'It's so sweet that Ruby and Addie will be starting school the same week, isn't it?'

'Is Addie really starting this year?'

'You know she is. Her Montessori teachers said that she's ready.'

'It's just that Ruby seems so much older than her, doesn't she? I mean she's just so much more articulate and mature. I'm worried that she'll be bored. She knows all her letters and numbers.'

'She's already reading, that's great.'

'No, of course she can't read. I suppose Addie can read, can she?'

'Well, no. I'm not saying that—'

My face was hot with irritation and hurt but I didn't have the stamina for a row. I felt flabby and spotty by the time our main courses were cleared. She had triumphed, she was king of the castle. I was lost. My one attempt at a big word – discombobulated – was seized upon, challenged, laughed at and finally spat out, like the one odd-tasting mussel that was discarded and put her off the rest of her linguini. And then there she was, standing up at her chair at school, pointing at me and roaring with laughter, toffee from break time still coating her train tracks, because I couldn't spell the word 'because'.

And then neither of us could think of a thing to say. For five deeply uncomfortable minutes the only sounds coming from our table were the clink of cutlery and quiet mastication. This had never happened before and made both of us uneasy.

We were also being made to feel sober and dull by the girls on the table beside ours: shiny, bleached-blonde women, glistening lipstick, Brown Thomas bags wedged between their legs, who were either leaning in towards each other whispering, or sitting back on their seats, mouths thrown open, teeth bared, howling at some outrageous revelation.

All evening I'd wanted to tell her the compliment the ticket collector had given me, but I knew it was a blatant boast and that it would bug the hell out of her.

I stuttered it out at a time that seemed natural – we were talking about getting our first grey hairs and how often to dye them. I said it as if I'd just thought of it. And why shouldn't I? She'd been releasing little boasts, like odourless flatulence, all evening. 'Yeah, right!' she said. 'As if.' She slapped her hand on the table, then looked at me earnestly for a second, 'Sorry, of course, maybe you were the best looking. God, what a compliment. Must have made your day.' I was embarrassed by my boast, by my one-upmanship and ready to pay *her* a compliment to regain equilibrium.

'Your hair looks really good,' I said, wiping a bit of sweat from my upper lip. She saw straight through it. 'What do you mean?' she said, grabbing a bit of it. 'It's a mess. I'm getting it done this Friday.'

I excused myself and went to the Ladies. When I returned it was with a sense of purpose, beginning my sentence before I was back in my seat to make up for the awkward moments of getting reacquainted – best thoughts always come when you're on the toilet. I confided in her, having decided on the train in that I would not. I only did it to improve our evening, to give us some sort of connection, a reason to lean in towards each other. I told her about Joy sketching Addie in the dark. I didn't want to make a thing of this incident because I knew as soon as I did that Joy would become another problem that I would then need to sort out.

'And she keeps telling me Addie has asthma. It's so irritating. I mean I think I'd know if my own child were sick. I even Googled Munchausen by Proxy; imagine if she were making Addie ill?'

Ruth looked underwhelmed. She took out her lipstick and reapplied it without needing a mirror. I felt dirty, it seemed gratuitous. At the end of the revelation her eyes were still wide with expectancy, but I had no more to say. 'I think that's very creepy,' was all she said, and then, that she was 'bursting'.

I had a need for closeness, for some sort of statement of friendship, for sympathy, for help, for some warmth that just wasn't there that night. I felt a soreness at the back of my throat.

After coffee I saw it in her face. The exhaustion, the pursed lips, sentences hanging with a vacant 'so, anyway'. No more questions, no more anecdotes. Then she took out all her irritation with me, with our night, on the drip that was still coming from the ceiling.

The next train to Bray was in twenty-seven minutes. This information was almost unbearable; I was cold, I had nothing to read. I put two Euro in the vending machine which it swallowed without giving me the bottle of mineral water I'd wanted. I paced up and down the icy platform doing the things you do to stave off boredom: walking on my heels; not stepping on the lines; looking for mice between the tracks; imagining other passengers naked; checking and rechecking the time on the board.

When the Dart finally crawled into the station, I pushed forward in an un-lady-like manner, such was my need to get warm and to get a window seat on the sea side. Not that I would see much sea at that time of night. Joe was always astounded at how I couldn't work out the geography of where I needed to sit to get a seat on the sea side and how ridiculously often I got it wrong. Astounded but charmed, I'd always assumed, by my silly, sweet, lousy sense of direction.

It was only when I'd found a free newspaper and got comfortable: bag on the floor beside me, coat off, only when I'd brushed against the knee of the person opposite me and had looked up to say sorry, that I realised how attractive my fellow passenger was – dark, large, broad-legged, scruffy-haired.

I tried my old trick, finishing the complex crossword incredibly quickly, filling in the squares with any old nonsense, to make me appear intelligent. I wasn't sure if he was watching. His legs were so broad that I had to sit neatly to prevent them from touching, which on two occasions they did.

Although she wanted me to forget all about Joe, Ruth didn't want me to rush into anything new either. She had seen this pattern all my adult life – always starting a new relationship as soon as the last one had ended. She never came out and said it, but I knew how she felt from the way she talked about other friends of hers who had done the very same thing: making poor romantic choices, being bad judges of character, going for the wrong men, like Joe, just because they didn't want to be on their own. 'It's good to be single. I was for years.' She had always been this certain with her advice.

I slid forward in my seat until our knees touched again. I felt him look up but I didn't apologise or move. I kept them there as I filled in the final squares.

Chapter Twelve

A triumph. Unprecedented. An astonishing result. Adjectives had been tossed around the national airwaves since ballot boxes were opened at the first count centre, in Athlone at seven a.m. that Friday morning. Meltdown, wipe-out, tsunami for the old regime and a record number of seats for the new. They would get down to work straight away. State cars would be abolished. Ministers' salaries cut. The callers to Joe Duffy on RTE One were not complaining for once.

All the citizens of Bray, it seemed, were out that sunny afternoon: Old Arthur trundling along the path ahead of us in his motorised wheelchair, off to do errands on the high street. A happy train of red-bibbed toddlers from the Montessori chattering on their way home from ballet class, Pamela pulling weeds from the brickwork of the Cherry Glade. She and her hermaphrodite sibling, Edie, both in their eighties, lived four doors up from us. Pamela was out and about every day with her brush and barrow, sweeping, cleaning, chatting in her Ugg boots and mini-kilt, always tending to others homes while neglecting her own – her way of keeping abreast of developments on the square, and a means of staving off loneliness. Edie was quieter, more reclusive. I'd seen him/her once waiting for a bus outside Bray station – a man from the top in a flat cap, glasses and short white hair, but large breasted under a sweater and hippy in high-waisted slacks.

Juliette Larson was squatting behind a car parked just outside her house, in last night's city shorts and diaphanous top, waiting for her father to leave for his Italian class so that she could sneak back indoors. I smiled and sort of winked at her as we passed, hoping to convey from my expression that I'd been there before, that I knew just what it was like and that her secret was safe with me.

Mr Norman, the unacknowledged head of the residents' committee, a cheerful, round-faced man who lived in the house directly opposite the park's entrance, arrived at the playground with two bowls of cocktail sausages. I didn't know him well but sometimes we would chat on our way to the beach, him with a towel tucked under his arm, Addie tucked under mine. He swam in the sea every day to keep busy, to keep strong, while his wife faded with Alzheimer's.

Irenka took the bowls from him and added them to the assortment of refreshments she'd arranged on the picnic bench on top of which she had spread a checked red-and-white tablecloth. Her own contribution was bottles of juice which she had taken some time to individually label in case a child put one down and picked up another by mistake, thereby risking contamination.

'OK, listen up, everyone.' Frank, the youth worker, was balancing on the see-saw, the residents of the square and their children in an attentive group around him.

'No child is to be excluded from joining in any game,' he said, following his finger along the line of rules which Irenka had typed up, trying to keep the sheet from folding over in the wind. 'So, none of that crap, OK?' he said, looking over at the teenagers. The girls were giddy and identical in fashion, blonde hair extensions, fake tan, pink tracksuits, lip-glossed and giggling about something so 'random' it was 'super embarrassing'. The boys had their hoods up, were chewing gum and spittle, or sucking on cigarettes, not sure of anything, wanting a grab at something fleshy or a glimpse down a top.

'Where was I? OK, so any attempt at excluding a child will not be tolerated. And piggy-backs are forbidden. As is play-fighting. Any questions?'

'Sorry, Frank, can I just add a rider to that please?' Joy said, reaching out for his hand, forcing him to pull her up onto the see-saw beside him. She laughed as she wobbled; he held her around the waist till she'd steadied herself.

Irenka wasn't looking one bit happy about these adults' flagrant violation of park rules (no child over twelve was permitted to use playground equipment) and she had no room left on the table for Joy's gluten-free vegetarian dumplings. Her husband, Donal, a swivel-eyed, curly-haired, furtive little man, was a fat lot of use. He was kneeling on the ground beside her deliberating over whether to sort through a pile of luminous bibs first or to separate plastic cones. He'd been reeled in by Irenka's foreign accent when they'd first met and had been paying the price ever since.

'Hide and seek is not permitted,' Joy said, hands on copious hips.

Oh, for crying out loud.

'It promotes secretive play. The nature of the game is to not tell anyone where you are or what you are doing and that's plain wrong, isn't it?' she said, asking the children. And then looking for adult agreement, 'Hide and seek asks children to hide and not come out; telling children to hide so they can't be found. That is not what we want, is it?'

We were all too bemused to argue. Sophie and I shot conspiratorial glances at each other, then she was pulled away by Ben – a beautiful, white-haired, brown-eyed little chap. I had never seen him still, he was always running, his parents always tearing after him, trying to catch him and keep him safe. He was forever trying to escape and they were forever in pursuit. Sophie grabbed hold of the hood of his coat as he took off down the hill. Once again I examined with envy the perfectness of her figure. The curves and lines, the way her jeans were a little loose around the thighs. She had buttoned them with ease – no squeezed in flabby skin, no red indentation marks – and as she grabbed Ben before he scooted out of the park and under the wheels of a passing jeep, I could see there was even a shadowy space at the top, between the material and her concave stomach.

'OK, everyone into two teams! Let's go!' Frank said, resting his hand for a moment on Joy's shoulder then jumping down and jogging into the centre of the park. 'You going to join us?' he shouted at Billy who was watching from the far side of the railings.

'You're all right,' Billy said, sitting up on his saddle and cycling away. Belinda was working late at the library that evening and had warned him to keep out of trouble.

'Red Rover, Red Rover, we call Addie over!' Frank shouted, winking at my little girl.

'Mama, Mama! Come with me!' She was beaming, frightened and excited at the same time.

We took off running, hand in hand, Addie and me against the playground, against the world, her little face animated, looking ahead and then every few seconds up at me, her hand rigid with determination in mine. We pushed against the linked arms of Frank and Dylan and we made it, or at least they let us through, knowing that defeat would make Addie cry. We landed on the ground on the other side of the human wall, giggling, victorious.

'You run just like your little girl.' This was Dylan's mother, Mimi, standing beside me, cleaning the inside of her thumbnail between her teeth. I'd caught my breath and was back by the swings. She was a raspy-voiced, sexy woman with cropped blonde hair, in a fake fur coat. I'd only met her a couple of times, and on each occasion she hadn't remembered me. I considered my running style, recalling the slight limp I used to affect when I was a child; I thought it made me appear boyish, tough, suggested I'd been through a lot.

Now Dylan was playing five-a-side with his dad and some of his friends. When the ball rolled off course, across the path and down towards the flowerbeds, he let Addie get it for him. She ran down the muddy slope and straight into the daffodils that had been planted the previous week, picked it up and kicked it a few inches and not in his direction, but she shrieked with her sense of achievement and he cheered at her.

'He's very sweet,' I said to Mimi.

'Dylan's a dream child, so he is. Never given me a day's worry, not like that little minx,' she said, referring to her toddler who was coming down the slide head first; a cut above her right eye and holding a filthy toy dog.

'It's good to see him down here to be honest. He doesn't seem to be interested in football any more, it's all about girls now; all about Juliette.'

'I just saw her,' I said, stopping myself before I gave anything away. 'Is it quite serious between them?'

'As serious as anything can be when you're seventeen. Doesn't seem that long since he vomited when they played a video of a couple having intercourse in his biology class at his school. He was so innocent. I had to leave work early and take him home.'

I laughed. I liked her.

'But, God, it's causing a lot of strife – Billy Flynn is wild about her too, always has been. They were going together for a little while, but thank God she broke it off.'

'Really? I can't picture them together, the pretty, popular girl with someone like Billy?'

'I know, it's a strange one, isn't it? I think they got close when both their mams had cancer at the same time. They used to hang out together at the hospital while they had their treatment.'

Belinda had had cancer. Why had she not told me? Had she told anyone? Even Joy didn't appear to know.

'What sort of cancer was it?'

'Of the breast, for them both. You wouldn't have met Christina, would you? Well, she passed away when Juliette was only thirteen. Belinda beat it, but now it's back. The poor woman.'

I was still reeling from this, as Mimi went on. She was 'over-sharing' a little now, as Joy would say.

'It was sweet seeing them together, so it was, Billy and Juliette, playing Monopoly, cards, you know, that kind of thing, but I'm going back five years now, they were only kids. Then Juliette grew up overnight, the way girls do, and didn't want anything more to do with Billy. And when her mam died she went off the rails altogether, riding all around her, so she was. But this will make you laugh,' she said, moving nearer and clutching my elbow, 'Belinda phoned Juliette's dad one day, a few months after her mam had passed, and said Billy was crying himself to sleep at night he was that in love with Juliette and did he think they could maybe go out for dinner together? They were both only thirteen years old, for Christ's sake!'

Her phone rang then and I heard a tiny disembodied voice say, 'Hey, Mam, can you call me back?'

'Sorry. That's the other one. No credit. The usual! Excuse me.'

I looked about for Addie. She was running across the playground, shouting at Ben who was charging the other way. 'No, let's go back to the sandpit!'

'Where?' Ben said. He stopped, changed route, ran after her.

'The sandpit, where we first met.'

She sounded just like an old movie. 'You wore blue,' I said to Sophie, seeing her laugh.

'All those years ago,' she said and we stood side by side watching our children in the autumn sunshine.

Irenka was clearing up the picnic table while talking to the bicycle-mounted policeman who'd just done a circuit of the park. She held her hand out towards me to let me know she wanted a word when she'd finished with him. Now she was striding towards us. That day there was not a single thing she could criticise about my mothering: no sucky blanket, hair clips in, fleece top and padded coat, new shoes.

'Excuse me, Sophie,' she said, while gripping me by the forearm. 'Listen, Eve, I need a big favour. Donal and I are going to London in the morning, he has a job interview. Could you please open the park for me?' I was a little surprised that she trusted me to do this job, but I agreed – I couldn't wait to tell Addie. 'You are my superstar,' she said. She hugged me, handed me the keys and explained the procedure in too much detail. She and Mr Norman were the only residents of the square who possessed keys to the park. Quite how this had come about, no one was sure. They liked the control but not the tiresome responsibility, so between them they had drawn up a new opening and closing rota and had asked the council for more sets of keys. Residents of the square would from now on take turns with this duty – women in the mornings, men doing the more challenging night shift – picking up rubbish and keeping an eye on the teenagers.

My name hadn't been included on the official list, perhaps they were seeing if I were up to it.

I sought out Sumita. I had some drugs for her. She was talking to Jayani, a plump Sri Lankan ten year old, while eating the wax from a Babybel cheese that Irenka had just given her, having never seen one before.

Beside them, two little boys had buried themselves beneath a pile of leaves with just enough space for their serious faces and ginger hair. They were perfectly camouflaged in autumn shades of russet, saffron, gold. Rashi was busy covering their faces, making tiny exhales of effort as she did. This frightened the boys and made them cough and soon the three of them were bickering. Park diplomat Jayani went to sort it out. 'And wad did you say to heem?' she asked, serious and cross, before taking three lollipops from her pocket and distributing them.

I waited till then to pass Sumita the small cellophane package I'd been fingering in my pocket. 'These will help you sleep – they'll make you feel so calm. I'd take them every day if I could.'

She examined the pink capsules in her hand. 'Thank you, but I cannot take them. My doctor says these are very bad thing. Now I am thinking what we need is bunk beds.'

'Bunk beds? Maybe I could find some for you, I could email around my friends if you'd like?' I said, putting the Xanax back in my pocket, feeling a little hurt by her rejection and also a little addicted and unstable. Never mind, all the more for me.

'That would be very great,' she said, then she told me about her three goals. She wanted to one day buy a house – she had told her husband that this was a good time – she wanted to learn how to drive and she wanted to have another baby. I told her as much as I could remember about our attempts, tried to reassure her.

The little bugger from number three had found a branch and was trailing it around the path in one hand, holding onto his scooter with the other. He collided with Rashi and knocked her to the ground. 'Sinita,' one of the other mums shouted. They all seemed to have problems pronouncing her name. Rashi had slipped on the dried mud edge of the playground and was bleeding; a group of older boys, including the little bugger, stood over her pointing and laughing.

'They always give her a bad time. It's the same at school; she's not happy there,' Sumita said.

'You should hear what the older ones call me sometimes!' It was Lars, the German, up off his bench, helping Rashi to her feet. 'Nazi, Kraut, Adolf.'

I breathed in his whiskey breath. He was more buoyant than usual today, he'd just been offered some extra work up in Ardmore Studios.

Frank and Joy wound up the games with clapping and shouting and orders to clean up. It was dark and starting to rain and the kids were sweaty and exhausted. Addie bit me because I wouldn't do roly-poly down the hill beyond the gardener's shed. 'Joy said it's a good thing to keep crying and crying,' she said when I told her to quit her crocodile tears. 'That's why because you have to get it all out.'

As we waited to cross the road for home, I noticed Arthur outside our front gate. He was sitting in his motorised wheelchair, his neck leant over to one side. One cloudy eye was watching us from under his woollen hat, too high on his head, exposing a bald bit above his ears. He looked like he needed our help.

'Could you give me a push, missus?' he asked, talking into his chest.

I'd met him before though I wasn't sure he recognised me. My favourite part of my job in the library was travelling in a van, driven by Pete, the head librarian, once a week to deliver books to nursing homes around the area. The residents of the Cherry Glade liked large-print romance and audio books best, but Arthur loved Westerns – 'better than the telly,' he said. 'John Wayne, *Laramie*, the *Lone Ranger*.'

Pete said he smoked one hundred cigarettes a day. 'He must get up early for that. One hundred a day, sure that would kill you dead. Bang-bang.'

'The battery's gone on my cart. Could you get them to open the door?' Arthur said, gesturing with his head. His hands were purplish around the knuckles and looked very cold. A large translucent droplet was hanging from his left nostril. I didn't know many elderly people, aside from the one my mother had become, but Joy had told me all about Arthur, about how he'd been born into a broken family and had been in care homes ever since.

I pushed him across the Tarmac as far as the ramp, talking a little louder and slower than usual. Addie trotted along beside us. I left them there, walked ahead and pressed the bell. A nurse from the north opened the door; I'd seen her before, a pink cardigan over her shoulders and a warm smile.

'Ach, Art, it's yourself. Hold on a wee minute and we'll get you sorted.'

We stepped into the warmth of the hall. 'Ach the wee dote,' she said about Addie.

Tired souls were slumped in a variety of chairs in the large room beyond where we stood, just hanging on, attentive nurses around them. It was bacon and cabbage for tea. 'What happened to your wee cart?' I heard the nurse say, as she pushed Arthur up and over the ramp and back into the solace of the home.

'Maybe we could come and visit Arthur again some day? Bring him some buns? What do you think, sweetie?'

'That's a good idea. He's my best friend.'

'What's it like to be a big lady?' Addie asked me once. 'What does it feel like in your head?' A bunch of keys, that's what I remember as a child. It was the most grown-up thing. And now I had keys to the playground in my hand.

I was a helpful, trustworthy member of the local community. I gave my jeans a quick tug as we passed Nathan's house, in case he happened to be looking out the window. He was. He waved at me and smiled. I smiled back, made Addie wave too. We finally belonged in Bray.

Chapter Thirteen

I undid the chain to the park, with some difficulty, and we pushed open the gates in unison, Addie and me, as if we owned the place. Alfie bounded in ahead of us, did the circuit, sniffing and peeing, then stood still in the centre of the grass, ears and tail erect, waiting for a non-existent ball to be thrown.

I looked around me in the stark winter light at the blackness of the branches, felt the cold coming up from the sea. Overnight the clocks had gone back and winter had arrived. I folded my arms, tucked my icy hands under my armpits. We'd make this expedition quick.

Little Miss Muffet pushed her buggy straight up the muddy hillock to the playground. Alfie charged after her, over his disappointment and back to his happy default setting, scattering crows as he ran.

It took the two of us twenty minutes to get him on his lead, the day we adopted him from the animal refuge. He was too excited to see us, leaping vertically behind his cage, desperate for human contact, desperate to be free. He'd been abandoned twice in his short life already, once as a puppy and again as a young dog. We'd gone to bed at nine o'clock that first evening, leaving him lurching from sofa to chair in the sitting room, unable to calm him, wondering if we'd done the wrong thing. We bought him a bed, which he humped for two days before eating, we took him to obedience classes where he was always top dog – walking beautifully, sitting, fetching, rolling over – until the class had ended and he pulled us the whole way home like two idiots at the end of a chain. He's the image of Robert De Niro, Joe used to say, the very same beauty spot on his cheek. He liked to sleep on his back in the armchair, his legs pointing up in the air, like cartoon roadkill. He was such a perfect caricature of a dog, he was like a dog in a dog outfit. I used to wish that he could have spoken to us, even once, to let us know that he was happy in his new home. We imagined his accent. Deep and American, Joe thought.

Once a substitute for all that we didn't have, when the baby arrived Alfie dropped right to the bottom of the pecking order. He got shouted at more often, more often ignored. 'Don't shake!' Joe used to say. 'He can't help it, it's what dogs do,' I'd say in his defence. 'Get down!' we'd both roar when he jumped up on us, arriving home from somewhere, because he was just so happy to see us.

'Keep your dog under control!'

There was a man and a child standing beside the swings – how did they get in? His hands were resting on his girl's shoulders. Both of them were very still.

'Come again?' I said, trying to sound casual and cool.

'Keep your dog under control.' The man, early-thirties, long-haired, handsome, leather-clad, was a grown-up version of exactly the sort of guy I would have snogged as a teenager in town. He jabbed his finger in the air and backed away from us towards the cherry tree, the one behind which all the kids peed.

'He is under control. He's allowed to be here without a lead.'

'Just keep him away from my kid.'

'He has no interest in your kid, he's nowhere near her! We come here every day, I live just over there.' I said, indicating with my finger, which he didn't follow. 'We have every right to be here. I open the gate in the mornings,' I said with some pride. Adrenalin was shooting through me; as I spoke I could feel it affecting me physically. I felt a weight on my bladder, on my womb.

'Just keep him away from my kid.'

'How dare you speak to me like that? Our dog is entitled to be here. Why are you being so ignorant? He's friendly. What sort of life lesson are you teaching your child, to be afraid of a friendly dog? I mean look at him, for Christ's sake.'

I forced him to follow my shaking finger as I pointed at Alfie who was reclining beneath a tree, attending to his testicles.

'Keep him away from my kid,' he said again and again.

'Come on, Addie. Let's go home. We don't have to listen to this nonsense.'

I was trembling with the injustice of it, with the shock of the fight, shaken by the sound of my own raised voice, stunned at how I'd shouted at him, at this complete stranger, who was just afraid of dogs or had had a bad experience with one at some time. The anger poured out of me. It must have been there, below the surface, biding its time, waiting for such a juicy moment.

'Look what special thing I can do,' Addie said, showing off to his little girl who had climbed to the top of the monkey bars and was peering down at her.

Addie grabbed hold of the bars and with quite a bit of effort lifted her feet a few inches off the ground.

'That's so easy,' the girl said, unimpressed.

'Maybe not when you're only three,' I said. 'Come on, Addie, let's go.'

'She's three?' she called after us, her eyes cartoon wide. 'She looks like she's two and a half.'

'Really,' I said, returning, standing taller, hating her. 'So, what age are you exactly?'

'Seven,' she said with some pride, getting to her feet as if to prove it.

'Well, you look six.' Ha! Put that in your pipe, you little cow.

'Why was that man talking so crossly?' Addie asked, on our furious march back around the square, unsure of what to do next. 'And why does she have up hair if she's a girl?'

'I don't know, darling,' I snapped. 'Girls can have up hair or down hair, can't they? We've been through this before.'

'What's after happening there?' Nathan was standing by the small boundary wall of his house, worrying a bit of wood with a crowbar. I wasn't going to go over to him; I was feeling too upset and too shy.

'There's a total d-i-c-k-h-e-a-d in the playground,' I shouted across, wondering if I'd spelt it right.

He hauled himself onto the wall to see for himself and walked along it for a while, his arms outstretched for balance, like a little boy. He stumbled when he jumped down and landed on our side. I pretended not to notice and tried to dissuade tears of injustice as I told him what had happened.

'I just don't want Addie to see that sort of aggression. Her dad used to lose his temper like that – shouting the same thing over and over. She's going to grow up hating all men.'

'You don't hate me, do you?' he said, leaning down and squeezing her round the waist and then, looking back up at me: 'Want me to have a word with him?'

Did I? Probably not. I found myself nodding all the same.

'OK, come here, boy,' he said, holding out his hand to take Alfie's lead. He crossed the road to the playground, the crowbar still in his free hand. Poor Alf didn't understand why we weren't coming too and stopped every so often to look back at us, head bowed.

I watched Nathan from across the street as he circled the swings, the monkey bars and the slide, which the man was now sitting on top of, beside his little bully of a daughter. It was really quite clichéd to have a crush on him – he was such an alpha male. I was also punching way above my weight. See, I was even thinking about him in clichés. I sounded like something you'd read on a Love Heart.

'Is there a problem?' I heard him shout. 'There's a woman and a kid over there who are real upset.' I quite liked the way he left the 'ly' out of 'really', it made him sound like a cowboy.

I couldn't hear what the man said back, but his voice sounded low and intimated, not so full of bravado now.

'Ah, would you ever cop on!' Nathan roared up in response and started waving the crowbar about, marching away and coming back with more. He seemed to be enjoying this a little too much. I knew he was showing off – he'd watched one too many episodes of *The Sopranos*.

'Why don't you wise up or clear off?'

Alfie wasn't doing much for our case with his nose in the base of a buggy, reappearing seconds later with a ham sandwich between his teeth.

I left the dog at home and dropped Addie over to Sumita's for the afternoon. She said she'd take her and Rashi down to the aquarium to see the octopus (who, having mated, was unfortunately dying, the way octopuses do; I asked her not to tell the kids), then back to theirs for tea.

I set off for the library. I was looking forward to my shift. To sit in the warmth under its comforting artificial light, the sort of light that always brought me back to school – sprayed snowmen lit up in the little square windows of our classroom as we practised for the nativity play, excited by the promise of parents and applause and of being in school at night, when it seemed like a far more exciting place.

I'd borrowed a charcoal-grey trouser suit from Ruth for the interview.

'Of course I'm not saying you're fat,' she'd said, chewing on her bottom lip as she'd watched me yank at the zip. 'It's just that we're different lengths.'

'Be enthusiastic!' Mum had enthused over a poor phone line from Perugia. I'd asked endless questions and had sat forward on my seat, feeling confident that I would get the job; I generally did, it was only after interviews that things tended to go downhill quite swiftly.

I said hello or nodded and stood back to let people pass as I walked along the high street. I needed to feel that I was a decent, functioning member of society after my fight with that idiot in the park, needed to know that I got on with most normal human beings. I smiled at dusty old Mr Ledwidge who was standing in the doorway of his home services store, waiting for customers, at Mrs Dicker, humming in her little red electrical shop, as she reorganised her window display. To the bad-tempered baker who was wagging his finger at his young Asian employee over a black forest gateau, keeping one eye on the junkies at the door moving in slow motion, the way they do, looking for change for a bun, him on crutches, his baseball cap pulled low, her holding onto him, pregnant belly exposed. To the stylist with cobalt-blue hair, resting her backside on the window ledge of Hairbox, waiting for her nine o'clock curly blow-dry.

Belinda sucked in her stomach and lifted her breasts to squeeze through the tiny gap between the filing cabinet and her seat, knocking the key for the toilet off its hook, as she did several times a day. She bent to retrieve it, cursing at herself for her clumsiness, and hung it back where it belonged. I breezed past, all business, with the newspapers in one arm and a decaf vanilla soya latte in the other. I'd entered the papers in the ledger already and was on my way upstairs to display them along tables in the 'quiet' room. I quite liked this bit of my morning because it meant I could have a very quick read of them out of sight of my colleagues while enjoying the rest of my coffee. Then I'd thump downstairs, efficient and eager, and check the door count; an invisible beam you stepped across as you entered the library that recorded the footfall on any given day. Three hundred and fifty people had used the library the day before: to read, to research, to play, to keep warm, to use the facilities, to hang out with friends.

I was on shakier grounds, mathematically, totting up the fines, but I'd snuck in Addie's Hello Kitty calculator for anything tricky. Request fees, photocopying money, fees for lost books – click, click, clickedy click – and then another excuse to escape, to lodge these fees at the Bank of Ireland on the high street.

I snuck into Tesco for a takeaway tuna and sweetcorn sandwich on the way back from the bank. The automated voice at the self-service till told me, told everyone, in a chipper, approving tone that my Clubcard had been accepted. I was not just an organised librarian, careful with her money and always remembering her Clubcard when shopping. I was a fully functioning mother of one and people approved of me.

Back at my desk, I dealt with two queries. The first was from Charlie, a drinker and loner, who always came in to read the sports pages in the mornings and when the weather was cold or wet. He considered this place home, even brought his own cushion, because his haemorrhoids made sitting uncomfortable.

'Can I use the phone, please?' he asked me, smelling ripe.

'It's for emergencies only, I'm afraid.'

'This qualifies as an emergency, believe me, young lady,' he said, his words sliding all over the place. He leant over the desk, helped himself, knowing I was too new and too junior to stop him.

'Dave? It's Charlie. Listen, come here to me,' he said, then cupped his hand over the receiver. 'Did I leave a six-pack at yours?'

Mrs Stanley phoned as soon as Charlie had hung up, to enquire about her account. She was ninety-four and profoundly deaf. Even a question like 'Can I help you?' had to be repeated and yelled. 'It's all right, dear, no need to shout,' she always replied, quite irate.

I opened the double doors to the library at precisely ten o'clock. It felt good to let in some air and some natural light. It seemed deprived of both: a squat, seventies-style brick and stone building with brown carpets, porridge-coloured walls and the library staff in their taupe turtlenecks and beige cardigans perfectly camouflaged behind ancient grey hulks of computers. The peace lilies and spider plants by the information desk were drooping and looked like they couldn't breathe. Even the children's area was gloomy despite all its colour: the giant Duplo blocks dirty and old, the stuffed elephant saggy and depressed. And the smells: old books mixed with squiffy socks.

'It's mayhem up there,' Pete said, his eyes behind thick glasses turned skyward. He was balancing a great stack of books in one hand. 'A young fella trying to get on porn.' There was always trouble in the computer room. Pete had been at the library for twenty years and filed everything in a system and order that he alone understood. He loved to be asked about this system and he loved explaining it in detail, to those less clever than him, but he was so bright he found it impossible to put it into simple language and much as they wanted to understand, one by one the communal eyes of the library staff glazed over.

'Chemical Ali's just arrived too. High as a kite this morning.' This was a skinny, jumpy junkie who was in every day, getting agitated with the machines. We were all a little afraid of him. 'He's wiping his nose on his sleeve and spreading snot all over the keyboard. Disgusting, so it is. The red-faced auld one keeps complaining.'

I wasn't certain if he was telling me this so that I would go up and sort it out or whether he intended to see to it himself. In the children's section a small girl was pulling pages out of a *Mr Men* book while her mother checked her phone. This I could tackle more easily.

'Imelda, what am I after saying?' her mother said, sleepily, when she saw me approach, then went back to her frantic two-thumb texting.

A woman, gaunt, ponytailed, tired, hurried in with a small boy and girl. She sat them both on one chair in front of a computer, turned it on, found the game they liked.

'Now, no messin', d'ya hear?'

The little girl nodded. The boy looked upset.

'See yas later. OK?'

'I want to come with you,' he said.

'Ah, don't start that, Sean.'

'I'll bring back a surprise if you're good, OK?' she said and turned and left.

'On her way into town again,' Pete said. 'Just watch and see. She'll leave them here for the day. I've confronted her before but she keeps doing it anyway and sure I've no power to stop her.'

I was in non-fiction filing returns when Belinda wheeled her trolley along my row. She made more noise than any of the regulars, humming, complaining and reminding everyone of the rules: 'No eating, no drinking, mobile phones off', always ignoring the golden one – to be quiet.

'God, my shoulders are bleedin' killing me, they're so knotted,' she said, hunching and relaxing them. 'I'd love one of those deep-tissue massages. Billy got me into a headlock in the chipper last night because I wouldn't buy him another Coke. I think he's after dislocating something.'

'God, that sounds humiliating. And sore.'

'It was both, believe me. Then he lost it completely when we got home. He smashed the Batman lava lamp I bought him for his birthday. He loved that stupid thing.'

'What do you think's bothering him?'

'Can't tell you. Who knows? The full moon? That makes kids go mad, I read somewhere. And Billy just has these crazy moods where no one can reach him – "incredible sulks" his dad used to call them. So how did the games thing go the other night?' she asked, wanting to get off the subject of her son. 'I'm on next week, any tips?'

'It was good fun, though Irenka and Joy were pretty overbearing. Were you stuck here all evening?'

'I was in, my eye! I had my last session of radiotherapy that afternoon. I was too wiped out, to be honest.'

'You look so well. I didn't realise.'

'Really? Thought I was the talk of the playground, assumed everyone knew. Breast cancer. I had a lumpectomy thing and then some radiotherapy. That was my last treatment, thank Christ.' She carried on stacking, then stopped, sat back on her ankles, looked at me, rubbed her hand on my back.

'Don't look so worried. I'll be OK. I've beaten it, I think. I wish Billy could believe it though. Every time I so much as cough he's fussing over me. The poor lad's angry because this is my second time with it. And I had scans and a mammogram that didn't catch it. He's blaming the doctors, the machines, everything. He's trying to get me on a raw vegan diet that he read about online; he's been on that computer for hours. He's terrified that it's going to kill me. He lost it when his dad left, now he's blaming himself for the stress he put me through around then; he thinks that's why it's after coming back.'

The cleaner, Mary, was making a remarkable amount of noise beside us, throwing old papers into bin sacks, to show that she wasn't earwigging, which of course she was.

'I'll do next Wednesday's games shift with you, if you'd like? It's the same day as Addie's birthday but I thought I'd bring the party over to the playground.'

'Ah lovely, thanks, Eve.'

The system crashed that afternoon, something to do with 'comms' – a word, an abbreviation, that meant nothing to any of the staff. For the first half an hour after it went down everyone was irritated, particularly Pete who took pride in his organisational skills and was now unable to record late returns. Two hours later and with no sign of the technician, we had all begun to enjoy our inability to do any work.

The disorder was infectious. No one was even attempting to whisper. Kids were plunging into the bean bags, screaming, amazed at not being told off. The local drunks had reinstated themselves on the bench outside the back door, and were happily inebriated. The elderly, always noisy with their groans and coughs and heavy breathing and unable to find their mobile phones with the incredibly loud and incongruous ringtones their grandchildren had selected for them, chatted at the top of their voices about the news, the weather, the result of the general election.

The chaos had seeped as far as the toilets. 'You'd want to see what they've done in there,' Mary said, on her way back with a mop and bucket and a slippery surface sign.

'Spare us the details, would you? Please?' Belinda said.

It was that time of the afternoon, three forty-five, when the Leaving Cert students arrived: coats hanging off, dragging their bags behind them, the girls, flatfooted in Dubes, the boys behind them in beanies, slumped shoulders and spotty chins, pretending they were there to do homework when really they just wanted to hang out.

As soon as they sat, the sniggering and loud whispering began. Then snorts of hysteria, swapping places, dragging chairs across the floor, lots of little rebellions. They were too full of hormones and too keen to impress to sit still. Next were the endless trips in and out through the swing door for cigarettes or to the shops for coffee and sweets. One girl thought it was hilarious to continuously clear her throat, as if to sit silently doing your homework was deeply un-cool. Had I ever been this silly? A whole lot sillier actually, but that wasn't the point.

'Hey, guys, can you keep it down a little?' I said, from where I was standing in Health and Beauty, the sound of my voice reverberating horribly in my ear, the snorts of suppressed laughter from the two girls down the end making me cringe. It still came as a shock to realise that I was no longer young, but someone's mother, middle-aged, invisible. 'Snazzy,' I heard myself say about a new coat one of Addie's little school friends was wearing the other day—I could have sworn the toddlers rolled their eyes at each other.

My phone beeped in my pocket, causing a student to look up from his computer and tut. Two new messages, the first from Sumita letting me know that Addie was 'very great but didn't eat much her carrots'. The second from Mr Norman:

Thank you for opening the park this morning. Just two things to note for the next time: open the LEFT HAND GATE only (this is safer so that kids can't run out onto the road), and please can you LOCK the chain to the RAILING rather than the GATE. PS: you may not have noticed the new sign – dogs are no longer permitted.

'Library's closing in five minutes,' I said, working my way around each section, at exactly five minutes to five. The small girl and boy that had been deposited in the corner that morning were still there. The boy was lying on the floor on his belly, colouring in a photocopy of SpongeBob SquarePants; his sister was above him, curled into a chair, sucking her thumb as she read a book.

'We have to wait for our mam,' she said as she stood up, bookmarked her place in her novel, grabbed her rucksack.

'That's OK, sit tight. She'll be here soon, I'm sure,' I said, trying to be kind. She opened her book again, slotted her thumb back in her mouth, told her brother it was OK.

With Joe it was always his glasses, but there was something about me and keys. If you were to pile up all the keys I'd lost in my life they would reach a great height. I must have left them in the library which was now closed. It was Addie who noticed the open window by the balcony. Joy must have forgotten to close it when she'd left monkey nuts out for the squirrels that morning. She'd now gone to spend a week at an artist's retreat in County Monaghan, to work on the themes of loneliness and sexual longing, so there was no point in calling her about keys.

Mr Norman, who always kept a close eye on happenings around the square, was straight over to assist. What we needed was a ladder. I hitched myself over the wall of the porch and knocked on Mr Larson's door. I knew he had one, I'd seen him use it for the hedge that separated our two homes. He appeared in his dressing gown for some reason, didn't acknowledge Mr Norman, who was leaning against the wall, arms folded, and he was at the front gate moments later with the ladder, still in his dressing gown but having swapped his slippers for wellington boots.

I'd forgotten that the two men didn't get along. Irenka told me that they'd fallen out years earlier over a strip of land between their two homes. Mr Norman had wanted to develop the land but Mr Larson wouldn't give it up, so Mr Norman sold, moved to the opposite side of the square and for a while Mr Larson used the land to grow rocket, turnips and potatoes. Now it was a no man's wilderness, a rubbish dump for the neighbourhood, great hunting ground for cats. 'That bastard' was how the two men had referred to each other ever since.

It was hard to imagine Mr Norman being bad-tempered, a little easier with Mr Larson. Though outwardly jolly, jogging indoors instead of walking when he came back from putting out the bins, I sometimes heard his raised voice through the walls, and he'd shown a flash of anger the other evening when I'd charged round the corner with my umbrella and we'd collided, the spokes of my brolly poking him on the head (I was in heels and he was quite short). His expression had changed as soon as he'd recognised me and I'd smiled and said hello. He'd smiled back, asked how I was, folded his arms and settled into a conversation. I liked that I might be mending old wounds – that I was bringing them together, forcing a truce.

The two men stumbled around the front garden, trying to manage the ladder, looking like Laurel and Hardy. They were attempting to balance it against the balcony – neither one of them seemed particularly excited about the prospect of climbing up and neither had volunteered when Nathan arrived. He took the ladder from the two men, propped it against the balcony and climbed up the side of the house in seconds. I stood there like a silly girl, shouting at him to be careful. The other two men stood back, impressed but somewhat emasculated by his confidence and agility.

'Do you want me to put that up while I'm here?' Nathan asked, once we were safely inside again, tapping his foot against the side of an Ikea box that was lying on the floor in the sitting room beside the TV. It was a bookshelf that I had bought for Addie several months before but had yet to assemble.

'Could you? That would be wonderful, if you're sure you have time? Can I get you some tea?'

'No bother at all. Milk, two sugars, please.'

'Now, you show me where you'd like me to put it, little lady,' he said, taking Addie by the hand and letting her lead the way.

He also replaced a door handle that afternoon and fixed a leak in the toilet, lifting Addie up when he'd finished to show her how the cistern worked.

'So, I'd better get back to it . . .' he said, all his jobs done. I thanked him. Told Addie that he had to go home.

'Would you like to play a game with me?' she asked, her invitation so simple and earnest it was impossible to refuse. He threw her up in his arms, caught her and tickled her until she could bear it no more, the way Joe used to. Then he rooted in his pocket, took out a small green bouncy ball that lit up when you squeezed it.

'OK, I know a good game, come with me.'

He stood at the top of the stairs in the hall while Addie stood at the bottom and they threw the ball to each other. Every so often it bounced against the Memory Foam mattress propped in the hall for Irenka to help her bad back, which caused it to ricochet off the walls. This made Addie giggle so hard that she got the hiccups and then she had a little accident.

'Nathan's so silly,' she said that evening, as I lifted her into her bath. 'He's my best friend. That's why because he makes me laugh and laugh.'

'You are more relaxed than you've been in a long time. You are in complete control of your thoughts and your feelings.' Nonsense.

'Your mind is very centered and calm. A deep feeling of inner calm begins to resonate through your whole body.' No it doesn't.

Why was I being deliberately self-destructive? Why wouldn't my mind just shut up and let it work? Bella had recommended this meditation CD, *Creating Inner Peace and Calm.* She'd tried it out for her fear of flying and she made it the whole way to Boston and back without the help of alcohol or drugs; she'd just listened to the CD over and over and practised diaphragmatic breathing techniques.

I tried again to quiet my mind, I breathed slowly and deeply. I tried to shut out Addie's little snores.

'You are strolling through a meadow on a warm summer's day. The air is clean and fresh. You feel the pleasant warmth of the sun on your head and shoulders. You feel so good. You relax, deeper and deeper. Drifting down, drifting down, drifting down. You reach a secluded spot by the edge of a stream

where you can rest. You gaze into the gently flowing water and feel a deep connection with the effortless flow of nature. You lower yourself down onto the soft grassy bank and gaze up at the bright-blue sky. You lie back on the grass. And relax, deeper and deeper. Not a care in the world now. You feel yourself drifting off into a relaxing sleep. A deep, dreamy sleep. Sleep, sleep, sleep. You gooo to sleep. You gooo to sleep . . .'

'Come here,' Nathan said, leaning against the edge of the picnic table in the park, holding his arms out, beckoning me.

'Why?' I said grinning, chewing my lip, moving towards him. He linked his arms around my waist, pulled me close and kissed me hard on the mouth.

'Jesus. I've wanted to do that for days, months. Since you moved in,' he said between kisses. Then we fell back onto the table in the darkness.

'Oh God, I need to shave, need a shower.'

'Shush. You're perfect. Delicious.'

He smiled and squeezed me and kissed me again on the warm skin of my neck. Then he lifted me up, carried me away from the table, lowered me onto the grass.

He lay above me, slipped his hand under the material of my skirt and rubbed the sticky-hot area between my thighs, sending aches of pleasure shooting through me. He prodded with two fingers, then fed them deep inside me and tugged my knickers to my knees. We kissed more, harder lips, entwining tongues. I undid his belt, pushed his stiff denims . . .

'Mama! I need you. My elbows are bursting!'

Chapter Fourteen

'It's absolutely infuriating, she never answers her phone. No, no. Just milk, please. That's enough. Thanks, Margo.'

There was a muffled noise that sounded like the phone being dropped.

'Hi, Mum. Mum? I'm here.'

'I'll try her again later. She might be – what day is it?'

'Mum? I can hear you. Mum?'

'Oh, hi, pet. I thought you weren't there.'

We began the conversation as we always did, both talking at the same time and staying silent at the same moment. We couldn't get the timing right.

'Sorry, Mum, you go first. Are you having a lovely holiday?'

'I'm sitting here looking at the most glorious view – fields and fields of sunflowers around me, all in bloom. All's fine. Yop. Yop. Now listen, tell me, how did Addie get on this morning? That was the most smashing photo, by the way.'

It was her first day at school. She had stood, proud and mischievous, while I'd taken her photograph outside the front door, in her new blue shoes and bumble bee rucksack. She had let me down a little when I'd introduced her to her teacher, Miss Meredith, refusing to speak or to even look at her. She'd just kept whacking me with her koala bear. Then she'd wanted to paint, which I'd been pleased about;

this would impress the teachers and the other mothers (I hadn't said it to Ruth, but I thought she had quite an aptitude for her age). What she produced was a huge black scrawl, disconcerting in several ways.

'She's still there, the poor little thing. I'm collecting her at one.' All her bravado had evaporated when the moment came for us to part. She had clung onto my leg, then tugged hard at my hair, begging me not to go.

'Well, I must say I feel terribly sad to be missing all these occasions, but I'm home first thing Wednesday morning and I've got her a lovely Pinocchio puppet.' Mum didn't do surprises, I was never sure why.

'So how are you getting along?'

'I've had a bit of a stomach upset but other than that I'm having a marvellous time.'

'Oh no, Mum, are you OK?'

'Of course, sweetheart, don't be silly. I'm absolutely fine.' She hated, hated being asked about her health. She moved on to her plans for the rest of her trip; I moved towards the window and looked out. Someone had left one of those enormous blue Ikea bags just outside my front door. It was filled to the top with timber. My first thought was that it was some sort of joke; Billy and one of his pranks or perhaps something Joy had ordered for an art installation. Then I remembered Nathan's promise to bring me firewood.

'Mum, you're breaking up a bit.'

'Hello? I can still hear you.'

'I'll see you in a few days, maybe we'll drop round on Friday? Oh and, Mum, I forgot to say, your hall ceiling's leaking again.'

'Oh, dash it. Well, there's precious little I can do about it from here,' she said, irritated by the news and by me for imparting it.

Then she was seized by a coughing spasm. It started with a simple clearing of her throat and became a chesty, phlegm-filled, breathless thing. On and on it went. When she was able to talk again she sounded a little fainter, a little further away.

'Are you OK, Mum?'

'Yes. Yes. It's nothing. It's just a morning thing. Just a crumb,' she said, still wheezing.

I looked outside to see if I could spot Nathan so I could pop over to thank him once I'd hung up, but the house was empty, his jeep gone. The playground had been colonised by a thousand school kids in green uniforms, all of them screaming. At least six of them were on the net swing together, moving wildly to and fro; a boy was surfing on the middle of the see-saw, while two others balanced on either end. Some were climbing up the slide, making arches of their legs, while others slid down between them. Two were dangling out of the chestnut tree, clinging onto its leafless branches. They must have been on a half day.

'Sorry, Mum, what time is it?'

'Well it's nearly two o'clock here but we're an hour ahead of course.'

'Oh, God, I have to go, I've got to collect Addie.'

'All right, love, off you go, you can't be late on her first day. Bye bye bye bye bye.'

'Bye, Mum. I can't wait till you're home. I always feel happier when you're here.'

This was something I always said and always meant. I think she only half-liked hearing it. She liked to know that she was loved and missed, but it also made her feel guilty that she was so often away. Whenever she was abroad I felt disconcerted, worried that she was in too much of a hurry. Worried that she would trip over on a kerb, slip on the step into the swimming pool, like she'd done before, become careless in her competitiveness and drive into a wall, exhaust herself by being up before anyone else, by taking charge of the day's itinerary, always agreeing to share a room with the snorer, or with a person so eccentric or extreme that no one else could tolerate them. She would always take the discomfort, put her own needs last. And I was worried about us at home without her. Often I couldn't put my finger on my unease but as soon as she was home, it evaporated and my world felt safe again.

I stood outside the classroom window watching Addie. She looked serious and a little sad in a queue with her classmates, smaller than the others and not quite managing her school bag, lunch box, coat and a still-wet painting. When she spotted me, everything about her became animated, her eyes, face, body. She began jumping on the spot, waved and blew kisses and gave me the most luminescent smile, then she nudged the child beside her to show her that her mama had come back, that all was right in her world.

'I got a sticker! That's why because I ate my lunch all up. And do you know what else? I got a happy helper silver star.'

'She's had a wonderful morning and just one little accident,' Miss Meredith said, handing me her wet knickers in a bag.

'OK, what'll we do?' I said, with a sudden surge of energy and love and enthusiasm and that strange childhood excitement that gave me a metallic taste at the back of my throat. I picked her up and swung her around in the air.

'How about the playground?' she suggested. 'That's a good idea,' she said, complimenting herself.

'Or we could take your bike down to the beach front?'

'No. The playground,' she whined.

She won as she always did. We returned home to collect her bike and some gingerbread men biscuits to share (if we met anyone we knew).

All the school kids had gone and the playground was quiet. Billy Flynn was the only one there, standing at the top of the gardener's hut with a supermarket trolley: sweaty-haired, red-cheeked, a hand down the front of his shiny grey tracksuit. He let the trolley career over the edge when he saw us, jumped down and landed by our feet.

'Hey, are you the mam that lost the toy?'

'Yes. Addie's toy rat. A few weeks ago.'

'I think I know where it is. Will I show her?' he asked, offering Addie his hand.

'OK, great! Thank you. Where did you find it?' I said, keeping up with them.

He led us to the sandpit, kicked off its plastic cover.

'There you go now. There's your ratty.'

We peered in at a rotten carcass. Its stomach was oozing purple, black, grey. Its mouth was open; sharp, yellow teeth exposed. Maggots scattering. Addie sought out my arms.

'Oh, for fuck's sake. That's disgusting, you twisted little bastard!' I pushed my child backwards. God, my language. I was going to have to bring this up with Belinda; he couldn't go on terrorising Addie like this.

He burst into laughter, backed off grinning.

We made our slow, ambling way around the square. Most of the windows of the houses were dark, their driveways empty of cars. I'd never seen a single person come or go out of the new colonial-style homes in the small estate at the corner. With its white pillars and Tarmac driveways, it was like a cardboard facade of a developer's vision.

I got ready to smile at the small Filipino nurse who I recognised from the Cherry Glade. She was shuffling towards us, accompanied by a large man with a handlebar moustache and beige slacks belted too high. I recognised him, I'd seen him from my bedroom window smoking and pacing like a depressed polar bear outside the garden shed next door. And on sunny days, out with his fellow inmates, propped beside the picnic table, under a lopsided sunhat. I put my hands on my child's shoulders and tried to direct her out of their way.

When they reached the gates of the nursing home, the nurse held him under the elbow and attempted to guide him back indoors. 'Fuck off!' the man shouted, flailing his stick at her. 'Get off me. I'm not going back into that fucking place.' He pulled away from her and made his way, limping, spitting, bilious, towards us while the nurse ran across the concrete drive of the home, pressed the bell and banged on the door shouting, 'I need help. He's really bad this time.'

I carried Addie and her bike across the road and away from him, to the far side of the square. My nerves were jangled already, I really didn't need this. I eased her down on the pavement outside number five and felt the warm sweat of clean clothes on my face, heard the comforting drone of a tumble dryer. I glanced through the yellowy light of the basement window: Sophie was at the kitchen sink with her back to us, in loose-fitting Levi's, a dusty-pink sweater and trainers. Her little girl, Lauren, was dancing about behind her in a tutu.

As if sensing our presence, Sophie turned around at that moment and looked towards the window, lifting her chin. I gave her a smile, a half-wave, but then she ran her hand through her hair. She was only examining her reflection.

'Come on, Addie, let's go,' I said, ushering her ahead of me. Then we heard a door open and Sophie calling after us.

'Hi, Addie's Mum!'

'Oh, hello. Hi.' I turned and walked back towards her, holding my hand out behind me without looking to beckon Addie in that absent-minded way of mothers.

'Lauren wants to know if Addie would like to play?'

'Now?' I glanced at my watch, which wasn't in fact there – it had begun to cause a rash on my wrist so I'd given up wearing it – but I took a few seconds so it would look as though I was deliberating over appointments and routines.

A kerfuffle had broken out opposite us. At the gate of the park the man who'd escaped from the Cherry Glade had been cornered by three male members of staff, two of them had hooked their arms around his elbows, the third was standing in front of him, pressing his hand against the old man's chest. Humiliated, all his energy gone, he allowed them to lead him back to the home without any further struggle.

'Look at the chocolate cups Mummy's made for dinner,' Lauren said, leading me by the arm over to the fridge: a double-doored, chrome-coloured American monster decorated with kids' paintings and photos. She pulled it open with some effort and there on the top shelf were a row of small, gold-rimmed china cups in pale-blue, pink and vanilla, all filled to their tops with chocolate. She went to shut it again, soon distracted as little girls are, but I held it open with my foot to study the cups further. Six of them, the chocolate settling on top, glistening with a layer of frost. I complimented Sophie and she laughed, readjusting the bra strap that had slipped over her shoulder.

'They're for a dinner party we're having tonight. Work colleagues of Mark's and a sort of birthday celebration for me. I've no idea what they taste like!' Was it then that I noticed that her eyes were wet, as if she'd been crying? Though not the sort of crying I did which left my eyes small and swollen and my cheeks spotty and raw; if anything, their wateriness made her look even more attractive, in a vulnerable, waif-like way. I wished her a happy birthday and asked her age. 'Thirty-seven,' she said with a groan.

Addie was so at home in Sophie's house; we both were – it was like getting into a warm bubble bath. The kitchen smelt of cinnamon; the playroom was filled with colourful toys and tents and dolls' houses and princesses' castles and a table for colouring and another with animal-shaped cookie cutters and playdough. The walls were covered in framed photos of the children and weddings and parties, and curled in the corner was their giant poodle, Buddy.

Sophie explained that Buddy belonged to an old lady who could no longer care for him because she'd had to go into a home. 'I told the vet that I'd take anything,' she said, watching Addie and Lauren kneel beside him. 'That I love all dogs. I forgot to say, except poodles that is.' We laughed together, I knew just what she meant.

'Oh, she's so juicy,' she said, watching my little girl.

While the children played together, we drank tea and bitched about Irenka and Sophie told me all about a drama class that she was going to sign Lauren up for ('though it's quite expensive, but on the other hand they sometimes get picked to do TV ads which would be quite exciting, wouldn't it?') and about a little chefs' cookery class that she'd heard about in Greystones. I wasn't sure if she was telling me about these classes just so I'd know or if she was suggesting that we enrol the kids together. I didn't want to be too forward, so I nodded and enthused but didn't commit. Then we got on to the problems with Billy Flynn.

'Gosh, he's completely wild! I heard that he drank the contents of a fish bowl at a party for a dare last Christmas – the whole lot, including the two fish and the ants' eggs. Isn't that vile?' Sophie said, crinkling her nose and giggling.

'What are you saying about that boy, Mama?' Lauren asked, looking up from her playdough ice cream.

'Oh no, nothing, sweetheart. Just that he has issues.'

She considered this for a moment, came up to the kitchen table. 'No he doesn't. He has black shoes.'

'Would Addie like to stay for tea?' Sophie asked then, moving the clothes horse that was positioned in front of the Aga out of the way.

'Look at these,' she said, without waiting for my answer, holding up a tiny pair of black lace knickers that had been drying beside some rather large white M&S ones.

'The au pair's. Unbelievable, aren't they? Don't mine look grotty beside them?'

'Not at all. They look comfortable.' I said, all middle-aged and mumsy. I considered my own 'panties' as Joy referred to them, the word making me wince every time she uttered it. She'd surprised me one evening by washing them for me, then ironing and folding them in a tidy stack on my bed. A few days later she'd asked if the cheap material they were made from 'didn't chaff my skin?' As if she'd given it some serious thought.

'Do you think it would be rude to ask her to move them into her bedroom to dry?'

'Of course not. I'd move them myself if I were you.'

'Would you? You know this morning I couldn't find her or Mark, do you know where they were? Sharing a cigarette in the back garden. And she wasn't even wearing a bra under her sweater.' She pulled out the chair beside me, took a Ben 10 toy car off it, and sat down. 'Do you think I could ask her to start wearing one? I'm so sick of Mark ogling them over breakfast, but I don't know how to say it without offending her.'

'Why don't you ask him to keep his eyes on his breakfast rather than on her poached eggs?' This made her laugh.

I told her we'd be delighted to stay for tea. Then I reassured her with flattery. Beatriz was certainly no more beautiful than she was. I'd seen her with the kids a few times. She reminded me of a gymnast, always in the same pale-blue tracksuit, thin, blonde hair tied back in a ponytail, sunken eyes, no make-up. Although I was surprised she'd got the job; au pairing was surely the only profession where being too good-looking counted against you.

'Mama!'

Addie was in the downstairs toilet, tights around ankles, door open.

'Are you so proud?' she asked, her voice strained as she pushed. She'd been constipated for the last two days.

I told her I was extremely proud of her and turned to leave.

'Will you stay with me?' she said.

I leant back against the radiator and waited.

'Lauren says her dada's getting her a black Furby for her birthday.'

'Lucky Lauren.'

'Can I have one? Except only a pink one with purple ears?'

'We'll see, Furbies are very expensive. Are you nearly finished?'

'OK, I've got a deal! How about I ask Dada to get it for me for my birthday?'

'Maybe, sweetie.'

'Can Dada please just come home for a sleepover and a playdate?'

'We'll see about that too. Now call me when you're done and I'll wipe your bum bum, OK?'

'*Mummy* stop asking me that, it's so embarrassing. When can he? In one sleep or two sleeps?'

'I'm not sure when.'

'Mama, don't tell anyone I said this, but is Dada going to be in our house again, every day properly?'

'No, sweetheart, you know he isn't. It's you and me now, OK?'

Her face got serious, little eyebrows arched.

'Don't tell anyone I said that, OK?'

'I promise I won't. You know I love you up to Jupiter and back, don't you?' I rested my hands on her knees.

'Well, I love you up to Jupiter and back a thousand and one. Can you go now, please?'

I offered to help lay the table but proved useless, having to ask Sophie where everything was and setting a place for myself too, which was a little awkward when it became clear that she'd only meant tea for the children. Of course, she would be eating at the dinner party later, with her adult friends. I had become so used to having tea with Addie at five in the evening that this hadn't even occurred to me.

'No. I insist! There's enough for all of you, and to be honest I'd love the company. Mark's been away in Europe for most of the week. It gets quite lonely. God, I hope he's not late tonight. I'll kill him if I'm left entertaining his friends on my own,' she said, lifting a bunch of white hydrangeas in a huge glass vase off the kitchen table and over to beside the sink. They were so perfect they looked plastic and something about them seemed a little desperate, as if they had been put there to convince you that all was well. They reminded me of the ones I'd bought when I was selling the house in Sandycove, to give the impression that our home was a happy, fragrant, positive place, not that I was moving out because Joe had abandoned us and I could no longer afford to pay the mortgage, or that things were so bad I'd had to borrow fifty Euro from my mother to pay for the flowers in the first place. The American couple who fell for them, and for the house, had two blonde children with huge eyes and smiles. I'd since heard that they'd got married. Getting married after kids, when you knew each other, seemed so much more romantic than doing it in the early days, when everything was easy and you were both still in love.

'Listen, I'm taking the kids for a picnic tomorrow if you'd like to join us?' Sophie said as we ate our ice cream and jelly. 'I have to go to the dentist to get a crown first thing but I could meet you around twelve?'

'Oh we would love to, thank you, but poor you!'

'I know. Lauren's got to come with me and she's far more excited about it than I am.'

'She may have a very different idea of what a crown is to you. Did you clarify that it's not a princess crown?' I said, making her laugh.

There was another awkward moment that nobody saw, when Addie tried to hug Ben who was lying on the sofa, watching *Fireman Sam*. He kicked her hard in the stomach with both feet, and I whispered a warning at him – 'you must never, ever do that again' – surreptitious but sharp.

'Can I tell you a secret?' Addie asked, taking my hand as we walked home, both of us with a spring in our step, loving the idea that we had new friends that lived just across the square. 'I like Ben only a tiny bit.'

Chapter Fifteen

I sat in front of the mirror and examined myself, stroking the single black hair growing from the mole on my chin. I wished it wasn't there and yet there was something pleasurable in its vileness. I liked to try to catch it and pull it between my thumb and first fingernail, but it would always slide away, until trying to catch it became unbearable, made me nauseous.

I rummaged about in the chaos of my dressing table drawer for tweezers, found them, turned my head to the side so that I could see what I was doing in the mirror, angled the prongs and tugged at the hair until, with a sharp little sting, it came free. And as I sat there, poking and pulling, my mind was whirring, preparing trial runs of possible conversations, trying to think of things Sophie might find interesting, stories that might make her laugh, and wondering what to wear, what she had seen me in before, the sort of thing she might like. I dabbed a generous amount of Preparation H on my eye bags and rubbed it in.

The outing began quite perfectly. It was a beautiful, clear, unseasonably warm October day. A strange time of year for a picnic on the beach, you might think, but we often had picnics in the winter growing up, and anyway, the children needed airing, as Sophie said. And Billy Flynn had defecated on the picnic bench in the playground the other day so we didn't want to go there.

I found the second last parking space, and was easing into it when I spotted my new friend driving into the last one, two cars down from mine. We waved at each other, then she disappeared into the darkness of her car to sort out her children.

I felt animated, aware of the small smile on my face as I helped Addie out of her seat, but shy too with the sense that I was being watched, which of course I was not. This was just what I wanted for me; just what I wanted for Addie. A lovely, warm, straightforward, easygoing new friend we could depend on, who lived nearby, with children Addie could become close to. I imagined sleepovers, shared childminders, maybe even holidays together in the future. If we spent enough time with Sophie's kids, perhaps Addie wouldn't feel so much like an only child. And Sophie's husband was away so often; we could do lots of things at weekends too.

I unpacked the boot, worried again that the picnic blanket and rucksack full of food was a little too much, but I needn't have fretted because the very first thing Sophie said was: 'Oh brilliant, you've brought a blanket.' We hugged hello and I crouched down to Ben who ignored me and my smothering embrace. What she didn't yet know was that it was even better than that: I had a wicker basket full of goodies and under that pile of goodies was a wrapped belated birthday present for her which I'd alternated between thinking was very kind of me and the appropriate thing and far too much and a little bit creepy.

'Oh, hi,' Sophie shouted, turning and waving at a passing jeep.

'You always know everyone,' I gushed, loading my arms with buckets, spades and a fishing net that I thought might be good fun.

'Oh no, that's just Nicola. Lauren wanted to go in their car. They're going to join us for a while. I hope you don't mind?'

I tried to hide the feeling I had of being winded in the stomach.

Nicola. Dull Beige Nicola was coming to our picnic with her horrible pink-clad, whiny kids. She was a cardboardy woman I'd met in the playground a couple of times who spoke in a sleepy monotone and had a habit of letting her voice trail off at the end of a sentence, as if she weren't expecting anyone to be listening, which we weren't. And she was so boringly diplomatic and fair about everything: I'd once complimented her daughter's brown eyes, 'but Addie has nice eyes too,' she'd said, sounding irritated, as if I should know never to compare children. But the very worst thing about all of this was that Sophie's kids knew and liked her girls a lot more than they knew or liked Addie, and now my child would be left out.

Out the kids came, whining already as Buddy bounded over to sniff them. Oh, for fuck's sake, they were both frightened of dogs. Brilliant. I just couldn't be bothered even saying hello to this woman or her girls, but of course I did, amazed at how adept I was at sounding sincere.

On the beach Sophie was like a child, so happy to be by the sea, long-legged and giggling, apologizing to strangers about her wayward dog, helping her little girl out of her socks and shoes and trying to find Ben's spade. Her hair looked different – had she had it cut? Surely not since yesterday? And she was wearing a cozy-looking navy-blue duffle coat with a checked lining that I hadn't seen before. I smiled at her while Beige Nicola got herself comfortable on my picnic blanket before I'd even straightened it out. She wrapped her arms around her girls, all three of them watching Buddy's every move and whimpering any time he came within sniffing distance.

One of her girls thought it would be a good idea to cover the blanket with pebbles from the beach. And did Beige Nicola do anything to stop her? No, of course she didn't. I soon gave up trying to organise things, took Addie's hand, encouraged her to go and play with Lauren who was skimming stones into the sea, while I caught up with my new friend and tried to get a conversation started. I moved in close and whispered, 'Her kids are afraid of dogs.'

'I know. It's a tiny bit awkward, isn't it? But they won't be staying long. She has to get back to bake biscuits for the school cake sale.'

'Ah no, it's lovely to see her.' I said, all blasé, carefree. I couldn't let her see how put out I was, how them being there changed everything, never mind that I'd only packed for three:

3 x packets of Snacks crisps

3 x cartons of smoothies

3 x packets of chocolate buttons

1 x bag of Babybel cheeses (that Sophie and I could also share)

3 x blueberry muffins (which hadn't quite worked out. The first two attempts had burnt and these ones were crumbly and underdone, less muffins, more of a doughy mush in tinfoil, but I thought they tasted yum.)

Lauren had become naked from the waist down; her Love Heart knickers abandoned on the sand because of some problem with them. Her bum looked too large when compared to the rest of her and somehow too adult-looking to be on view. Addie was annoying her, mimicking her every move. 'Stop copying me,' she shouted, interested only in running away from the waves with Beige Nicola's little, but bigger, girl.

'They're not playing with me, Mama,' Addie whined.

'How do you do it like that? It's amazing!' Sophie said, about Addie's hairdo. Joy had styled it that morning into two tidy plaits that formed a perfect heart shape at the back of her head.

'All Joy's work I'm afraid.'

'God, she seems amazing – you're so lucky to have someone like her.'

'I am lucky, but—'

'But what?'

'But nothing. Joy is a lovely human being,' I said, not wanting her to think I was a bitch.

Another family was making their way through the sand towards us, encumbered with buckets and blankets. We weren't the only mad ones, it seemed. And where did they sit, with the whole great spread of beach before them? Right beside us. Staring, smiling, encouraging their children to play with ours as they organised themselves. Why couldn't they all just bugger off and let us be by ourselves the way I'd planned it?

I told myself to snap out of it. The sun was warm on my neck and Beige Nicola's kids had begun to relax; both had ventured a few inches away from their mum and were occupied with the fishing net. I would try to be a little more flexible, to forget about my original plan.

I battled on. 'Did you hear that Billy Flynn climbed over the railings the other day, when he couldn't get in by the gate? He ran through the flowerbed, uprooting all the flowers Irenka had planted, just for the heck of it. She went berserk!'

The story fell flat and Sophie didn't even hear the best bit about Irenka wounding him with her garden shears because just at that moment Beige Nicola started shouting at her daughter, who was down at the seashore, trying to remove her clothes too. 'No, darling. It's too cold for no knickers,' obscuring the crucial part of the rather amusing remark I'd just made.

Other things I'd been planning to say to Sophie – things that might have interested or amazed or fascinated or made her laugh – were never said.

And I was developing the sort of headache, just above my left eye, that I always got when I was talking to mothers I didn't really know about things I wasn't really interested in. The conversation was unsatisfactory and left me feeling the way fast food does, filling you up for a short time but leaving you hungry half an hour later. There were so many missed opportunities, so many unheard jokes and distracted half sentences and meaningless conversations about shoe size and toilet training and all of those other things that had become such a fundamental yet dull part of my life.

And then, far too soon, there was talk of home. Not from Beige Nicola of course, no such luck, no mention yet of the biscuits she had to bake, she was just settling in, her hands propped behind her back, her face upward towards the sun, her legs spread out on my picnic blanket. There was a hole in her left sock; an unpainted, yellowing-at-the edges toenail was toying with the tassels of *my* picnic blanket.

No, it was Sophie who'd said it. 'Oh, you can't go yet,' I said, sounding a little desperate, 'we haven't had the picnic.' And when was I supposed to give her the birthday present? A honey-scented bath cream that I now considered to be wasted on her, on us, on the development of a friendship that wasn't developing the way it should because Beige Nicola was there beside us, listening in, so that I had to dilute everything, make it general, censor myself.

'God, of course, Eve. Thank you for going to so much trouble,' Sophie said, settling down again, beckoning her children.

And out came the picnic. And great news, Beige Nicola. I had miscounted; I had in fact FIVE smoothies, enough for everyone. Now I was in control, I was mother hen. The children gathered on sandy knees and wet knickers around me. Beige Nicola's kids dove in and she sunk her teeth into a Babybel, her horrible big toe still fiddling with the tassels. Not one mention of 'thanks' or 'I shouldn't really', or 'you're so generous'. All she said was, 'You know, these are just full of sugar. I mean you might as well be giving them chocolate,' as she read through the ingredients on the side of the smoothie carton.

Sophie had brought some snacks too: homemade flapjacks in a recycled shoe box, hazelnuts and a large bag of cashew nuts, as well as some popcorn in a Tupperware container that made my shop-bought chocolate and juices look wasteful, artificial and unhealthy. She sat sideways on the blanket in her duffle coat, felt about for a tissue and wiped her nose – I hadn't realised she had a cold.

'Guess what, Ben, in the car on the way over, Addie said you were her best friend.'

'Well, actually, Chloe's my best friend,' Ben said, shimmying over towards her, 'because she has prettier hair.'

'Ben, that's so rude!' Sophie said, giggling. Addie folded her arms in a huff and turned her little back to them.

I hadn't meant it seriously, Addie said it about everyone but I could see what Sophie was thinking: best friend, but they've only met twice. It also occurred to me for a disconcerting moment that she might think I was a lesbian – ridiculous for so many reasons, I know, but you never know – or just in some way obsessed with her. She complained about a cold sore on her lip and I told her I hadn't even noticed it and then that it made them look bee stung. And I interrupted a story she was telling to say that she had a lovely speaking voice. I was just trying to be nice.

We heard roars coming from the other family who had inched further down the beach to give us some space. Buddy was happily defecating on their son's sandcastle.

'Oh God, let me deal with this,' Sophie said, getting to her feet, shouting 'just coming!' and checking her pockets for dog bags.

'Eve, could you mind Ben for a second?'

'Of course. Have fun!'

Ha, she had entrusted me rather than Beige Nicola with her son's safety. That had cheered up my day. God, I was being pathetic. Before I could say, 'Are you OK, little man?' Ben had taken off like a bullet, towards the waves. I cursed and charged after him, dropped my keys, retrieved them and yelled at him to stop, fighting images of his death by drowning as I ran.

Still out of breath with the captured and crying child, I sat back down on the picnic blanket, held him on my lap, found a game for him on my phone and shoved it into his hand.

'So, how are things? It must be so hard for you.' Beige Nicola asked as she examined her fungus-riddled toenail. Of course Sophie would have told her about the tragedy of my situation, how could she not? What woman wouldn't mention it, even in passing, but did Beige Nicola think I needed her pity? Did she expect me to open up to her? She who wasn't even supposed to be here. Who had – at last – started saying (giving me hope, giving me hope!) that she needed to get back to bake biscuits for the school cake sale. Well off you go then. Stick your head in the oven, frost up those glasses and bake, bake, bake.

'You know, you might not believe it now but you will love again,' Beige Nicola, not the world's most profound woman, said then, leaning back on her forearms, squinting at the sun. Pass the bucket. Why was I being so mean?

Neither she nor Sophie noticed Buddy coming up behind them as they stood together watching their children play, both with their arms folded in the cold. He had the fishing net in his mouth. He ran between them and knocked them to the ground. Sophie roared laughing at Beige Nicola, grabbing hold of her arm to steady herself, before struggling to her feet again. 'Goodness, what a scamp!' she said, between howls. I didn't make her laugh like this, had never seen her throw her head back this way.

But we got our moment. I got mine. Beige Nicola's children were easier to organise than ours and of course she had nothing to carry as she didn't bring anything, so she set off towards the car. As Sophie gathered up the last of her things, saying what a brilliant day it had been and how we must do it again soon, I grappled for the gift, stuttering over my words as I tried to pull it out, playing it down, apologising, 'Oh, God, it's nothing. Just a tiny thing.'

It was a wonderful success. She was thrilled, she was touched. I blushed and stammered and told her that I used to love it, that Joe used to buy it for me, and then we hugged and our sunglasses hit off each other's but we didn't comment on that, we just both rearranged them so we could begin the challenge of getting everyone from the beach back to the car. By now we were all freezing and I was so frazzled with everything that I picked up Ben instead of Addie and carried him over to where I had parked. It was only as I went to lift him into the car seat that I realised I had the wrong child. The Preparation H had seeped into my eyes, covering them with a greasy film and had made everything sepia-edged and fuzzy.

And through the muddle and chaos I didn't get the opportunity to say goodbye to Beige Nicola or her two pink girls. Never mind. Tra la la. My bag was light when I hooked it over my shoulder, everything that was in it now eaten or given away.

I replayed the afternoon on the drive home, trying to reassure myself about how it had gone, recalling a few of the witty things I'd said, things that had got an unexpected laugh. Then cringing that I'd suggested dinner when it was far too soon for that. And about my hand touching a red patch on Sophie's arm where I thought she might have grazed herself when she fell. And for calling her children by their nicknames and hugging them or helping them when it wasn't my job. 'No, I want Mummy,' Ben had said when I'd tried to put him into Addie's car seat.

The gift. Had it been too much? Like the Elvis poster I'd bought to make Carla Brogan like me at school. It was in thanks for the torn newspaper cutting she'd given me of Bruno from the kids from 'Fame'. I pretended I'd found it at home; little did she know that I'd forced Mum through every shop in Stillorgan searching for the perfect one.

Though the election was long over, Labour Party candidate Teresa Ferris was still staring in at us from the telegraph pole opposite our flat, with her painted lips and set hair. Her eyes followed me around the sitting room, always seeming to look away just as I turned to look at her.

'Squirrel!' Teresa didn't flinch, but Addie was over, her small fingers smudging the window pane. 'Hey, Mr Squirrel,' she said, delighted, her exhales leaving little patches of condensation on the glass. She thumped at the window as he made his way – scuttle, scuttle – over the thick twine of the telegraph wire. And then he was gone, our excitement short-lived.

'OK, say night-night to the playground,' I was slowing down as I always did at this time of the evening. I contemplated the countless small battles we would have between now and bed.

'It's not bedtime?' Addie said, releasing a bit of wind.

'Excuse me, Little Miss Stink-a-lot.'

''Scuse me.' She giggled at my giggling.

'It *is* bedtime, I'm afraid. It's cold and dark. Look, the park's empty.

All the children have gone home. Everyone's asleep. Even the squirrels are off to bed.'

She examined her reflection in the window, moved closer and gave herself a long, wet kiss. 'Joy says I'm in charge about when I go asleep.'

'Does she now?' Joy had returned from Monaghan creatively revived and more controlling than ever. We'd had an argument about my parenting skills before she'd even unpacked; Addie had been half-naked and happy on a chair by the kitchen sink, doing the washing up, singing an old country song her dad used to play for her. (*Bottle of wine, fruit of the vine, when you gonna let me get sober?*) Aside from the inappropriateness of the lyrics, Joy felt this was a further sign that Addie needed some professional help to come to terms with her father no longer being part of her life. Then she suggested that she (not I) take Addie to see a wonderful therapist she'd met at the retreat. She'd left a brochure for Oasis Counselling on my bedside table, told me to 'find a quiet moment to consider it' and had disappeared into the bathroom with a bucket of Epsom Salts.

'Is Granny asleep?'

'Yes, Granny's asleep.'

'Is Alfie asleep?'

'You can see he's asleep. Now, that's enough questions.'

'Is Daddy asleep?'

'You don't have a daddy any more. Just like you don't have a little brother.' That was not a sensible thing to say. I wasn't handling this well.

'Or a crocodile,' Addie said, grinning. Addie was fine. Addie was going to be OK; we were going to be OK.

I turned away from her, tried to think of other things, tried to catch the headlines on the six o'clock news.

'Mummy, Mummy, peoples there.'

'Really,' I said, kneeling on the ground, balling up a bit of newspaper and throwing it onto the fire. Another of Joe's old jobs. He always seemed to be passing me on his way upstairs or down, with a bucket full of logs, always on his knees, sweeping the grate, forehead creased with industry, engrossed in this, his favourite daily ritual. I'd become quite adept at it.

'Peoples. No clothes on!'

'Silly-billy,' I said and stood, wiping my hands on my jeans, leaving great black streaks along each leg. I walked over, bent down behind her, held her around her waist, blew on her neck. Reflected in the window, the flames from the fire were licking the telegraph wire. It took a moment to see what she was pointing at, and then to make sense of it, but there on the bench beneath the oak tree in the playground, was a boy in a red sweater, his bare backside moving up and down, a girl's legs bent either side of him.

'Jesus.'

'What happened, Mummy?'

'Never mind. Silly people. They'll get very cold. Now, how about a cartoon?' I said, pulling her away and turning on my computer which I'd set up on the coffee table beside the window.

'I love you. You're my best friend,' she said, settling into her seat, thrilled at my inconsistency.

She pointed at a thumbnail illustration on YouTube for an episode of *Peppa Pig* she hadn't seen and settled into her seat. I turned back to the window – they were still at it. Then the girl must have seen me; she pushed the boy off. He stood up, tugged at the belt of his jeans. It was Dylan Freeney, Mimi's 'dream child', the boy all the mothers loved. Dylan and Juliette doing it in the park. Juliette grabbed her bag, sat back down on the picnic bench. No wait. Not Juliette.

Juliette's hair was longer, blonder. It was Dylan and some girl I didn't know. I closed the shutter, turned back to the TV, tried to concentrate on the news.

The beautiful female newsreader, so polished and coiffed, always made me feel grubby. Too aware of my unshaven legs, my dirty, bitten nails. Two hundred jobs were to go at a factory in Roscommon. There would be Social Welfare cuts in the budget. House prices had fallen again.

'Come on, Peppa,' says George, 'I want to rape you.' I looked over Addie's shoulder to see the two little cartoon characters ice-skating, and then the sound of kids giggling and a thumb over the camera, and more giggles. *'Peppa's dad wants to fuck you.'*

'God, what's going on this evening? OK, that's enough Peppa.' I stretched over, slammed the lid down and pulled her away.

''Nother one,' she said, holding up her hand, voice cracking. 'Look at my thumb, it says one.'

I carried her protesting down to the bedroom.

'I want more cartoons! You're hurting my tummy's feelings. Is it school tomorrow?'

'Yes, sweetie.'

'But I don't like school.' She started to cry.

'Do you want to see me hop?' she said, with a quick change of tactic, jumping from foot to foot. 'I'm not very good but it's the bestest I can do.'

'Fantastic. Now, off we go.'

'But I didn't do whining and crying.'

'You *are* doing whining and crying.'

'But I want to be happy. I want to be good.'

'OK, be good then, please.'

'But I don't know how to be good.'

When she was calm, I crept back into the sitting room. The playground was in darkness. Definitely Dylan, but not Juliette. The little creep. I then spent one hour and fifteen minutes trying to remove the security tag from the bottle of wine I'd bought at Tesco using the self-service till, such was my need for a drink after a very long day with a very short person. It took three screwdrivers, one pair of scissors (now kaput), a pair of pliers and Joe's Swiss Army knife to remove the plastic.

I texted Sophie, my fingers still sore and cut, to tell her how much we'd enjoyed our day at the beach. Of course just after I'd sent it, I thought of a joke I could have made about the au pair, but a second text would be a bit needy.

And then I didn't hear back from her. I checked my phone every few minutes, feeling a bit put out by her casualness, re-reading my sent message to see if the tone was right. She'd have read it by now for sure. Maybe she didn't enjoy our time together as much as I had? Maybe the gift was too much after all. Maybe she'd wanted to hang out with Beige Nicola instead, maybe she'd just invited us to be polite.

And then it happened. My phone rang. 'Hello?' I said, heart galloping.

'A disaster striked!' It wasn't Sophie, it was flipping Irenka. I could hear her in stereo, on the phone and coming up through the floorboards.

'Those leetal bastards. I'm sorry, Eve, but can't you not see? They're burning the bloody rope bridge out there. The leetel shits.'

I looked out the window, saw the flames.

'Can you come and see me, please?' she said, sounding like a headmistress. 'I can't leave Charlotte, Donal's out at a Tidy Town's meeting.' I knocked on the bathroom door, and called out to Joy in a loud whisper, trying not to wake Addie. No reply. I imagined her like Ophelia, ears under water, swishing her salt-and-pepper hair about, deaf to everything. I grabbed the baby monitor from the hall table, trudged down the stairs.

'You know we have no fire service here in Bray?' Irenka said, holding her door open. Her hair was standing on end – it looked hacked at, as if she'd taken a pair of scissors to it in a premenstrual rage. 'It's bloody dangerous,' she said, negotiating furniture on her way to the window, her mobile phone in her hand.

We stood together watching the kids, who were now trying to put out the fire, but I sunk back behind the shutters when one of them turned around, terrified of being spotted. I wasn't going to tell her about the sex. Her reaction would be exhausting and I couldn't be certain of what I saw.

'What can we do? We can't confront them. Two women on their own.'

'What? And why nod?' The spots flared up between her eyebrows. 'Should I be afraid in my own home?' A bit of her spit landed on my lip. This was just what she didn't want to hear; what everyone had always said to her before. I had hit her Achilles heel, I could feel a rant coming on, but I didn't have the energy for it. All I wanted to do was to go back upstairs.

'I tell you, Eve, when we get those hedges cut – the council said Monday for sure – we can keep our kids safe and we can keep an eye on those pigs.'

Her mobile phone began playing 'Eine Kleine Nachtmusik'.

'Yes, Sergeant. Thanks for returning my call. The boys, the three boys I told you about, they're back. They're setting fires in the park. I'm watching them as we speak,' she said, picking a bit of fluff from my sweater.

I looked around at her remarkably clean and orderly home. The handles of all the tea cups along the shelves in the kitchen were turned in the same direction; the tea towels lined up at the same length on the rail in front of the cooker. This wasn't going to be a quick conversation with the police; Irenka had settled on the sofa with the phone and was flipping through the pages of a notebook, looking for something else to complain about to the sergeant, now that she had him. I felt sorry for the police, however ineffectual they had been in sorting out the problems with the playground, Irenka was on to them almost daily; she must have had them on speed dial.

I was restless; it was difficult to see anything in the park now that the fire had died. I moved away from the window and occupied myself looking at framed photographs of Irenka and her family that were arranged on a mahogany side table. Donal in a mortar board, receiving a degree, everyone huddled together and beaming on a family skiing trip, Charlotte and her grandparents beside a Christmas tree. Something about all of them seemed a little odd, but I couldn't say precisely what.

'You'll notice a white space in each of them, yes?'

Irenka had finished her call, without my realising, and was now standing behind me.

I looked closer. In each photograph there *was* a strange white space.

'That was where my sister, Jolanta, used to be. She's no longer part of my family. I had her professionally airbrushed out. They did an excellent job, don't you think?'

'That was a bit radical,' I said, laughing but at the same time thinking she was insane. 'What on earth did she do?'

'That is none of your concern, Eve. You understand me, eh?'

'Diddle, diddle, dumpling!'

We couldn't make out his shape in the darkness, but Irenka recognised his voice. There was the chime of a stick on the park railings, the top of his ginger head. Billy Flynn was marching across the road towards us. He stopped and stood still, legs spread, hands on hips, outside our gate, looking in at us. 'My son John went to bed with his trousers on. One shoe off.'

And he bent on one knee, yanked off his trainer and hurled it at us. It flew at the window like a strange white bird in the dark of night and thumped against the glass. We both jerked our heads backwards. It fell into the mud below the hydrangea bush. How our faces must have looked, silent and scared, frozen in that moment when he had absolute control over us.

'Oh, I'm sorry, Irenka. I'll be a good boy now, I promise.' He said in a mocking tone. He rooted through the bushes to retrieve his shoe and made his way, hobbling, laughing, away from us, down the dark avenue that lead to the seafront and under the dank bridge of the train station where pigeons mate and breed and die under the wheels of jeeps and men from the pub take a piss or a snog or a quick fuck or feel.

Back upstairs, I closed the shutters and double-locked the front door. And in the next five minutes I undid everything that that very expensive sleep trainer had taught us and Addie about sleep. I not only took her out of bed – and she was at that stage of deep sleep where she wanted to stay there, wasn't fighting it any more – I carried her up to the sitting room and gave her some ice cream.

Unable to sleep that night, I got up and logged onto Rollercoaster. Pink Panther was getting her Spanx in a twist. A mother had had such a stressful afternoon with her three children in a supermarket that she had left them sitting on the wall of the car park, reversed out of her space and pretended to drive off without them. They had got such a fright that they had run after her screaming. All the other mothers sympathised, said they had been there. Pink Panther said she would be reporting her to Social Services.

I logged out, got up, opened the shutters, looked out at the night. Its stillness and quiet was comforting. Then a small flicker of light caught my eye. And there Billy was, standing still in darkness, holding a lighter under his chin, his face lit up by the flame, his satanic, twisted smile broadening and just as soon fading again.

Chapter Sixteen

We woke to the sound of chainsaws and opened the sitting room shutters to see men cutting the hedges that lined the park, lunging and retreating as they worked, lifting their snarling guide bars in the air. There were sights and sounds of industry everywhere: teams in Tidy Town T-shirts had begun raking leaves, heaping piles in specified points around the park. Neighbours I'd never seen before, in checked shirts and baseball caps, were working with yard brushes and spades along the south side of the square. Children held bin bags open while others climbed into the bushes to retrieve things – umbrellas, beer cans, socks, crisp packets – that had blown up the avenue from the sea.

We got dressed and went across the road to help, me casual in grey sweatshirt and jeans, Addie with a toy rake and her bumble-bee rucksack containing one unicorn, two fairies, a box of princess plasters, in case she had an accident, and her little book of wild flowers. It was worrying that she was expecting misfortune but the book of wild flowers made me happy. She used to potter after Joe around the garden, trying to match things with its black-and-white photos and in the early days after he'd left she had it with her all the time. Soon she abandoned it for some new obsession – her musical jewellery box that she'd filled with 'sapphires' or her plastic

Fisher Price laptop – but it had left her with a lasting interest in nature (when she wasn't playing Candy Crush Saga on my phone).

As soon as we'd reached the gates, Addie let go of my hand and ran across the grass to Dylan who bent and lifted her into his arms, swung her around a couple of times, then carried her back over to me, and got on with edging the borders, Juliette stuffing his hoodie with leaves while he worked. I tried to get the image of his naked backside out of my head.

Assiduous as ever, Irenka was on her knees by the flower bed, her slim, dexterous hands planting bulbs of daffodils and tulips. 'Flowers uplift our spirit, well at least mine, anyway,' she was saying, though no one was listening. She didn't need a second person in order to have a conversation.

Donal was standing above her, handing out trays of bulbs to the other volunteers. No one whistles any more, Joe used to say, but Donal was whistling that day, and there was even singing: Mr Norman in his high, tenor voice as he cleaned graffiti from the slide with his special 'graffiti attack pack'.

The local kids were raking with such enthusiasm that they were ripping out grass, leaving patches of dirt where they worked. Around the playground mothers hovered over their offspring, trying to keep them out of trouble.

Joy had wheeled Arthur over from the Cherry Glade and had propped him beside the slide, the Yankees baseball cap on his head askew, the blue-white sheen of his shins exposed. Now she was up in the tree house attaching a homemade American flag above the wooden door. Billy was watching her from outside the park, a brown paper bag over his head, Ned Kelly-style, holes cut out at the eyes. Lars was there in his usual red-and-white striped top, settling on his bench beneath the oak tree. 'There's Wally,' Addie always said when she saw him.

'Come on, ladies, Sumita, Eve, let's get to work!' Irenka said, striding over to us. We'd been looking for an excuse to escape; we'd got stuck in the middle of a conversation with Beige Nicola and the mother who was always in riding boots and was too tall for me to consider making friends with.

'I mean, at the end of the day, I personally feel there's absolutely no point in buying environmentally friendly nappies if you're going to dispose of them in a Tommy Tippee bin bag which takes about one hundred years to decompose,' Beige Nicola said.

'You could always buy some recycled nappy sacks,' the horsey one said. Sumita listened, keeping her head down with a small repertoire of interjections which alternated between 'Oh my gosh!' and 'really?' with a roll in the 'r', using both often. I had nothing to add.

Irenka grabbed Addie round the waist, watching as she escaped her and ran away. 'Look, see. I still think she is walking a bit funny, on the inside of her feet. Her weight is not balanced, it's not good for her spine. She needs better shoes, like Charlotte's,' she said, pointing at her own child's feet. It sounded like she had done a lot of thinking about it. 'They're from Ecco. They have very good elasticity. Very good for their developing bones.'

I took this with a nod and a smile. She wasn't going to get to me that day. Also I'd asked her to mind Addie while I took my driving test that afternoon so I couldn't fall out with her before then.

'This is a public park. Open up, you spaz!' It had been Mr Norman's decision to lock the gates while we worked. Billy had hoiked himself up onto the railings and crossed to the chestnut tree beside them, where Mr Norman had nailed a sign with the new opening and closing times. He tried to yank it free.

'If you don't get out of that effing tree now, I'm going to come after you with my shoe,' Belinda said, reaching over her solid midriff towards her foot, to show she meant business.

'And you watch your language, young man. There are small children here,' Irenka said, striding towards him.

'That woman's a pain in the arse.' Nathan had come up beside me. 'She deserves a slap. I saw her chase a kid round here the other day with a Twix wrapper in her hand. I mean, for fuck's sake. She needs to wise up.'

I was finding it hard to meet his eye, as if he really had had sex with me recently.

'Your house is coming on. You know we're so close, I can see right into your bedroom. Oh, sorry, that sounds a bit strange.'

'No it doesn't. It sounds very exciting,' he said, leaning over and squeezing my arm.

'Mama, can I make an apple tree with these? I know how to do it. Barney showed me,' Addie said, holding an apple core in her hand.

'Would you like me to help you with that, little lady?' Belinda asked, rocking back on her heels, her cheeks flushed from digging. Addie handed her the apple and watched, mesmerised, as she teased the seeds out of the core, then the two of them knelt together and planted the seeds.

I smiled at people whose names I didn't yet know but whose faces had become familiar and I met some more neighbours that morning: a Chinese couple whose little boy was the same age as my girl, a homesick South African woman who worked for the bank and was always getting abuse from customers, and the lady from number fourteen who told me about a cookery course up the road.

'Why does your mummy never put clips in your hair?' Irenka

asked Addie, as she led her away and I went home to get ready for my driving test.

'What's the minimum tyre tread depth?' Nathan shouted over to where I was standing in the front drive. He was on the other side of the park railings, above a row of daffodil bulbs he'd just planted, leaning on his spade. I hadn't realised he'd been watching me. I hoped he hadn't seen me wave up at the sitting room window, as was my habit, to pretend we didn't live alone.

'Erm . . . one point six millimetres?'

'Very good. And name three people in authority for whom you should stop.'

'Garda, school warden, person in charge of animals.' I knew the answers to all these questions, Joe had asked me them a thousand times, it was like reeling off prayers at Mass. In theory I was great, in practice, a little less so. He'd tell me ten reasons I'd failed before I'd turned the engine on and the tensest of hours would follow, Joe jamming his foot on an imaginary brake every few seconds, gripping the handle above him, not daring to look away from the road ahead. We'd always finish early, swapping places in silence so he could do the tricky parallel parking bit. I'd slam the garden gate on him with my L plates in my sweaty hands and we'd both swear never again. I was going to pass this test all by myself.

'You're all set, best of luck.'

'Bye!' OK, I couldn't mess this up. I got into the car, began reversing out the gate. Concentrate. Concentrate. Not only was Nathan watching, but there was a car idling on the road waiting for me to exit. Back I reversed, but too far, forcing the other car to reverse a few yards as well. Then I stalled. And stalled again, pulled myself together, ploughed on and grabbed for the indicator to thank him – that quick, confident flash of competent drivers – but turned on the windscreen wipers instead. I put my foot down hard on the accelerator not wanting to delay him further and also maybe to show off a little bit. On I went through sun bright streets, picking up speed, passing a sweet old man and his little grandson. The old man, though I didn't recognise him, held his hand up as I passed him. I waved back, it was like *Sesame Street*. This really was a wonderful neighbourhood.

As I approached the junction where our road and the main road out of Bray met, there was a sudden sound of sirens. I tried to recall what you're meant to do when an ambulance is behind you; it always made me emotional when I saw cars pulling over to let a sick person through. The siren was getting nearer and nearer. I looked in the overhead mirror but all I could see was myself: my arched eyebrows, my shower-wet hair. I readjusted it, and saw that it wasn't an ambulance after all, but the car that had been behind me, now with a rotating light on its roof, and it didn't seem to want to pass. It pulled up alongside me.

'Do you know what you just did?' He was a policeman. He wasn't smiling, he had soft brown eyes that were not looking softly at me. I had no idea what he was upset about. Oh God, please don't ask to see my licence.

'Do you have any idea how dangerous that was?'

'What was?'

'You just went straight through a red light.'

'Did I? No I didn't. When? Where?'

'At the pedestrian crossing behind you. And they hadn't just turned red either. You could have killed that old man and the child.'

'I had no idea. I'm sorry. Sorry. Sorry.'

The old man's outstretched hand – not a wave at all but a

warning – telling me to slow down. To stop. To take heed. His other arm had been held over the little boy on his tricycle with his helmet, having learnt all about the green man.

'Just show a little more consideration in future.'

He was letting me go. I was not just reckless. I was selfish. And I was breaking the law.

I drove on, still shaking, feeling like an admonished child. Everyone I passed on the high street, every single resident of Bray; Mrs Dicker always in soft focus in her bottle-thick glasses and beiges and creams and the folds of flesh of her fallen face, outside her bits and bobs shop; the school kids waiting below the graveyard for a bus, on the kerb, not out on the road, not about to kill anyone, not doing anything illegal, or reckless, seemed sane, more sensible, less selfish than me.

I pulled into the test centre and parked. Was my examiner standing at some unseen window, picking at his teeth, draining his coffee, pulling at the crotch of his slacks, waiting for his two-thirty? A time, not a name. One of ten to get through in the day.

OK, what did I need? I leant over, opened the glove compartment and fished around for my learner's permit, my hand shaky as anything. Not there. Cursing I pulled everything out: the boring old car manual that Joe was always trying to get me to read, two pairs of sunglasses, one with a broken arm, Joe's gym membership for the Riverview Club. I turned the laminated card over in my hand. He looked tired in the photo, his eye bags, a family trait, very pronounced. It had expired of course. I think he went about twice, then pulled a muscle in his chest when lifting a too-heavy weight after not warming up. He blamed his trainer and never went back after that. That was so like Joe. He gave up on everything as soon as it got hard, just like he gave up on us. My permit was stuck to the underside of the card, the adhesive between them an ancient, fluff-covered Chupa Chups lollipop. I wiped the permit as best I could, stuffed it in my back pocket, took five deep breaths, checked my teeth for lipstick, got out and slammed the car door. I was going to get this, I was different from Joe, I was going to see this through.

I sat in the waiting room that brought to mind failed Irish exams, the bitten lips of disappointed teachers and parents, slammed doors, tears of not understanding, and then sought out the toilets, always the toilets before the terrifying thing.

I watched the swing doors to the interrogation room and when he appeared I could not believe my bad luck. The German. Not the damned German! The one who'd failed me the third time, when I'd been convinced that I'd driven beautifully. When I'd had to hold my fingers over the edges of my lips to suppress my smile as I'd followed him back into the test centre with warm thoughts of telling Joe, my mum, my sister. When I could just see myself emerging triumphant, punching my hands in the air, like that man on the *Rules of the Road* DVD.

He didn't seem to recognise me. This was probably a good thing. I resisted the temptation to remind him. We were the last of five cars to pull out. I followed the others, all terrified, all cautious, along the main road, feeling like a cartoon character of a perfect driver, looking in the mirror, indicating to change lanes, hands correctly positioned at ten to two. Observation, observation, observation. I wanted to talk to him, to get him on my side, but I knew that was against the rules. The air in the car was too sweet, too close.

At the end of the street, there was a roundabout, a peculiar one with a church in the middle of it, one that had confused me before. It was a busy Saturday afternoon. Qualified, mature, sensible people were driving into town to shop or picking up their children from playdates. We all slowed, prepared to stop. A neat row of driving school cars, the drivers behind us, tutting at their misfortune.

There was a break in the traffic. The first car, five ahead of mine, nudged forward and out, but instead of driving clockwise around the roundabout they indicated to the right and moved on. The next car did the very same thing. As did the three cars behind them.

'What's happening? Why are they all driving the wrong way?'

'Drive on, please,' said the German, his expression giving nothing away. Were some roundabouts different to others? Oh, God, what should I do? I followed my instincts and turned left. I did my own thing and went the right, correct way around the roundabout and when I reached the other side, the German settled back in his seat. The four driving school cars were in an untidy arrangement along the road ahead of us, doing three-point turns, not as part of the exam but in order to get their cars facing the right way to drive back to the test centre having all clearly failed. The German told me to overtake. I indicated to the right, pulled out and well clear of them, put my foot on the accelerator, drove over a speed bump and on into the traffic, confident, watchful, a taste of freedom in my mouth.

Chapter Seventeen

Simply Delicious Carrot and Courgette Muffins

We stood over the recipe, reading it together, me in my Avoca apron, clean hands, hair tied up; Mum with the sleeves of her cardigan rolled to the elbow, eyebrows arched. She was reading aloud to herself, using the little finger of her left hand to keep her place in the text. Addie had her apron on too but was taking a break, sitting on her little red horse, sharing her grapes with Alfie and watching *Charlie and Lola* in Spanish. Joy had shown me an article about a mother who only let her kids watch cartoons in foreign languages – better for their brains apparently, so I thought I'd give it a go. Not that there was much wrong with her brain. She had stood beside me moments earlier as I'd tried to remove the plastic cellophane wrapper from the DVD. First with my fingers, then with my teeth. 'No, Mama, you're doing it wrongly. How about scissors?' she'd said.

'Maybe you could beat the eggs, pet?'

We had the kitchen to ourselves for my cookery lesson; Joy was down on the promenade with Solly sticking crudely created plaster casts they'd made of people's faces along the harbour wall with the strong sense that they were giving to the community rather than taking from it, by defacing the pretty harbour with ugly effigies.

I shadowed my mother as she worked, sniffle-nosed and simple, following her around like a useless sous chef, getting in her way, asking silly questions. Cooking was so instinctive to her that she didn't understand how I hadn't picked up these skills by osmosis, particularly considering I'd been under her feet in the kitchen for most of my childhood, licking the mixing spoon of her chocolate cakes, cutting myself huge, jagged heels of Ballymaloe bread, which she'd have left to cool for a dinner party, standing tent-like on the breadboard, slathering them with butter I'd shaped with my fingers into ornate curls in the silver dishes with the blue inners that only came out when we had guests and made me think of priests and Mass.

Addie and I had begun to bake most afternoons. This was how I was learning; Addie was teaching me to cook. The other afternoon we tried some Annabel Karmel veggie burgers. The recipe said twenty-five minutes preparation time – we were still grating carrots three hours later, but she loved it and even tried two mouthfuls for tea that evening before saying they were yuck.

I broke three eggs into a bowl and tried to drag small fragments of shell out along its side using a teaspoon and, when that didn't work, my fingers. I dropped a great lump of butter into a Pyrex dish filled with cool flour. If all my ingredients had been laid out in front of me in clean little Pyrex dishes, all measured and ready to go like on an old TV show, I think I might have been quite a good cook. It was the measurements that confused me – you'll need maths all your life, my mammoth-breasted teacher had warned me – and then the ingredients. I was nervous of going into delis or organic stores where mothers who knew all about food queued behind me, stretched over me, asking about sweet potatoes and organic yams.

Someone left the cake out in the rain. I don't think that I can take it cos it took so long to bake it and I'll never have that recipe again. Ohhhh noooo!

Joe's mother baked. Joe's mother sewed. Joe's mother made a needlepoint tapestry to mark the queen's visit to Northern Ireland. He was disappointed to find that I didn't possess any of these skills. 'You weren't brought up proper,' he used to say.

Mum stood up from the oven, having slid the muffins in on a baking tray, her face red from being upside down and from the heat coming from the opened door. 'So now we just leave them for twenty minutes,' she said, wiping flour from her sweater, retrieving a tissue from up her sleeve, dashing it across her nose.

'I want another cartoon but in Bray language,' Addie said, and then seeing that she had our attention, she changed her mind.

'Watch this!' she said, up from her seat, slamming down the lid of my laptop. She twirled around on the kitchen floor.

We whooped and applauded.

'That's why because I've got so much energy!' she said, giving us an encore.

We carried cups of tea out onto the balcony, along with a couple of deckchairs and a tin watering can for Addie that I'd bought in the two Euro shop. It had immediately leaked, leaving a trail of water from the kitchen sink to the sitting room window.

'Ah, this is wonderful,' Mum said, holding her head up to the sun, her chair sinking a little beneath her in the uneven Tarmac.

It was one of those lovely October days, bright and cold, when you could see your own breath; the sky was cloudless and everything was clean-edged and cartoon-coloured. Mum was talking but I had gone, back to college classes I'd never taken in Oxford, with my black bicycle and striped scarf, past the steamy-windowed cafe on campus and the lamp-lit library behind ivy-covered walls and on to meet an imaginary man for a walk by the river and then, when it got dark, to a fireworks display on some misty old heath or hill.

'Do you know what might look rather fun there?' Mum was up off her seat peering over the balcony's stone edge.

'Ivy?'

'Yop. But no. I was thinking more of something like a clematis – you could start to train one up along the pillars,' she said, excited that she'd had a better idea than the one I'd suggested.

'I'm just renting, Mum.'

'Of course you are. I'd rather forgotten that. You could always mention it to your landlord . . .'

Mum paused, gazed at the ground, the way people do when they're trying to recall something, as if the answer will come from there.

'To Mr Lyons.'

'Maybe – look, there he is now.' Nathan had just got out of his filthy jeep across the road, and was on the phone, surveying the house. He was wearing a luminous bib and holding a hard hat in his hand. The concrete, walls and roof were all in. It looked like they were fitting the windows that day.

'Oh, he's quite dishy, isn't he?'

'Do you think?' I said, as if it hadn't even occurred to me.

'Well, I must say, I think it's wonderfully optimistic to be building a house in the middle of a recession,' Mum said, rooting in her bag for her sunglasses.

'Isn't it just?' I said, sounding exactly like her. 'And he was so sweet about me having got a lodger.' As soon as I'd said it I remembered I'd told her a little lie. I'd said that I'd cleared it with him before I'd placed the advert. It was the sort of harmless untruth you tell your mother so she won't worry about you, or worry about you a little less.

She let it go. 'Well, I'm jolly glad you've got that straightened out.'

'Though now that it's all above board, I'm having a few doubts about Joy.'

This was not what she wanted to hear. Why do you do it, Bella would say. Why do you say things that you know will annoy her?

I told her how she had taken over with Addie and about how I was starting to find her a little bit creepy.

'Ah, listen, pet, it's too late for that now. I really wouldn't bring up anything that might offend her.' She approved of Joy, she was older and more sensible and, most of all, Mum liked that someone else was looking after me so that she could have a little more peace.

'I've got the best idea for Addie's birthday,' I said to distract her.

'I feel desperate about this, love, but actually I'll be in Cephalonia that week,' she said, her voice rising a little towards the end of the sentence with happy thoughts of her trip.

'Ah, Mum, that's the second time you've missed her birthday in three years.'

'But I'm sure I told you?'

I shook my head, though no doubt she had. 'And what about Maud?' She was an old school friend of Mum's who was on her way out. 'You'll probably miss her funeral if you go.'

'Well yes, but I'm no good at funerals.'

'It's not a matter of being good, Mum, you don't need to say anything, you just need to be there.'

'But I can't possibly let Vivienne down; it's all booked and paid for and she's expecting me and I go every year and—'

'Mum, please don't go. It's just one holiday. Why are you always travelling? Don't you like being at home with us?'

'Now stop that! I'm perfectly happy at home. Addie will have lots of other birthdays and I'll bring her back a surprise. I do feel awful about it, sweetheart, please don't go on.'

'My turn,' Addie said, noticing Mum's sunglasses for the first time.

She abandoned her watering can and stretched out to grab them from her face.

Mum obliged, bent down, helped slot them onto her grandchild's little snub of a nose. Addie held her head high and jutted out her chin to hold them in place. 'Look at me, Mummy,' she said, walking straight into the wall.

She whimpered, we reassured her, watched her, admired her and returned to our disjointed conversation. 'And you can just about make out the sea.' We stood together so that I could show her the triangle of blue that was visible between the two chimneys of the house opposite. 'Yes, and when those leaves have gone, you'll have a great view of it.'

When Mum sat again, exhaling as she lowered herself, the way older people do, Addie was beside her chair. She'd become bored of the sunglasses game and was trying to hand them back to her.

'Oh, thank you very much,' Mum said, bending to retrieve them. Then somehow they slipped out of her hand. 'Let me do it,' Addie said as Mum felt around for them beneath her seat. It was at that moment, as she tilted sideways, feeling for them blindly with her fingers, that she lost balance and toppled over, still in the chair, trapping Addie beneath her.

'Oh God! Mum! Addie!'

Mum couldn't move and I couldn't move her. I tried to pull my child free but she was stuck under my mother and under the chair legs. Addie was screaming. I was screaming. Mum was telling me not to panic as she tried to hoist herself up, away from Addie, but the weight of her own body and the chair was too great. I had no choice but to push her backwards. I shoved against her soft, padded skin; I shoved as hard as I could to get her off my child, and she tried to assist me, jolting backward, trying to get into a rhythm where she could launch herself upright again. 'Sorry, Mum,' I heard myself whimper. I pushed, I flailed, I screamed, until together we made her fall backwards, still in the chair, with her back on the ground and her legs and arms in the air, the ridges of the wicker chair imprinted on the underside of her thighs. I cried with fright and relief, hugged Addie in my arms and checked her for damage. 'Everything's fine, she's fine, I'm fine,' Mum said, trying to comfort us from her position upside-down in the air.

'It's OK. Honestly,' she said when she was upright again, though I could see that she'd snagged her skirt on the chair leg and that the skin beneath was bleeding. I sat down beside her, holding Addie, still trembling. Mum rubbed her hand along my leg, then wrapped her arms around both of us.

'That's my favourite smell. Firewood burning in the autumn. Can you get it?'

'Not really. Though I do smell burning coming from somewhere.'

'Oh dash it. The buns.'

In a few seconds we heard Irenka's quick footfalls on the carpet and her questioning call of my name, smoke travelling up nostrils as flared and keen as a dog's. I anticipated her knock before she'd had a chance, opened the door and sent her on her way.

Help! Advice needed!

I typed into Rollercoaster as Addie sat beside me not eating her pasta that evening.

My mum fell on DD today. She seems to be OK but she's not eating and she's a little bit wheezy. Do you think there could be internal damage? What should I do?

There was a plethora of responses, most of them reassuring:

OMG, you poor thing!

How frightening!

Hugs and xxxxxx!

Then one pinged in from the Pink Panther:

What sort of mother are you, wasting your time posting on here instead of bringing your child to Casualty?

How dare she? I was still thinking as I bundled Addie into the car.

The hospital was an awful Victorian institution, the sort of place that makes you feel frail, with threadbare seats and walls the colour of panty pad packages and grey-faced, pyjamaed people in wheelchairs tugging at cigarettes outside the automatic doors and the Virgin looking down on us by the vending machine that didn't work. And the smell, of illness, of death, sprayed over with antiseptic, made my limbs weak and made me want to take my beautiful, healthy, strong-hearted child home again to keep her safe and uninfected.

The waiting room was full of people who looked like they'd been waiting forever: a large woman in a pink nightie in a wheelchair by the door, a packet of cigarettes on her lap; a bristle-haired rat boy walking in and out of the automatic doors, one eye so swollen he couldn't open it. A woman who'd swallowed a fishbone that had got stuck in her throat, an elderly lady with her mother – sticks and bandages and plastic bags of belongings. I watched with envy and pity the people who were called to be seen by the triage nurse, while Addie lay listless in my arms.

'Be brave, Mama, hold my hand.'

It seemed impossibly small and soft in mine.

'Now do this,' she said, lightly stroking the top of my own hand with her finger to show me how.

'Sorry, Mama,' she wheezed, when she saw me sitting with my head in my hands, half an hour later. 'Sorry,' she whispered again, leaning forward to kiss me. Sometimes she would lean too hard on my shoulder as I tried to dress her, digging her sharp little nails into my skin, and I'd feel irritated by her physical closeness. At times our games, so exciting to her, were tedious to me. Some mornings, tired, hung-over, worried, I wouldn't be with her at all. 'OK, last time,' I'd say, always hurrying her up, always with something more important to do. Or I'd yank her out of her chair when she'd spilt her milk by mistake, and squeeze that top over her head when it was six months too small for her, because we were in a hurry and because she looked cute in it, even if she wanted to wear the sparkly one. And then I'd sit her in front of yet another episode of *Peppa Pig*, because I wanted to do a workout, text someone, make up my face. I held her tight in my arms and nuzzled my nose in her hair, drifting in and out of conversations around me.

'Do you ever get scared?'

'They caught it in the early stages.'

'Lovely lady.'

'Very hard though, if you've children.'

'Not funny, really.'

'Always thought he was seeing someone else.'

'It's not good news, I'm afraid.'

'It's not good news, I'm afraid.' Those words brought me right back there. The doctor had been smiling as she said them, it was what bad news did to her face. Seeing that I was going to cry, she'd nudged the purposefully placed box of tissues a little closer to where I was sitting. 'Your embryo didn't survive the defrost.' How many times had she been through this? How many couples had sat opposite her, devastated, crumpled, beyond hope. And still she'd smiled. An empathetic sort of smile, but a smile none the less. She'd made phone calls, took notes. She'd written out our options on a green Post-it note. There was one more embryo they could defrost, though the quality wasn't as good as the one that hadn't survived. Alternatively, we could embark on another fresh cycle but that would be quite costly. Joe had had a big presentation at work that day so I was on my own. She'd told me to think about it.

I'd walked out of her office and across the city into a large department store. Clothes were like my comfort food. I'd tried on a skirt in a size bigger than usual, but I couldn't even get the zip up I was so bloated with fertility drugs. I'd looked at my face in the changing room mirror: baggy-eyed, worn-out, washed-up.

I'd hung the skirt on the side of the cheese counter, left and wandered back to the clinic, praying and terrified.

'It looks like a really good one!' The consultant had said, beaming.

Our final little ice baby had survived the defrost. I'd watched it throbbing and swelling on a monitor beside me and saw the catheter enter, deposit the embryo and slowly exit again.

'You have a beautiful uterus,' the embryologist had said, looking up at me from between my legs.

We'd been waiting to see the triage nurse for almost an hour: standing, sitting, texting, lying my child down across the plastic, easy-wipe seats, then lifting her up again. The woman with the fishbone that turned out not to be a fishbone at all but a small bit of wire, was now wire-free and wishing us luck as she escaped into the clear air and the land of the free and the healthy. The man beside us told me he was dying of lung cancer as he opened a packet of crisps. Then he told me that we were in the wrong hospital.

'The X-ray shows no bruising to the ribs,' the paediatrician at the children's hospital said, as he listened to Addie's chest, 'but I agree that she sounds a little wheezy. Does she have a history of chest infections?'

'No, she's never really been sick,' I said, holding her close to me.

'It may be some sort of allergy. Do you have any pets?'

'Yes, just a dog, but he's been with us since before she was born. I don't think he could be causing the problem. I'm pretty good at brushing him, picking up his fur.'

'Well, he may or may not be. It isn't so much their fur, more their dander and saliva. Dogs shed tiny flakes of skin as it replaces itself, just as our skin does,' he said, in that simple sort of tone adults adopt when they are in the company of small children. 'Does he shed a lot?'

'Yes, but he's short-haired.'

'Short-haired breeds shed the most, I'm afraid. It's possible that she has developed an allergy.'

'Do you mean asthma?' I asked, panicking.

'Don't panic. It's very common in small children. And also very manageable. I'll prescribe an inhaler for her as a precaution. Here's an information leaflet, it should tell you most of what you need to know.'

'And what should I do about the d-o-g?'

He spelt out his response.

'I can't do that I'm afraid. It's just not possible.'

'Well, I can't make that decision for you but if your child's wheezing gets any worse and you find yourself using the inhaler more regularly it's something you may have to consider.'

Chapter Eighteen

Alfie got out of bed, stretched, straightened his legs in front of him, shoved his rear end in the air. As soon as he saw me take his lead from where it hung on a hook at the back of the flat door, he began yelping, pacing and jumping in circles, eyes alight, frantic – a crazed beast on LSD.

He tried to sit still so that I could slide his collar over his snout and ears, he raised and jutted his head forward to help, but he was too excited, he couldn't do it. He kept knocking the collar out of my hands.

'Please, Alfie. Stay. That's it. Good boy.' His big eyes were pleading, filled with expectation. This was all he wanted in life, a walk and a master to obey and love.

I put on my coat and rooted in the hall drawer for poo bags. Now he knew it was happening. He couldn't contain himself; he grabbed his squeaky giraffe and charged down the stairs ahead of Addie and me. And when we were down, he thundered through the opened hall door, and leapt with unabashed glee into the boot of the car – the car always meant a long walk. There he sat alert, in a tidy position, only his paws still moving, pacing from side to side.

'Where are we going?' Addie asked, as I strapped her into her seat.

'Alf's going on his holidays.'

'To America? On the airplane? Can I come too?'

'No, not to America. Alfie's going on holidays to a special place in the countryside with lots of other doggies.'

'Al*fie*,' she shrieked and giggled when he came up behind her, sniffed the back of her neck and gave her a big, paternal lick.

The dogs' home was a two-hour drive from Bray according to Valerie – the brusque-sounding woman I'd spoken to on the phone. I was nervous of the trip; though I was now a fully qualified driver (my round-the-corner reverse didn't go very well – the German said I'd have needed to take a bus to reach the kerb, but he let it go) this was the longest trip I had ever attempted on my own. I didn't trust either of my companions' bladders for this length of time and it made me anxious that they were so trusting of me, so sure that I knew what I was doing. They both looked very contented to be going on an expedition. The more I looked in the rear-view mirror, the more I couldn't stand it. 'I am strong,' I told myself. 'I am making decisions. I am in control.'

For the first few years he'd been so noisy in the car, howling with such misery on even the shortest journeys, that Joe used to drive with a water pistol over his shoulder, ready to douse him. Now he sat upright, attentive, and silent in the boot, only standing when he needed some air, sticking his snout out the side passenger window, which Addie was controlling with the automatic button.

I babbled away, sang songs, recited nursery rhymes, tried to keep things upbeat.

In autumn the leaves come falling down
And children go back to school
Some mothers are sad
And some are glad
And that's the end of my tune.

'Do it again.'

I don't know why this poem had stayed with me. It had beaten my own short story, *Killing Time* – a dark and worrying essay about varying ways to top yourself – in our first-year creative writing competition.

The road wound out, undulating; great hills and huge dips. We drove on through a valley, through a picture-postcard scene: the dense forests on either side of us coloured orange, red, saffron-yellow, gold, the light coming through the clouds above us into the blueness, biblical in its intensity. Ireland does autumn so well.

On and on we went into the never-ending distance, the mountains ahead of us always moving away. The car dipped, hit rocks and potholes on roads too narrow and unknown to be safe and strewn with leaves turned to mulch around the edges.

I listened to the radio, Addie chatted to herself. Alfie was no longer visible in the rear-view mirror; he must have gone to sleep.

A lone goat ambled in muddy ground outside the entrance to the shelter, which I found after several wrong turns and pulling over to ask strangers. Addie laughed at the perfect white head and orange beak of a goose, dipping and reappearing behind a hedge.

Our arrival at the home set off a cacophony of noise: warning barks, dejected wails, cries and howls. Dogs leapt in muddy compounds against grey metal fencing, knocked over feeding bowls, tore up newspaper; others, older, more jaded long-term residents stayed curled up in the back of their cages.

Alfie was awake now, standing, ears erect. I parked on a patch of grass gouged with tractor wheels, got out, released him. He took off, nose to the ground, cocked his leg on the side of the rusty entrance gate for a prolonged pee. I lifted Addie out of her seat, let her hot head rest on my shoulder.

'It's too noisy,' she said, looking up, one cheek angry red. 'I want to go home.'

'You know what? So do I, let's go.' I called Alfie, walked back in the direction of the car. It had started to spit with rain. An unidentifiable animal was whining. A gate was banging somewhere. Little pockets of hens puck-pucked in the mud around us.

'Hello.' I turned to see a manly woman in a fleece top, tracksuit bottoms and gum boots, stepping down from a mobile caravan. This must have been Valerie. We walked back towards her. She addressed me as 'Ava', which I didn't bother to correct. She didn't seem to notice Addie, but immediately bent to pet Alfie, rubbing him on the back, then clasping her hands around his face, letting him lick her on the mouth. 'Oh, aren't you a handsome fellow? Aren't you, aren't you, aren't you?' she said, getting him excited.

She looked up at me from where she was still crouched over, petting him. 'Has he had his breakfast?' she asked, running her free hand through her own cropped hair.

'Yes, about an hour ago.'

'And some buttery toast.' Addie said, kicking to be free.

Valerie began filling in a flip chart. I tried to answer her questions, inhaling to keep from getting upset, as I'd done so many times since Joe left. But once they started, they wouldn't stop. Hot, salty tears filling my eyes, then spilling down my cheeks.

'Don't be sad, Mummy. Feel better,' Addie said, anxious, her own bottom lip protruding, her little brows arched in confusion. 'Alfie's happy. He's going on an airplane on his holidays next week.'

'I think it's easiest for everyone if you just get on with it,' Valerie said. I could hear the disapproval in her voice, sensed that she felt we didn't really need to do this. The last thing the refuge needed in a recession was another dog.

Before she said anything further I tried to explain, 'Like I said to you on the phone, if there were any possible way.'

'I know. I understand,' she said, though she didn't. I couldn't bear that we were doing this; that I was tearing our little family apart.

'Oh, Alfie,' I said on my knees now, as he licked my face, gave me his paw. 'You're such a good boy. Such a good boy.'

'Don't worry, we'll take good care of him.'

'Do you think it will be long, you know, till he finds . . .'

'Impossible to say; it's a little more difficult for older, large dogs. Puppies are what everyone wants, though they don't even want them at the moment.'

'Where will he sleep?'

'Last cage on the right, with Lily, a lovely old Basset Hound. I'll show you.'

Valerie took Alfie by the lead; he snuffled along beside her, head bowed, looking back at us. The rain was heavier now, stinging our faces. She led us through a yard where a long line of aluminium dishes were laid out in a row, to a huge fenced cage, partitioned into small runs and a covered area at the back of each, where the dogs slept. There was a toy teddy on the grey concrete of the Basset Hound's cage and a dish of uneaten food. The Basset's eyes glowed out at us from where she was sheltering in her kennel.

I handed over Alfie's feeding bowl and his favourite squeaky toy, the plastic giraffe that was once Addie's, the one that all French babies have. Alfie sniffed at it, then looked up at me, eager, keen-eyed, trusting, loyal, loving, velvet-eared, waiting for his walk. Valerie handed me back his collar.

'Let's go, Alf. Hurry up, Alfie. Let's go home,' Addie said as we turned to leave.

I carried her away, but her arms were outstretched. She was kicking me in the stomach, screaming.

'No, Mummy, no. Wait for Alfie. I want Alfie, Alfie home. Alfie home.'

'Shush, shush.'

'No, Mummy, don't say shush. Let's go, Alfie. I want Alfie,' she said, her little face collapsing.

I could hear Alfie cry too – that soft plaintive sound he sometimes made when he was dreaming.

Addie let her body go stiff, refusing to get into her seat, then she bit me hard on the arm. I had to push her into submission. I held my hands on her stomach, forced the straps around her, while she flailed about and kicked and hit me. 'I need Alfie. Need Alfie,' was her mantra till her voice became hoarse. Somewhere along the road back to Bray she faded with exhaustion to sleep.

I pulled over at a lay-by near a scrubby field and rested my head on the steering wheel. Another member of our little family gone. Addie's face was dirty with tears and snot, her hands gripping Alfie's collar, her eyelashes fluttering in sleep. How could I keep doing this to her? Consistency, love, routine is what all the books said and in her first years of life, two things had already left her. I sat there, at that lay-by, somewhere south of Wicklow for I don't know how long, but till the light had faded and evening was on its way. Then I indicated, pulled out and moved on. I turned on the radio, picked dog hair off my coat.

Chapter Nineteen

Joy was carrying a bale of hay and a box of small pumpkins through the garden gate – she stood well back and out of our way when she saw us approach and helped to direct my car into its space. I'd forgotten all about the pumpkin patch she had organised in the playground that day. I'd even forgotten it was Hallowe'en.

Addie had been excited about it for weeks, putting her sucky blanket over her head, making little 'whooo' sounds, like all the best spirits do, as she walked around the sitting room with her hands in the air, stopping and holding up the bottom of it every few seconds to see where she was going. Joy had made her a homemade witch's costume for the occasion.

'It was awesome,' Joy said, thumping up the stairs ahead of us. 'There must have been thirty kids there. I was worried we might run out of pumpkins but they all got one. And Sophie brought cupcakes along for everyone – oh, she's such a kind girl. She's invited us to go trick or treating with her tonight. Irenka's coming too. Where were you guys anyway? Oh listen, I got some posters printed up for Ratty.'

Now she was at the top of the stairs, rooting in her pumpkin box and trying to catch her breath. She unfurled a poster on which she had illustrated an image of Ratty with the words LOST and REWARD OFFERED in capitals and her phone number beneath.

Ratty had been missing for weeks and I was hoping Addie would forget all about him. 'And I picked up some sedatives for Alfie – NaturVet Quiet Moments, they're the best they say – the poor guy's going to be freaked out by the fireworks,' Joy said, holding the flat door open and letting us in ahead of her.

'Alfie's gone on holidays,' Addie said, almost in inverted commas, as if she no longer believed me, stomping past us into the sitting room like a teenager. I waited to explain my decision till she was absorbed in a cartoon and Joy and I were out of earshot, in the kitchen.

'You're kidding me, right?'

'He's going to have a good life. A much better one than he had with us. They're going to find him a lovely home in Sweden or maybe even in Italy; lurchers are a novelty over there because they don't breed them nationally,' I said, knowing that this scheme was really for retired greyhounds. I was lying to make both of us feel better. I tried to picture Alfie in his new home in Europe, sprawled out on a chaise longue, with a sparkling, diamanté collar.

'I can't believe what you're telling me,' Joy said, taking her brown rice off the boil. I sat at the kitchen table; she stood over me, hands on hips.

'Look, please don't give me a hard time about this. I'm miserable enough about it as it is.'

'And how do you think Alfie's feeling right now? And what about your poor kid? She adores that dog. I just don't know how you can do that to her.' I had never seen Joy angry before and it was alarming, so much more so with her than with anyone else because I was seeing her for the first time without her armour: her warmth, her effervescence, her optimism. I tried to beam myself out of the room, as I'd done so many times at school or when I was being fired or shouted at or broken up with. I focused on the Celtic brooch pinned to her purple waterfall cardigan. It had come loose and was about to fall off.

'I've explained it to Addie, she understands.'

'Like hell she does.'

'I did it for Addie.'

'Oh give me a break.' The brooch fell to the floor.

'You don't have to believe me, but I did.'

'Dogs are good for kids. They're healthy for their immune systems,' she said, bending to retrieve it and pricking herself with her finger as she did.

'Not according to the doctor. I'm too worried to risk it.'

I got up. Moved to the window, shut it. Turned around.

'Oh, these Western doctors don't know diddly-squat.' She looked at her finger, put it in her mouth, sucked away the blood.

'And since when are you such an expert? You don't even have kids. Excuse me,' I said, knowing that that last bit was below the belt. I forced her to stand out of the way so I could open the fridge. I closed it again, opened the freezer and got out some Birdseye potato waffles for Addie's tea ('Might as well eat air,' she had said about these the last time she'd seen me buy them, 'zero nutritional benefit'). Tonight I didn't have the energy. Tomorrow I would start healthy living for both of us again.

She watched as I opened a can of beans, spilling some over the edge as I emptied them into a saucepan and stirred.

'I may not have kids but I know that all children do much better with stability and how much they benefit from regular contact with both parents, even after a split.'

'I'm sorry? What's that got to do with any of this?'

She said nothing. I took out two plates, put the waffles on. Poured beans over them.

I took a carton of apple juice from the fridge, poured it into Addie's plastic cup. You should really dilute that first, I could hear Joy think, and give it to her with a straw, so much better for her teeth – better still, don't give it to her at all; water is all she needs.

'That kid needs to see her dad is what I'm saying and, well, I think I should let you know that I've made a few calls on Addie's behalf.'

'Oh God, who did you call?'

'I knew you'd be pissed if I told you but I felt it was my duty as Addie's friend. I did a little research – Google's just wonderful, isn't it? – anyways, I found the agency you thought he'd joined and, well, I just went right ahead and phoned them, but I'm afraid I've got some bad news for you.'

'Off you go?'

'He's moved to their sister agency in Amsterdam. I don't think he's coming home, dear heart, to you, or to his precious child.'

'I am well aware that he's not coming home, that's hardly news.' I moved to the kitchen door, closed it over, continued more quietly. 'And how dare you make that call without telling me?'

'Oh, you'd never have had the balls to do it. Someone's got to look out for that kid.'

'That's complete crap!' I said, accidently showering her with saliva. 'I've accepted that I'm a single mum now and I know I'm doing loads of things wrong, but I am trying my very best, believe me,' I said, choking with self-pity. 'And you don't know the first thing about my relationship with Joe or about being a mother for that matter. It isn't all about organic quinoa and origami swans. There's a little more to it than that,' I said, squirting ketchup on the side of each plate.

I wanted her to retaliate, instead she just stood there, irritatingly serene, with a slight smile on her face, as if she'd seen all of this coming. She'd placed her hands together in prayer position, legs crossed, and was leaning against the cooker watching, utterly silent, as I put our TV dinner on a tray.

'Mummy!'

'What is it, sweetheart? Just give me a second.'

'But *Bubble Guppies* is over.'

'OK, I'm coming, darling,' I said, picking up the tray.

'You know what you need?' Joy finally spoke. She had given this some thought.

'Go ahead, tell me.'

'You need to do a course in anger management, dear heart. That's what you need.'

A car passed on the road outside, sending a shadow sweeping across the sitting room wall, lighting up the little figures on the Indian cabinet. Addie wriggled into her costume, struggling to keep her hat in place with one hand while holding her broomstick with the other.

'I don't want to blow away up into the sky' she said as we went down the stairs, counting them the way we always did, her small hand in mine.

'I promise you won't. I'll hold your hand very tight.'

I put on my own witch's hat at her insistence and we set off together across the road to join Sophie's party.

Out on the square, little skeletons, pirates and devils were being hurried through the murk, their costumes and plastic bags rustling. Fireworks were going off somewhere on the seafront; they whistled and rushed, great flashes of colour lighting up the night sky.

Some of the houses had made a huge effort: candle-lit pumpkins glowed from bay windows, scarecrows and witches hung behind them. 'Do not enter' signs and fake cobwebs had been stretched across front doors, tombstones made out of painted-grey polystyrene were positioned in gardens, skeletons hung from bare trees. Other homes looked ghostly enough without embellishment in the damp, foggy night. 'Dank,' Joy would have said. 'The weather in Dublin's so dank.' There were no lights on at the drug-dealer's house on the corner; both of us jumped at the teenagers who were kissing in the darkness in the mass of the leylandii trees outside. Juliette giggled, Dylan apologised and told Addie she was an excellent witch. Kids were running from the old sisters' house. They were a natural and easy target. Their game was to ring the doorbell and leg it; we saw a grey-haired figure retreat from the first-floor window but couldn't tell which sister it was. Billy, shifty-eyed under a racoon hat, was playing a more dangerous game; stuffing lit tapers through their letterbox. He'd had it in for Pamela ever since she'd driven her ancient Citroën to the high street knowing that his kitten, later to be christened Diesel, was stuck in its engine. Frank, the youth worker, said he'd come close to punching the old woman on Billy's behalf; Pamela said cat or no cat, she had to go to the post office to cash her pension cheque.

A few homes had made no effort at all and were not participating: the glow of a television set in the corner, unseen faces balancing dinners on knees behind curtains, watching the six o'clock news, ignoring the occasion, all knocks on the door.

We crossed the square and climbed down the steps to the basement of Sophie's house, cobweb-covered lanterns guiding our way.

'My bum bum's gone off,' Addie said, hiding behind me, as we waited for the door to be answered. It wasn't Sophie but her husband, Mark, who let us in. He looked like he'd been asleep, with his shoes off and his shirt hanging out over his jeans.

'Ah, you've just missed them,' he said, 'give me a second.' He padded back into the sitting room. I waved in at the au pair girl, Beatriz, who was sitting forward on the sofa, tidying her hair and tugging at her skirt, as though she were about to pose for a photograph. 'Hello, Eve! Oh, you look so horrid, Addie!' she shouted out, not getting up.

'Mama, why has he done his buttons up wrongly?' Addie asked while he was away. I shushed her but saw for myself as he tucked his shirt into his jeans on his way back to us with a basket. He held it down in front of her, apologising, 'It's been fairly ransacked, I'm afraid.'

Addie took a green lollipop.

He gave us directions to the big estate that they had all set off to collect around. I listened, thanked him, but knew we wouldn't be going there. It was Joy who Sophie had invited, not us. Those two seemed to have become great pals lately, as Mum would say.

On the way home we passed a house whose front door was opened wide: adults and children were streaming in, all in fancy dress, the host, Count Dracula, was beckoning them. Addie wanted to go too. I tried to explain that we didn't know them, that we wouldn't be welcome. She seemed to accept this and then was silenced by her lollipop, serious under her witch's hat. We headed for home, Addie's cape rustling as she moved beside me, her empty orange bucket swinging in her hand.

Chapter Twenty

I woke early that morning to the sound of smashing glass, then a man's shout from the park, ugly drunk and too near: curse, spit, vomit, the revving of a car, a female shriek. Unable to settle back to sleep, I got up, sat on the toilet and squinted through the blinds at the brick facades of the houses in the estate behind us. Their rooftops were slick with rain, newly planted cherry trees precarious in the wind, the pavements below lit up by the smudgy glow of street lamps. There was a light on in the kitchen of the end house, as there often was in the night. A blurred figure in a pink dressing gown was moving about – another lonely insomniac. A siren sounded from somewhere and I thought about death, sleepily stunned by its inevitability.

Joy said she'd been planning to tell me anyway. She'd been offered 'an amazing opportunity to care for two small children in a wonderfully creative family'. 'I'll miss that little girl,' was the last thing she said as she left, 'Addie fed my heart.' And Addie missed Joy. She called her every day on her Peppa Pig plastic phone, told her all her news. One morning I found her peering into the toilet bowl, examining her produce. 'They look like vege-matarians,' she said, before I insisted she flush them away.

I tiptoed down to the kitchen and began preparing for Addie's fourth birthday party, visualising how it would go as I tidied. I carried the kitchen table into the sitting room and set it, putting a paper plate decorated with balloons, a matching paper cup, a tinsel-rimmed party hat and a carton of Toothkind Ribena on each place. Into candy-striped bowls I emptied packets of Hula Hoops and dinosaur-shaped jellies. I made egg, cheese and cucumber sandwiches, cut off their crusts, sliced them into little triangles and arranged them on two larger plates which I put in the centre of the table, the imprints of my fingers visible on the soft bread.

I tied three balloons to the front door knocker, all pink, one long, two short, a bit phallic I could hear Joe say, so I went back upstairs to get a forth.

Then I sat alone in the kitchen, waiting for the kettle to click off. This day last year he'd been standing on the kitchen table in his socks, draping a Happy 3rd Birthday banner across the stained-glass window of the old house, singing along to whiny old Lucinda Williams – cheating and hurting songs, that's what he called them – blaring from the stereo.

I shouldn't have said it; it all went bad when I did. All I'd said was that they were 'a bit gloomy' for a kids' party and could we not have something a little more upbeat. He'd got down from the table, slapped off the stereo, grabbed the CD, charged out of the room and slammed the door behind him. I'd followed him, whining, pleading with him to leave it, saying that I didn't mind the music after all, but he'd already gone upstairs and was out of earshot and once again, with guests about to arrive, I'd had tears in my eyes and everything was broken.

I'd climbed the stairs to the top of the house to make peace, trying not to cry because I'd just put mascara on and if I cried my eyes would get small and mean-looking again and the spots on my nose would be there for all to see.

I'd found him where I thought I would; playing online pool against the virtual fat man.

'Please, Joe, can we not fight?' I said, 'Everyone's about to arrive.'

'Leave me alone. I'm fine.'

'Jesus, all I said was I thought your music was a bit gloomy. I don't have to like your music.'

It had been pathetic, he'd known it, I'd known it. I'd forced him to stop his game, to turn around and hug me. He'd stood and he'd done it, but he'd been stiff, angular, his face turned away, still focused on his computer. 'Sorry,' he'd mumbled into his chest. His apology had been genuine but I couldn't resist taking advantage of it and had sulked for the afternoon.

There was a black ball of snot up Addie's left nostril that she wouldn't let me get out. She slotted her own finger up to retrieve it instead – always such a perfect fit, a baby finger in a baby nose. 'Where are my wishes?' she asked, adjusting her feather fairy wings which were already moulting on the kitchen floor. I handed her the magic wand and she set off again, casting spells and attempting to fly but stopping to cough, every few moments, her head bent to her knees. I didn't understand it. I'd hoovered the entire flat the evening before, picked up every single remaining dog hair and still Addie's chest was wheezy.

I'd anticipated and planned this party with such determination and in such detail that by the time the doorbell rang, delivering our first scrubbed clean, brushed-hair party guests, at 2.30 p.m., half an hour early, I had used up all my excitement and was now out the other side of it, somewhat exhausted.

I bent forward, stuffed my hand down my top to perk up my breasts in their double gel push-up bra, fiddled with my hair, sucked in my stomach, grabbed a wet tea towel, smeared it over Addie's face, lifted her into my arms and trotted downstairs to answer it.

There was a frozen moment on the doorstep; a couple of seconds where no one said anything. Superman clung to his mother's leg, having forgotten what it was he was supposed to do. His white hair had been spit-licked into place and he had a scabby rash under his nose. 'In you go, Ben,' Sophie said, giving him a little push and stepping over the doorstep behind him. They bundled into the hall with their presents and compliments and coats. 'Oh, are we too early?' she asked, seeming to suggest that something about us or the house didn't look quite ready to receive guests.

'Not at all. So lovely to see you.'

We embraced, a stiff, self-conscious little collision that felt like we were children just playing at being grown-ups.

'You look fantastic!'

'God, I don't feel it. But you look amazing!'

'Hello, birthday girl! Don't you look pretty?' We flustered and gasped over each other's offspring. Exclamation marks everywhere.

She was looking as soft and warm and fertile as she always did. No make-up, freckles sprinkled across her nose, pert bum in slim jeans, trainers, round-neck sweater. I felt like Miss Piggy beside her, my low-cut T-shirt too tight, my make-up too much, my four-inch heels fooling no one. What was Mark thinking of, getting together with that teenager when he had such a sweet and gorgeous wife? I had already decided I wasn't going to say a thing – it wasn't my business, it may have been a one-off event, it wasn't what she would want to hear and I couldn't be certain about any of it.

I led them upstairs and into the sitting room, already feeling too tired to entertain. I took their coats, but just as I'd offered Sophie tea, the doorbell rang again and I had to excuse myself, laughing – 'busy, busy' – to answer it. Addie cried and ran after me.

It was Irenka and Charlotte, dressed as a princess. It was the first time I'd seen Irenka upright in ages; she'd been in bed with a slipped disc for weeks. 'My brain has gone into a "mash",' she'd said when I dropped down one morning with some paracetamol and a bar of chocolate. I'd had to let myself in with her spare key; she'd been completely unable to move. It had been strange to see her still and stuffy in bed, surrendered and useless and dependent for a change.

'Oh, have you just been swimming?' I asked all friendly, bending to rub Charlotte's wet hair.

'Lice,' Irenka whispered, 'they're everywhere in Bray, just like the rubbish and the rats.' I pulled my hand away. That would go down great with the other mums.

Back in the sitting room I didn't know what to do with my hands, to fold them seemed too severe, too authoritarian for a children's party. On the hips didn't feel right either. I needed a drink or a child to hold. I pulled Addie towards me, played with her hair.

The flat was now full of women and children, all a little expectant, all depending on me. Sophie was lingering in the kitchen still hoping for the cup of tea that she'd said would be great twenty minutes earlier. Someone must have left Sumita and Rashi in. They were leaning against the far corner of the sofa, looking tentative, Rashi wrapped around her mother's leg. Irenka was standing with a tray full of tinfoil-covered buns, unsure of where to put them. Ben, too hot in his Superman suit, was crying, saying that he wanted to go home. I kind of wished he would.

The children soon became a little braver, more used to their surroundings, taking tentative steps towards the table, looking up at their mothers for reassurance, picking up, examining and rejecting an offering, then taking another and cautiously eating. Irenka's banana bran buns were still untouched, aside from one indented with a child's teeth marks that had been put back. We hovered above them, analysing their behaviour, fixing their hair, complimenting another child's party dress, fretting, fussing, bending, stretching, holding, carrying, wiping, warning.

'Look at the height of those heels,' Ruth said, watching me as I tried to pull the cork from a bottle of white wine. 'For God's sake. How can you possibly walk in them?'

'They're actually quite comfortable.' I said, face burning, without turning around.

'Ha! That's what short people always say.'

Her little girl, Ruby, was sitting cross-legged on the floor, helping Addie to open her presents, taking vicarious pleasure from ripping the paper. Much cleverer than her four years, Ruby made me nervous: the last time she was in our company, she'd asked Bella if she was growing a moustache.

I felt a small panic as I realised that the gift they were tearing open, from Irenka, was something Addie had already been given and was calculating how long it might take to dash into the sitting room and somehow conceal the existing present when Ruby, pulling the last bit of paper free from its packaging announced in a loud, self-satisfied voice: 'Addie already has this.'

'I've always actually wanted two of these!' Addie said, saving the day. 'It's dus perfect,' she'd said at seven that morning about the gift I'd given her: a toy cookery set in a small red-and-white polka dot suitcase. And then, 'Will you tickle my back?'

Charlotte was crying because *she* wanted to wear the Minnie Mouse costume which Addie had been given by Sophie, tears staining her rashy cheeks. And of course I said yes to Irenka who was already hoisting her child onto the kitchen counter top, pulling off her princess dress and squeezing her too-large body into the Disney costume. The kettle was boiling, Ruby was looking for more Wotsits, standing on a chair to reach a cupboard to get them herself, someone else was asking me about where they might find a milk jug and Superman needed to do a number two.

'He feels very hot,' Sophie said, putting her hand on Ben's forehead, then hoisting him onto her knee. 'He'll only do them at home. He'll hold on to it now for the afternoon.' She squeezed him and felt his forehead again. 'I think he might have a temperature. Poor little lamb.'

'Maybe take off his Superman suit?' Ruth offered.

'What about juice?' I said, adding my twopence-worth, worried that the party might be broken up before we'd even had cake. 'You know Addie's always in much better form after she's had a number two.' I couldn't believe that I was now coming out with sentences like this.

'Do you have Milk of Magnesia?' Sumita turned in her chair to ask me.

'Or even just some warm water?' Ruth suggested.

'If you rub your finger around his anus, and massage his sphincter muscle—' Irenka said from where she was sitting on the sofa, spinning her own finger in a clockwise direction, while sinking her teeth into a piece of coffee and walnut cake.

'Would you not be arrested for that?' I said. No one laughed.

I went into the kitchen to see what I could give him and found Ruth opening and closing cupboards one by one, moving packets around, taking stuff out, sniffing at it, turning boxes on their sides to read their contents. Ruby was trailing her, whimpering.

'A-ha, peanut butter,' she said, holding a jar that Joy had left when she'd moved out.

'Oh, good. She likes that?' I said, shadowing her now too.

'Mmm, yes, but this is the wrong sort,' she said, studying the label. 'Crunchy. Ruby won't touch it. She only eats smooth.'

I flustered about the place, pouring wine, making small-talk, getting everyone to sit. On the whole, it seemed to be going well but I was already looking forward to the evening when it would be over and the enjoyable phase of remembering it and analysing it and playing with Addie's new presents would begin.

I hadn't witnessed the offence but Ruth grabbed Ruby by the arm and dragged her over to the corner of the room, wagging her finger and spitting intense, private threats and reminders of earlier deals ('What did Mummy say? Remember that surprise? What surprise was Daddy going to bring you?'). Then she was upright again, composing herself, straightening her blouse, her voice restored to the light, pleasant tone of the polite guest.

Ben, who until this moment had been sitting beside me, sucking apple juice through a straw with great concentration, oblivious of everything, now paused and turned to me, his eyebrows arched in consternation: 'I have all the Superman stuff, so why am I not Superman?'

I drew the curtain in the sitting room, switched off the light. Everyone squeezed into the small room together and sang 'Happy Birthday' and for that moment, for the five seconds it took to get through the song, everyone was united, the feeling was of love for my small child, sitting bashful and proud at the top of the table. She blew out all her candles with great, saliva-filled efforts, then sat back and waved at her fans as they cheered.

'No, Ruby!' Addie said, as the little girl tried to get her fingers around the first piece of cake. 'I'm saving that one for my dada.'

There were a few raised eyebrows, snatched glances, chewed lips.

'Sweetheart,' I said, bending down beside her, feeling the eyes of all the mums on me. 'Remember I told you that your dada lives in another country now?' I put my arm around the back of her chair.

She listened and nodded and squished a chocolate star into the wood of the kitchen table with her finger.

'He's not able to see you any more and he can't come to your birthday, but he still loves you very much, OK?'

'But what about my pink Furby with the purple ears?'

'Let's ask Santa for that Furby, OK?' I said, kissing her on the forehead and getting up.

'OK,' she said, not looking at me.

It was the right time to take the party to the playground; the kids were high on sugar; Addie had her foot in my carrot cake; flatulence was filling up the room, making everyone a bit depressed. Several children had been swept off their feet and lifted into the air in a process of elimination but it was Ben, who still needed a poo. At one stage, all the kids were crying; we needed to get out.

There was an odd moment at the doorstep. I was waiting for everyone to get out so I could lock up but they all seemed to be stalling. It was Ruby who in the end reminded me, her mother shushing her as she forced her into her coat, that I'd forgotten their party bags.

'Which hand?' I said, teasing her, fists clenched behind my back. She was disgusted with the sparkly bouncy ball I presented – Charlotte didn't want hers either and handed it back. Sophie asked if Ben could have bubbles instead.

We set out in the damp November air, an untidy group of put-upon mothers – several running back to their cars for bottles, baby wipes, coats – and scattering kids: Ben on Addie's new bike, Rashi, bouncing along on her Space Hopper, the girls all bossy and busy with their dollies and buggies, everyone flustered and tiring.

I was embarrassed that Sophie and I were wearing almost identical navy-blue duffle coats. I'd owned mine for quite a few weeks but so far I'd only worn it in parts of Dublin where I thought it unlikely that I would bump into Sophie, having blatantly copied her. As soon as Addie saw her in it she said 'My mama has dus the same coat' so there was no longer any point in pretending. If she asked I'd say it was an early Christmas present from my mother and just an amazing coincidence. It was irritating that the same coat could make one woman look Parisian and cute, yet another, kind of simple and a tiny bit musty.

I had to sort of shunt Addie along the path ahead of me as I was carrying a dozen multicoloured Chinese lanterns in one hand and three bottles of Prosecco in a Tesco bag in the other. Mum had dropped them around before she'd set off on her latest trip. I'd also packed a bottle of water in case things didn't go to plan.

I'd bought the lanterns on Amazon for nearly nothing – the Disney movie *Tangled* had inspired me. And the conditions were perfect that evening; there was almost no wind and the drizzle had eased. I couldn't wait for Addie to see them lit up in the night sky.

I gave a quick salute to Mr Norman who was outside his house, coiling up a garden hose, and a casual shout to Dylan and Juliette. He was sitting cross-legged on the ground near the gardener's hut, playing his guitar; she was lying on his leather jacket beside him, head in her hands, humming along. I was pretending I knew my neighbours a lot better than I did. I waved at Jayani, the little Sri Lankan girl, who'd got some new rollerblades and seemed to have somehow sprouted breasts since Hallowe'en. She gave me a shy smile then thumped along the path behind her mother, complaining that her training bra was digging into her. I even smiled at the skinny boy from number three, who gave me a cursory nod, grabbed his football and ran.

I strode along with my gang and soon we had engulfed the place, hovering a little too near the swings while we waited for a child to finish her go. Addie was always cautious at the playground. She found the slide too high, she wouldn't stay on the see-saw for more than two seconds and the swings frightened her since that first time, when I accidently pushed her off. She liked to throw stones in the thing that spun round and round but would never dare sit in it herself. Today she was different. Today she was showing off her domain. She charged up the slide the wrong way, dangled off the monkey bars, ran screaming through thick layers of dead leaves.

Sophie disappeared behind a tree with Ben. All of us took envious little peeks at her toned backside as she bent to help him. A relieved and somewhat lighter looking child emerged minutes later. Then Charlotte threw up on the see-saw. 'She's been eating sweets since Hallowe'en night,' Irenka said, mopping up the vomit with baby wipes proffered by Sophie. Ruby slipped and fell playing hopscotch and everyone got dog dirt on their shoes.

It was getting dark though it wasn't quite five o'clock; trees were silhouetted against the backs of houses around the square. Cars sped by on the road outside, their lights momentarily illuminating the railings and the smoky grey of the park. The children's faces were no longer clearly visible, they were identifiable now by their bright coats, their shouts and by the trainers some of them wore, that lit up when they ran.

I laid the lanterns out on the grass and told the kids to stand well away. They were immediately compliant, stepping backwards in a huddle, their faces curious and expectant, Ruby bursting, her hand clenched between her legs, but not wanting to miss a thing.

Sophie and Sumita helped me to remove all the packaging, Irenka had already gone home – she'd been opposed to the idea from the start because a permit was required to use Chinese lanterns in a public place apparently and because her back was at her again. She'd sent Donal over in her place; if I were going to carry out an illegal act, she was adamant that a responsible person, such as her husband, oversee it. I could sense her surveying proceedings from her bed, moving this way and that on her bony bum to get the best vantage point in the fading light, just willing something to go wrong so she could say 'see what I'm telling to you'. The other person watching us that evening was Billy Flynn. I hadn't noticed him until that moment, but there he was, sitting with his legs dangling over the edge of the tree house, as though he were about to jump.

Donal hovered above me, desperate to take over, feeling that this was a man's job. The first two lanterns tore, to general groans and offers of help, but I tried again with a third. I was determined to launch one myself. I lit the little candle at the bottom of a neon-pink one and waited a few moments while the flame took.

'This one's for you, Addie!' I shouted as I stood and let it go. We watched it float straight up until it found an air-stream and took off high above the roof tops of the square and away. I was moved almost to tears by the beauty of the moment.

'Aw, but I wanted the silver one,' Addie said, arms folded beside me, looking furious. 'Bemember? Silver's my favourite colour.'

'OK, little madam. Give me a moment.' I lit and launched a silver one, this time with a little more panache.

'Sail on, silver girl!' I said as it took flight.

'Sail on by,' Donal had begun beside me. 'Your time has come to shine, all your dreams are on their way.' God, how could Irenka tolerate it? He turned everything you said into a song.

We sent the rest of them into the night one by one and gazed at the beautiful, multicoloured display that danced above us in the darkness. The kids were shrieking, arguing about which one was theirs, which was going highest, running through the grass to keep up with their progress until they lost sight of them. One veered badly off course, brushed against Ruth's hair – more hairspray than hair as it turned out – and set it alight. She jumped about screaming, patting her head, mortified. This energised the kids further.

I hadn't seen her arrive but Joy had joined the celebrations. She was crouched behind Addie, embracing her, face turned skyward and silent. 'Look, Ben, aren't they just magical?' Sophie said, standing beside them, her hands clasped around her little boy's shoulders.

Belinda arrived with a jug of orange squash and a bowl of cocktail sausages, apologising for being late for her shift. 'I'm after missing them all, amn't I?' she said, putting everything on the picnic table. 'I saw one go over the roof of the library on my way out. Beautiful so it was.' Hands on hips, she turned around and scanned the park for her son. 'Would you ever get down from there and give us a hand?' she shouted when she saw Billy in the tree house. He lunged forwards, tumbled as he landed and slouched over to his mother who made him pass the cocktail sausages around.

Sophie popped open the bottles of Prosecco, Sumita gave everyone plastic cups. 'Happy birthday again, Addie! Cheers!' I said holding up my cup then stretching over to clink cups with all of my guests, spilling half of mine as I did. I was giddy, tipsy, getting on with everyone.

'I'm after forgetting your birthday present, little lady,' Belinda said, grabbing Addie around the waist and giving her an affectionate shake.

'What was it anyway?'

'A tray of cyclamen bulbs.'

'Huh?' Addie looked up at me, smiling, shy.

'Now, I've got a very important question for you, Addie – do you think you could mind them for me and help them to grow? I heard from your mam that you're a bit of a green fingers, is that right?'

'Yep, I'm the bestest at doing that.'

'No direct sunlight, not too much water and feed them every two weeks, OK?'

'I already know that! You don't have to tell me.' Addie said, proud of the responsibility being bestowed on her.

I strode along the path with a black bin bag chatting to Sumita as she helped me clean up. 'I'm still asking everyone I can think of about childminding jobs for you,' I told her as we worked.

She looked up at me, smiling and bashful. 'Thank you, that's very kind. Rashi tells me every day, "I want a baby, I want a big house, I want a car", but how can I give her these things?'

To our amazement Billy appeared to be helping us; he'd put the empty Prosecco bottles in the recycling bin and had carefully collected all the used lighters.

Seeing her son usefully employed, Belinda nipped back home with the empty bowls and to get the cyclamen bulbs for Addie who couldn't wait till tomorrow to receive her birthday gift as had been suggested.

What sounded at first like Juliette's laugh was in fact her scream. Billy had snuck up on her and Dylan where they'd been kissing by the gardener's shed. He'd tried to set Juliette's hair on fire. Dylan noticed too soon, before it took hold. 'Would you ever just fuck off and leave her alone?' he said, taking off his scarf and pressing it against the back of his girlfriend's head.

'What is your fucking problem anyway?' Juliette said, examining the singed ends of her highlighted hair.

Now Billy was chasing the smaller kids, catching up with them and flicking the lighter in their frightened faces. I thought a game of Hide and Seek might help to restore calm and bore Billy back indoors. Of course Joy wouldn't have approved of it, but she wasn't a mother, so what did she know? It was the perfect way to get a few moments peace. Addie had been hanging off me whining, pulling at my arm, wanting me to bring her home; but I still had some cleaning up to do. I'd also promised Sophie I'd look after Ben while she went home to oversee Lauren's school project on autumn which had to be in the next day. Donal had taken Charlotte home to bed and before she'd left, Ruth had finally lost it with Ruby. She'd grabbed her daughter by the elbow, lifting her off her feet, and had smacked her hard on the backside before carrying her back to their car. We'd all chewed on our lips, said nothing.

'Oh, listen, you're not going to believe this,' Sophie said, as she knelt to pull up the zipper of Ben's coat over his costume, 'but I thought that stuff you gave me for my birthday was honey! I spread it on my toast. It was Lauren who said, "It's for the bath, Mummy."

Ugh. I couldn't get rid of that soapy taste for hours. God, it was disgusting.' She told Ben to be good and she was gone. Joy joined her at the gate and they walked away together.

I began counting absent-mindedly as the children ran and hid, watching through spread fingers to be sure that no one was heading for the gates and that my little girl was safe. She was fully visible behind a sapling, standing as still as she could. Ben was making slow progress up the steps to the tree house. Rashi was running back and forth, holding her mother's hand, between the oak tree and the picnic table, unable to decide where to hide. Billy seemed to have joined in too – he'd followed Ben to the tree house and was hurrying him up by shoving him in the backside as he stood on the ladder behind him. I carried on counting to give Rashi and Sumita a little more time. Why had Joy left with Sophie? I wondered when she'd be leaving Bray for good to begin her new job. No doubt she'd been bitching to her all about my abandoning poor Alfie, and Sophie as a dog lover would not have been impressed. 'But he was so good with kids,' I could imagine her saying. 'And it's not like he ever even bit anyone or anything like Buddy has.'

'Ready or not, here I come!' I set off in a self-conscious jog towards a chestnut tree I knew no one was behind and pretended I'd found Addie there. She started shouting for me, still not understanding the game. I headed for the picnic table as if I hadn't heard her. I thought of Billy watching me from where he was hiding with Ben, a hulking sixteen year old crouched down and waiting to be discovered. I felt sad for him – even his silly prank with the lighter was a way of trying to fit in – he'd seen our reaction to Ruth's hair being set alight, he probably thought we'd all find it funny again. I turned around and began jogging towards the tree house. That's when I saw the flames.

The tree house was on fire.

'Oh God, Ben! Billy!' I shouted as I ran towards them.

They had both got down the ladder; Billy was yelling 'Stop, drop, roll. Go on do it. I seen it on TV!' Ben was beside him, utterly silent and still, his little arms outstretched, his white hair illuminated by the flames climbing his legs. He was too shocked to move. Before I could reach them, Billy shoved Ben, the flames dying as he hit the ground and rolled over.

'Mama!'

'Stay away, Addie. I mean it! Billy, get Sophie!'

Billy ran, Sumita rang 999. I lifted Ben and carried him across the path, away from the burning timber falling from the tree house behind us. He was quiet in my arms; he didn't cry or scream as I lay him on the grass. His Superman costume was charred and had stuck to him on both legs from the knee down.

Now everyone around us was shouting, running, coughing through smoke in the darkness. Donal and Dylan doused what remained of the tree house with saucepans full of cold water. 'What's after happening? Ah, Lord, you poor little man!' Belinda got down beside us and poured a bottle of water over his legs, her bulbs for Addie upturned on the grass beside where she knelt. 'I'm going to try to cool you down, honey.'

'Jesus Christ!' Sophie screamed, trembling, sobbing, when she saw what had happened to her son. 'My poor, poor baby.' She sat on the ground, nestled his head in her lap and rubbed her hand across his forehead again and again.

Sumita tried to provide the ambulance despatch with directions to the playground and to answer question after question about Ben; twice she'd had to tell them to hold on so that she could ask Sophie herself. 'Christ, I don't know. Why can't they just hurry up!' Sophie said, still rubbing her son's forehead. I imagined its halting progress along the narrow approach road into Bray, cars mounting the pavement to let it through. Joy was standing by the gate ready to flag it down. Everyone wanted to shine in the crisis, wanted to be the one who acted quickly, thought quickly, who was logical and helpful, the one who saved the day. I seemed to be doing nothing logical or helpful that night – I wasn't logical or helpful by nature, however much I tried to be – and all my suggestions were nodded at but largely ignored. I had my child in my arms and that at least gave me a role and an excuse of sorts. She had become silent and angelic, the way kids do when they aren't the one injured or in trouble. Sumita asked Dylan to take Rashi home and to put on a cartoon. Addie just gripped me harder when he asked if she would like to go too.

Joy was like an air traffic controller, doing huge two-armed waves as the ambulance approached, the sound of its siren both alarming and a relief. Mr Norman told everyone to 'stand back' and 'make room' as they came into the park, not that anyone was in their way. They came towards us, a strange, torch-lit procession, the paramedics in their bottle-green uniforms, yellow reflective jackets, regulation boots, Mr Norman earnestly leading the way. Belinda and I got to our feet simultaneously as they approached and we both began to explain what had happened when they asked for information. 'Could just one person answer, please?' they said. I stopped talking and let Belinda continue, irritated by her dominance, especially as she hadn't even witnessed the event.

'He doesn't seem to be in pain, isn't that a good sign?' Sophie asked, all snotty and shaking as one of them cut away what was left of Ben's polyester costume. The skin on his legs looked leathery and translucent white; it smelt like bacon in a frying pan.

'No pain's not a good sign, love, it means there's probably some nerve damage because the burns are so deep and these are flame burns – the worst type. Can you tell me what happened?'

'I've no idea; I was at home. You were minding Ben, Eve. Can you tell him? It must have been one of those lanterns.'

'We were playing Hide and Seek,' I said, watching as they applied water gel to the burns. 'He was absolutely fine and—' I looked down at Sophie, tried to explain, but she'd turned her face away.

I sought out Sumita for support. 'I'm sorry, Eve, I didn't see anything. I was hiding behind the slide with Rashi,' she said, looking at me apologetically.

'He was in the tree house. I got him out and told him to do the stop drop and roll thing that I seen on TV.' Billy said.

'That was pretty brave, Billy, what you did.' Juliette said, arms wrapped around herself with fright and cold.

I waited for him to tell the full story, to tell everyone – his mother, the paramedics, Sophie – the truth. But he said nothing else. He looked down at the ground, embarrassed but proud, dug his foot into the soil.

We stood at the gates of the playground dazed by the seriousness of a real-life ambulance: the startling white of its interior, the whirring flash of its beacon, the primary yellow of the handles, the easy-wipe bed. Ben was carried on in the arms of one of the paramedics, Sophie by his side gripping him with her hand, chewing hard on the thumbnail of the other, her cardigan hanging off her. Joy climbed in behind them, her hands heavy on Sophie's shoulders.

'I want to stay with Mama! Mama, wait!' Addie screamed, as I reversed out the gate. Belinda held and tried to shush her.

'Sweetheart, I have to go to the hospital,' I said, through the rolled-down window. 'Be good.'

'How about I be Doctor McStuffins? That's why because I have my new set. Please, Mama?'

'No, just stop it now, Addie! Sorry, Belinda, you've got my keys?'

'Go on, go on, we'll be fine. Now, you have to help me sort out these bulbs,' she said, gripping the soil-covered polystyrene and turning to bring her indoors.

It was the paramedics who said I should follow them in, so Sophie could get a lift home with me 'to get supplies, the child's favourite toy, that sort of thing'. I couldn't check with Sophie, she was already in the ambulance. I told him I'd go, I didn't know what else to do.

I drove behind them at speed, not at all confident of finding the hospital myself, the siren terrifying in its volume and proximity. I wasn't sober enough to be driving. I tried to concentrate on the traffic but my mind was filled with images of flames, the tattered remains of the Superman cape, Ben's brave little face in his Hallowe'en costume.

We careered over ambulance ramps down to the children's entrance, outside which parents were smoking, butts all over the ground. Disney characters beamed down at us, Tigger, Mickey Mouse, Winnie the Pooh, as we rushed along brown-painted corridors, past limp Hallowe'en decorations, Virgin Marys, a single wheelchair, framed photographs of children who hadn't made it.

I stood outside their cubicle in A&E and listened to the doctor trying to talk to Sophie over Ben's screams. He was now alert, terrified, clinging to his mother. 'We have to replace fluid to stop these getting infected. You're all right, you poor little man, lots of big, deep breaths for me now,' and then to Sophie 'we'll get the play specialist down to distract him once he's been assessed.'

He was admitted to the burns unit, put on an intravenous morphine drip and fluid. His little legs were cleaned and bandaged and when Joy suggested I leave them to it, he was heavily sedated and sleeping.

It was as I sat at a wobbly-legged table in the cafe, grease in the air, the TV just below audible, waiting for more news that I understood two new things. Joy and Sophie were now sharing a home – the creative family she'd described had been Sophie's – and both of them were blaming me, not Billy, for Ben's accident.

'I have all the Superman stuff, so why am I not Superman?' It was one of the saddest things I'd ever heard.

Chapter Twenty-one

'Oh, it didn't work out for you? That's such a shame,' said Shauna, proprietor of the loveliest and most expensive children's clothes shop in Dublin, once so full of women you could smell the oestrogen. Today she was having a closing-down sale. She could no longer afford the rent and mothers couldn't afford her clothes any more. I handed her back the pink chiffon tutu, still in its wrapper. All I needed to do was get my refund and leave.

The last time I was in this shop, a week earlier, Shauna had shadowed me round the room, picking up and refolding clothes as she kept a subtle eye on me. I'd known as soon I'd opened the chiming door that I shouldn't have been there and had only lingered out of a mixture of politeness and embarrassment.

'That one also comes in pink gingham,' she'd said in her Californian drawl.

And 'Isn't it just adorable?' when I'd picked up the tutu.

'Don't you think every little girl should have one? India wears hers all the time, don't you, baby?' she'd said, gliding over to where her child was standing, picking her nose, by the till.

I had somehow been seduced by her, by Bing Crosby on the stereo, by the scent of vanilla in the air, by the bobble hats and star-spangled tights hanging off pegs across the frosted windows. I'd bought the tutu and a heart-shaped decoration for the tree. But the tutu alone cost one hundred Euro and Addie had nothing to wear with it and if I returned it I might have enough money to replace the Christmas tree which I'd bought two weeks too early and was now dry as a crisp and drooping. I also wanted to buy a gift for Ben.

He had received third-degree burns to the front of both legs from the knee down. Forty-eight hours after the accident he'd had to undergo a skin graft. They'd taken some skin from his back – the donor site, as they'd referred to it – to replace what had burnt off in the fire. It would take at least two years for the scarring to heal.

I hadn't seen Sophie since the accident; she had been living in the hospital, sleeping on a mattress beside Ben's bed. And I'd only seen the backs of Joy and Irenka in fleeces and trainers power-walking their way up to Bray Head. I'd heard about Ben from Belinda, who couldn't avoid me at the library.

'He has a tube down his nose into his tummy and splints behind his knees at night to keep his legs straight, the poor little lad,' she told me on our shift the other evening.

'When do you think he'll be coming home?' I asked, too afraid to question whether she also felt I was culpable.

'Maybe around Christmas, but they'll only let him out when the dressing doesn't hurt too much – his mam will have to change it for him every four days after that. Lord knows, I don't often get a chance to say it but I'm very proud of Billy, he probably saved that child's life.'

Some of the children in Addie's class had asked if her mother had hurt Ben. She hadn't wanted to go in one day and had cried when I'd tried to leave. I promised her I'd wave from the window when I got outside, like we'd done in the early days. And somehow in the minute-long journey between her classroom and outdoors I'd forgotten my promise to her. She had stood by that window waiting to wave and blow kisses, instead she saw her mother hurry by without so much as a glance. And she had stayed there, patient and hopeful, waiting for me to come back until her teacher had led her away. 'Hello, head, is there anybody even in there?' she'd said when I'd collected her. Then I'd shouted at her for not eating her lunch before realising that the roll I'd given her was covered in mould.

Shauna put the tutu back on its hanger, then stood at the till, leaning on one hip, the fingers of her ringed hands touching the material, as she waited for me to find the receipt.

'Such a shame. It's *so* darling.'

'I know. It is. If only it had been fifty Euro cheaper. Oh, sorry, and can I take this as well?' I handed her the snow globe I'd chosen for Ben: three silhouetted children, one on a sleigh, one pulling, one running behind, playing in a wintery park.

I watched her wrap it in tissue. Joe loved snow globes, knick-knacks, dust collectors of any sort. During the months he'd had no work he'd come home with tat – ornaments, carved animals, religious iconography – from charity shops on the high street and present them to me, always adding how little they cost to justify the purchase. One Christmas, he decorated the tree with redundant surgical implements from the Royal College of Surgeons; another year he covered it with gollywogs – I'd take them down whenever we had visitors; Joe would put them straight back up. Now he would be spending Christmas in Amsterdam. We'd been there together once, in the early days and I'd loved it: the houses, all squished together and higgledy-piggledy set, the mist over the canals, people riding back and forth over bridges on upright bikes; it was like the lid of an old-fashioned biscuit tin. I stopped myself from imagining him there with someone else but I knew I didn't want to be there with him either; Addie and I would have Christmas together and I would make it special for her.

'Sorry,' I said, scrabbling around my bag, trying to find the receipt. 'I know it's in here somewhere.' I emptied everything out onto the counter top.

'Please. Take your time. And *relax* a little. You're upsetting India's energy.'

I glanced up to see if she was being serious to find her taking a bottle of Bach's Herbal Remedy from her shirt pocket. She opened her mouth, put a few drops on her tongue, then turned to her daughter, who stuck her own tongue out, while her mother administered the potion.

'Shall I move away from the desk?' I said, joking.

'You know what? Would you mind?'

I apologised, blushed. Fumbled about again for the wretched receipt.

'You know you're better than you used to be, before you were pregnant you weren't here at all.'

'Really? Where was I? What do you mean?'

'I'm just saying that you could sure do with some healing. I could do it now, if you have twenty minutes?'

'God, no not really, my mother's minding my little girl and she's going to a carol concert at five.' We checked our watches simultaneously.

'Five? You have oodles of time. Colette? Can you watch things here for me for five minutes?' Colette appeared from the store room – a skinny girl in black-and-green leggings that reminded me of Rumpelstiltskin.

'I'm not sure about this. What does it involve?'

And even as I was saying these words she was leading me by the hand into the white picket-fenced play area. We sat opposite one another on tiny children's chairs. She rested her hands on my knees, told me to close my eyes.

I did what she asked. I closed my eyes; tried hard to concentrate. What the hell was I doing? How would I get out of this? I'd been suckered by yet another mad American and now I was trapped.

I was aware of movement around me; of customers entering and leaving the shop. I wanted to look up. 'Keep them closed,' she whispered, as if she knew just what I was thinking.

And there we sat together, Shauna's hands on my knees, in silence, for several minutes. Nothing was happening. When I could no longer resist, I opened my left eye, just a fraction, and saw her face. It was screwed up, her eyes squeezed tight with concentration, as though she were trying to pass a difficult bowel movement. I wondered if it was all a joke, if at any moment she was going to jump up, howling, 'God, you Irish are so damned gullible.'

I closed my eyes. I saw Ben's face in the window of the tree house, his unheard screams. I tried to think of other things. I thought of Nathan. I'd received a personalised Christmas card from him in the post that morning. It was like something out of *Hello!*. Him in a navy sweater and jeans, holding a huge Christmas wreath over his shoulder, his hand solidly around the waist of his Spanish-looking wife (swept-back hair and huge gold earrings, big boobs beneath a festive red sweater – you get the picture). Each of them had one hand on the shoulders of their two little girls, who were standing in front of them in satin dresses and tights and black patent shoes, grinning with missing teeth. *Merry Christmas from all the Lyons!* it said. I saw Ben's little face again, the flames around him. Billy's face lit up by the lighter under his chin outside the window of our flat that night, Billy helping to clean up the lighters, Billy the hero, Billy pushing Ben.

'I know, it's *too* cute, isn't it?' Colette was talking to a customer behind me.

'I love it. I mean it's like an antique. And it's such a bargain at fifty per cent off.'

The tutu. They were talking about Addie's tutu. They were wrapping Addie's tutu in pink tissue.

I heard the ting of the till.

'Goodbye, happy Christmas.'

Why hadn't she told me it was fifty per cent off? I could have bought it. It could have been Addie's. Jesus, how long did I have to fucking sit here? When was I meant to start feeling something? This was ridiculous. I was full of rage.

'I'm sensing a lot of rage,' Shauna said. I opened my eyes to find hers wide open too, staring at me with intensity. She looked extremely concerned. 'I'm sensing vast amounts of rage deep down inside of you.'

'Really?'

'I dunno, I think you were about seven. You were looking for your parents' attention but they weren't listening? And you needed someone to listen. *Listen to me!* You were shouting but no one heard you. You need to take charge of it. Your little girl needs her mother's attention. She needs you to get rid of some of that rage.'

Chapter Twenty-two

Muchwood was the name of the house, but the 'd' had fallen off years before.

'Muchwoo,' I said to myself as I stood outside Belinda's with a bottle of white wine in a brown paper bag and a box of Green & Black's chocolate miniatures. I was regretting my choice of outfit; my legs were so restricted in my pencil skirt that I felt like a mermaid. And my heels were ridiculous, Ruth was right. One of these days I would just have to accept my height. I was small – five foot four in socks – and getting smaller.

They didn't have a doorbell; I knocked twice on the wood and waited.

'Give me a second, Mia!' I heard Belinda shout internally.

'Oh no, it's not Mia, it's Eve.' I called back to her. 'Take your time!'

I waited a while longer, listening to various thumps, curses and bangs.

'Ah, Eve, how's it going? I was just waiting on Mia,' Belinda said when she opened the door, kicking a sausage dog draught excluder out of the way and looking a little addled, I thought. She was wearing pink slippers, tracksuit bottoms and a white Nike T-shirt. She had a huge pile of sheets in her arms.

'Sorry. It's bedlam in here. I'm trying to sort out Billy's washing

231

and Mia, Oscar's mam, was going to pick up some alterations; don't know where she's got to and Bad Hair Day's gone missing again, but come on in!' I didn't know any of the people/creatures she was talking about but I wiped my feet and followed her.

She kicked more things aside as she led me through the hall, turned on the lamp above the blanket chest, told me to watch out for this and that, apologised, cursed at Billy, shouted at him to come downstairs.

The kitchen smelt of cat pee. There was a mound of sheets and pillowcases on the table – the kind we had as children, pale brushed cotton, candy-striped – a rucksack that must have been Billy's, rotting bananas in a bowl, some sort of medicine from the Dargle pharmacy, and a bag of blue tinsel from the two Euro shop. A small black dog was licking the counter top beside the sink.

'Jaysus, would you get out of it, Nigger,' Belinda said, grabbing him under the belly and flinging him onto the floor.

She saw my doubtful smile. 'Don't ask. Billy comes up with the names. He wants all these flipping animals and then he gets bored of them after two days. Bad Hair Day, the guinea pig, is AWOL again. Nigger will probably get him, with any luck. Gives me the creeps to think of a furry thing scurrying round the house.' She shivered; I did too with empathy.

'Sorry, now make some room for yourself there.' She gestured at the table. She lifted the wet washing away, leaving a huge circular ring on the wood.

'Think I need to cut the grass; I just spent twenty minutes stabbing the clothes line around the garden trying to find the flipping hole. Didn't find it, of course.'

'I love cutting the grass,' I said, just for something to say. 'I like that it's a job with a proper start and finish.'

'Well, don't let me stop you,' she said with her smoker's cackle. I noticed she was wearing blue eye-shadow. I'd never seen her wear make-up before; she would never bother for the library and she was such a tomboy that it looked quite odd, it almost gave her the appearance of a transvestite.

'A takeaway OK for you? Indian all right?'

'Perfect,' I said, hoping my relief wasn't too obvious.

'You're very good bringing me wine.' She put the bottle in the fridge, then lifted a box beside it on the floor.

'Look at these.' She held up some tan boots with tassels. 'I love them, they make my legs look slender, make me feel a little bit sexy and make me taller. They looked fab with the dress I was wearing last night, so what's the problem? I can't walk in them at all. How do you do it?' she said looking at mine.

Billy thundered in. He was on his way out, looking smarter than I'd ever seen him before in a blue checked shirt, cream chinos and his hair gelled into place; 'up hair' as Addie would say.

He stood above his mother. We were now in the sitting room where Belinda had kicked off her slippers and was leaning back in an armchair, balancing her glass of wine on its arm. It was a moss-green one which had one of those flip-out bits at the end for her feet. It looked like it was where she always sat.

Billy didn't say anything, just rubbed his thumb and forefinger together.

'Manners!' she said, shoved her socked foot at his thigh and inclined her head towards me.

He turned around, grimaced.

'How's it goin'?'

I smiled at him.

'Moolah, Mama?'

She groaned. 'My bag's in the hall.'

He reappeared, flouncing and mincing around with his mum's black leather bag on his arm and her scarf around his neck. 'This it?'

'Ah, Billy, would you cop on? You know that's it! How many bleedin' bags do you think I own? Give it here. OK, we said twenty, didn't we?'

'Thanks, Ma. See you later.'

'Eh, excuse me! Come back here, young man. Haven't you forgotten something?'

'Ah, Jaysus, Ma.'

'Come here to me.'

She offered her cheek for a kiss and wrapped her arms around him.

'Good boy. You smell only gorgeous,' she said, pulling him closer, and then, 'Do you have drink taken?'

'Just a few cans, will you get off my case?'

'Where are you off to, anyway?' she shouted after him.

'Just out!' He slammed the front door.

She made a face at me. 'What can you do?'

'I'm starting to think I'm just bad for men. They seem to begin life with me extrovert, healthy, full of energy, but by the end they are washed-up, sickly introverts.' And then, once they've left me, they get back on their feet and land big jobs in Amsterdam, I thought but didn't say. 'Do you think I'm an enabler? Am I making them that way?'

We were onto our second bottle of wine. The room was warm, I was cosy on the sofa, Belinda curled up in her armchair opposite me.

'That's crazy. Why do women always blame themselves for these things?'

'I'm just saying it's a bit of a coincidence. There seems to be a pattern. I remember when things were really bad between us, feeling almost envious of other separated mums – their bravery, their freedom.'

'Before Derek left, I felt the same way.'

'What do you think went wrong between you?'

'One word. Billy.' She looked at her watch and felt around for the remote control – she didn't want to miss *The X Factor*. I told her I'd been following it too.

'Really? I wanted to ask you something about Billy actually—'

'Ah no, I don't really mean that about him,' she went on, as if she hadn't heard me. 'Well, I do and I don't. We both adored him, still do, but he was an absolute terror when he was little and we were always arguing about the best way to deal with him. Derek was soft on him; I was strict. I mean it was me who was always apologising to other people. He used to bite other kids at creche. He'd be sitting on his own on the naughty seat, looking out the window, every evening when I went to collect him.'

'There's nothing worse than collecting your child and feeling them shudder when you hug them because they've been crying all day – that's what Addie was like on Tuesday because I forgot to wave goodbye to her through the window.'

'Ah the poor little lamb. What I dreaded most was when the teacher would say 'Can I have a quick word?'. I kept my head down with Billy, just charged in and got him, charged out again, trying to avoid anyone's eye.'

I wanted to eat my vegetarian dumplings while they were still warm, but it looked too casual to eat while Belinda was opening up to me, so I ignored them until we'd analysed the situation from every angle, at which stage they were greasy and cold. Then we opened the box of Green & Blacks, Belinda threw two more briquettes on the fire and we settled back to watch *The X Factor*. There was one contestant to go. The audience were on their feet screaming. Out came the dancers, on came the strobe lights, dry ice, special effects.

'This is a tiny bit awkward, but I did want to have a chat with you about Billy.'

'Go on,' she said, not looking at me, tugging at some loose stitching on the armchair.

'You know the way he has a thing about fire?'

No response. Just a cold-eyed stare.

'He's always messing with lighters and matches, isn't he?'

'Just spit it out will you, for fuck's sake, Eve?'

'Well, obviously I didn't see him in the act but I think, listen, Belinda, I *know*, it was Billy who set the tree house on fire. It wasn't a lantern or anything else, it was Billy. I mean I'm sure he was just messing, experimenting. He did it with one of the lighters he'd been picking up for me. Of course, I know he would never want to hurt anyone—'

'So you have proof of this, do you, Eve?'

'No, I just said I didn't, but it's clear it was him and I'm only even bringing it up because—'

'Ah, would you lay off him, Eve. If it hadn't been for Billy, that lad would be a lot worse off. I'm proud of what he's done so I am.'

She was out of her seat, clearing the table.

'You know he's been given a lot of grief around here and for once—'

'Well, we're getting a lot of grief right now,' I said, standing up to help her; she gestured with her hand for me to sit back down.

'Addie doesn't understand why none of the kids in the park want to play with her any more and I'm being ignored by pretty much everyone aside from the youth worker who seems to be observing us very closely.'

She had stacked everything and carried it into the kitchen where she was now rinsing plates with her back to me. 'Well, you were pretty distracted that evening, weren't you?' she shouted in to me. 'And you left those lighters hanging around, didn't you? And you did promise Sophie you'd mind Ben.'

'Jesus, Belinda, that may all be true, but I didn't start any fire.'

'That couldn't be him back yet,' Belinda said, turning off the running tap and standing still to listen. I hadn't heard the front door. She passed through the sitting room and went out to the hall. There was some sort of problem, she sounded upset.

Billy was green, eyes closed, leaning back against the wall, a vomit ring around his neck and all down the front of his new shirt. Belinda was apologising to the Indian taxi driver who had just delivered him home.

'Thank you, ma'am, I understand, but that will still be twenty Euro for the fare please, and one hundred twenty for soiling my car.'

'Are you listening to what I'm saying? I haven't got it. All right?' Belinda said, scowling at Billy.

'I cannot work now for three days because of your boy.'

I rooted in my pockets behind her, offered the driver a fifty.

'Stay out of it, Eve. I'll look after this. Will you settle for sixty? Please?'

He accepted Belinda's offer and said, 'That's the very last time.'

Belinda stood in front of Billy, who had now moved to the sofa in the sitting room. He was holding his head between his hands and looked like he might vomit again.

'I think I should maybe head.' Both of them ignored me.

'Would you look at the state of you?! You stink. Get out of my sight, will you?'

'Leave me alone, Mam. I'm not in the mood.'

'*You're* not in the mood—' She paused. 'What happened tonight?'

'You mean what was *meant* to happen? What was meant to happen was a date.'

'And?'

'And she didn't fuckin' turn up, the bitch. She forgot or something, who knows, who cares? She doesn't give me the time of day any more.'

'Who are we talking about?'

'Just a girl, Ma. You don't know her.' He ran his foot along the carpet, against the grain. Then he flung himself backwards on the sofa and started kicking at his rucksack on the floor in front of him. I could see he'd stuffed some flowers inside. They looked like tulips.

'She can fuck off, so she can. All she cares about is that floppy-haired dick, and he's fucking every girl in Bray. What's an emo freak doing with a poshie like her anyway? He doesn't give a toss about her.' He must have been talking about Juliette. Little did he know that she could never have met him, had no intention of it; she'd been at my flat all evening, babysitting. This explained why he'd gone off the rails outside our house that night. He must have seen Dylan with that other girl in the park.

He lurched forward, grabbed his rucksack.

'I even brought her these,' he said, pulling out the limp flowers. 'I was sat in the playground waiting for her for two and a half hours. She told me to meet her there at eight. I had a blanket and the crisps she likes and cans and everything.'

'You know, I remember following this guy all around the city,' Belinda said, sitting down beside him, her voice softer. 'I would sit on the ground outside pubs in the cold all evening waiting for him – I was underage so the doormen wouldn't let me in – and he'd be inside drinking and snogging and—'

'Snogging?' Billy said, laughing at the phrase, 'Jesus, Mam.'

'Well, that's what he was doing. Flirting with other girls and snogging them while I was outside asking the doormen to pass messages to him. And I'd stay there till closing time, till I knew I would see him.'

'That's so gay.'

I felt something move underneath me. I leapt off the sofa screaming.

'Ah, Bad Hair Day, it's yourself,' Billy said, lifting the guinea pig. It was easy to see how he got his moniker. He wasn't the smooth sort you normally get. This one looked like he'd been blasted by a hair dryer, with his brown static fur in all directions. Billy turned him around in his hand to inspect him for damage, then kissed him on the nose.

'He's after eating two good-sized holes,' he said, bending to examine the sofa.

'Ah Jesus, Billy. I'm only after getting that upholstered.'

'Must have used the stuffing to make a nest for himself. Now don't be doing that again, do you hear me?' he said, dropping him back into his cage.

'You should have seen you! It was classic,' he said, laughing at me and doing an impression of my fright. And then, 'I think I'm going to be sick.'

He stood up from the sofa, went to the kitchen sink. Belinda followed him, waited. He burped a few times. 'Sorry, false alarm,' he said, then farted heavily.

She poured him a glass of water, rested her hand on his back. She said something to him in a whisper.

'No I feckin' didn't, OK? Stop asking me, will you?'

'There's a child very sick in hospital.'

The sound of more retching into the kitchen sink.

Chapter Twenty-three

'To your very good health.'

'Very good health.'

'Very good health.'

'Very good health.'

Murmur, Murmur. Clink. Clink, Clink. Bella said something that made the small group of guests around her chuckle. A child shouted. And then, somehow – who saw it? How did it happen? – my mother's champagne glass slipped out of her hand. It fell onto the drawing room floor and shattered into tiny fragments.

My aunt stepped down from where she'd been standing on the tile border of the fireplace. This was where she traditionally stood to tap her glass for the toast, balancing in a youthful way, to make her taller and to command attention. And all the other women swept into action, children were scooped up and away, furniture was pushed back, a hoover appeared, the lights were turned from dim to full. Mum stood by the drinks cabinet, shaking her head, red-faced, apologising. A few of the men bent on their hunkers and began picking up the shards of glass with their hands, their wives standing over them, cautioning and assisting: 'There's another bit there. Oh be careful! Now, I'd hoover the rest.' The party was paused, some guests shuffled around trying to look helpful; others stood quiet and still.

'Well, I must say, the tree is magnificent,' one of the women said, attempting to lift the mood.

'Yes, I'm delighted with this one. And do you know that it sings?' my aunt said, grabbing at a branch to get it going. 'Rather silly, I know. For the children, of course.' Then she turned to my mother who was still apologising, 'Oh, don't worry, Dot, it wasn't a good one, just one belonging to Bruce's great-great-grandmother,' she said and clomped away and down into the kitchen where the hired help – a Mexican brother and sister – were loading the dishwasher. She'd used them before and had found them very good, 'the boy in particular'.

'You stupid little man! Haven't I told you before? Don't put bone-handled knives in the dishwasher,' she roared, not quite out of earshot of her guests.

The 'adults', as we called them and as they happily referred to themselves, no longer enjoyed this party. It was an annual tradition between my parents and their relatives and oldest friends whose own children, flushed and awkward, neither knew each other or got along especially well, but felt obliged to be there, year after year, for the sake of their ageing parents. Rather than heralding Christmas, and what had once for them been two weeks of parties and drunken flirtations, it was now a sad reminder of all that they had lost. Almost all the men had gone or gone to seed, and the last one standing – who everyone, including himself, seemed a little surprised to find still alive – flushed-cheeked, stomach bulging against the belt of his high-waisted flannel trousers, was now so deaf that he only spoke in monologues because he couldn't hear what the other person was saying but was still determined to get his story told.

So this year, for the first time, the party was made up of women, the not-so-merry widows, with their arthritis, cataracts, hip-replacements, homes too big to live in but impossible to sell, catering, coping, laughing the loud laughs that once were their husbands, resplendent in purples and soft blues. They were now less characters, more caricatures of themselves: the barky, eccentric one, unsteady in heels, even before lunch had been served. The sporty, practical one, with her permanently suntanned legs, comfortable shoes, who had given up dieting, finally accepting her shape. The one with the new teeth that were a definite improvement on the yellow ivories she'd tolerated for so many years but that had yet to settle into her face. They were all here with the things they'd promised to bring: quiches wrapped in cellophane for the tricky vegetarians, a chocolate biscuit pudding for the kids.

It was our generation who supplied the men, but they were a less confident, less cohesive group. One of the husbands feigned a flat tyre because his carpet business was about to be wound up and he didn't want to handle awkward questions. He'd never liked the party in the first place, found it too stuck up. Another's partner couldn't get back from England because of a plane strike. There was much quiet tutting over the cocktail sausages about this ('Don't you think he would have come home to see his children? He said the ferry was for students, imagine that?') The shy one, who wasn't in fact shy at all but just couldn't be bothered to talk, was there as always, his silent and sullen presence making everyone uncomfortable; he was the kind of person who had to leave before a party could begin. And then there was the dashing West Brit amateur sailor who'd just come in from the sleet in his Barbour jacket, suntanned skin and thick hair. He examined the females in the room with great discretion, the girls who had become women in the year since he'd last seen them, the ones who'd put on weight, the ones that were looking radiant, all the while keeping his hand on the small of his wife's back.

I was not in party humour. Before we'd set off, I'd seen Ben arrive home. Sophie had held him in her arms, her hand protectively over his head as she'd lifted him out of the car and carried him down the steps to the basement of their house. I'd found and wrapped the snow globe, stuck the card Addie had made for him on top and had run across the square to drop it in, leaving Addie at home playing school with her new imaginary friends, Poppy, and her big sister, Serena. Joy had answered the door, told me Ben was resting. I'd handed her the gift and asked her to give it to him. 'I don't think so, dear heart,' she'd said, handing it straight back to me.

On our way I'd made the fatal decision to take Addie to a vast urban shopping centre. I'd wanted her to see Santa Claus and I'd still had three presents to get. We'd sat in a queue of cars stretching back to the M50 for an hour, parked illegally in a disabled spot and were then sucked into an overly warm world of materialism: waving polar bears in Tommy Hilfiger sweaters, hoards of addled parents, over-stimulated kids and endless Frappuccino-sucking teenagers and bewildered older people, stopping, standing for a moment, turning back in the other direction, *'So here it is, Merry Christmas'* hurting everyone's ears. The queue for Santa would have been another two hours in the sleet; we'd gone on the little Christmas train instead, Addie waving at shoppers too preoccupied to notice her.

We'd bumped into one of the old sisters, Pamela, in Urban Outfitters where I'd been attempting to find something to wear for Christmas day and Addie was pulling hands off mannequins.

'What do you think?' she'd asked me, this tiny woman in her eighties with freshly-dyed blue-black hair, a white made-up face and ruby lips, holding a sweatshirt decorated with a large red rose in front of her.

'I like it. Who's it for?'

'Me.'

'It's cute.'

'Really? But not too cute?'

'No. I like it.'

'Any news on that boy burnt by the lantern?' she'd asked, her voice travelling under the wall dividing our two changing rooms.

'He's at home. He's going to be OK,' I'd said, trying to escape from a too-tight white dress, getting make-up all over its neck.

I'd slumped to the floor of the changing room and replayed it for the millionth time in my head. If I told everyone what I saw that night, told them how I was sure it was Billy who deliberately set the tree house on fire, he would go back to being vilified by the community and I would lose the only proper friend I'd made since we'd moved to Bray. Belinda would do what any mother would do – she would always protect her own child.

'Is she very, very old?' Addie had asked about Pamela from where she was lying on her belly on the floor, straining to get a glimpse of her under the divider wall. Then I'd heard Pamela ask the sales assistant about the best place to get a tattoo.

'It's now or never,' she'd said.

On our way out, Addie had wanted to jump over the edge of the up escalator by herself but at the last moment she'd lost her nerve. She'd stood howling and frozen as I'd travelled away from her. I'd been damn tempted to keep on travelling – she'd just punched me on the nose in Starbucks because I wouldn't buy her a third chocolate coin. I'd had to let go of the buggy to grab hold of her and pull her towards me, feeling alarmed eyes all around me. The buggy had tipped backwards with the weight of the bottle of wine in a plastic bag that I'd hooked over the handle. I'd managed to get my child into my arms but the bottle had clunked out and rolled back down the escalator with no way for us to retrieve it.

My cousin was sent down to the shops for more wine and I snuck upstairs to the playroom with Addie, where an assortment of various-aged, awkward and silent children had been shoved together. They were all sitting around the TV, watching *The Wizard of Oz*. I'd handled several questions about the accident and now I was taking some respite. One of the women had come up and said, 'How *are* you?' looking me in the eye as she waited for a reply. So far this year no one had got my name wrong. The boy who'd grown a moustache since last Christmas, making him look younger than he was, had given me a hug that had lasted for far too long. Even my aunt who traditionally addressed me by my sister's name had got it right first time.

Children were a great social camouflage; you could arrive late, leave early, weren't expected to help or to provide stimulating conversation. You could sit in the playroom where you'd much rather be in the first place; where the magic started all those years ago in the big house at the big party with the dumb-waiter in the wall and the old black-and-white TV and the godfather who always gave you the most exciting presents – roller skates, that's what I got that year – breathing in all the delicious firewood, perfumey smells, the confusion and magic of it all and heavy black overcoats and things you saw that you shouldn't have seen. And trying again to understand why Christmas Eve – the evening of Christmas – came before Christmas day.

'I'm a little worried about your mother,' I heard my aunt say to her friend's daughter, as I passed them in the hall on my way to the toilet.

'Oh no, don't be. She's fine. She's doing much better in fact,' the daughter said, referring to her mother's recent hip-replacement. 'I mean she was a little grumpy for the first few days, but that was to be expected after the general anesthetic.'

'Well no, it's not that. It's just that she's meant to be bringing the fizzy drinks. She said she'd be here at two.'

And when she at last arrived at the door, my aunt gave her only the most cursory of welcomes and dived for what she'd been waiting for: two litre bottles of 7Up that were bulging from a plastic bag looped around her wrist, the handles strained and stretched and digging into her skin.

Our cousins were busy hosting and too many others were away from their seats helping them – never the sign of a successful party – or tending to a child and I always seemed to be the person with an empty seat beside me. I leant across a large bowl of uneaten Brussels sprouts to try and join a conversation Bella was having with another cousin, pretending to have read the book under discussion when I'd only seen the TV series. I said hello in a very animated way to a breastfeeding woman I'd had quite a long and intimate chat with about leaking boobs the previous year, but she seemed to have no idea who I was and just nodded and carried on the conversation she was having. I attempted it again a few moments later. This time she smiled in a detached, vague manner and even looked a little irritated. Then severing her nipple from her toddler's mouth with her thumb and forefinger, she told her child to say hello. Ruddy-cheeked, with a messy mop of brown curls, she was at least three and had a full set of first teeth. She looked up, surveyed her surroundings and finding nothing to amuse her, she whipped her head away and nuzzled back into the dark and moist comfort of her mother's breast. Bella and

I shot a glance at each other; we'd discussed this before. It just looked all wrong, like an Alice band on an old woman.

Ordinarily I would seek out the solace of my sister in these situations but I was a bit annoyed with her that day. She had already said that I looked exhausted – something I always hate being told; it's just another way of saying you look rough. Then the subject had somehow moved on to Joe. 'You really weren't well suited. It was always so volatile in their house,' she said to some of the other women in front of me just after Mum dropped the champagne glass.

'Was it?' I said, hurt and denying it – but then I recalled this day last year and the red toy kitchen for Addie from Santa that had taken me four hours to assemble with its tiny saucepans and microwave and little apron and telephone. That night, Joe had kicked and damaged it in a rage about me going to too many Christmas parties.

I felt out of sync with everyone in the room; the cadence of my voice was off-kilter. For an alarming half an hour I lost all sense of self-awareness or self-censoring – I couldn't judge whether I was being interesting or tedious. I was talking about an article I'd read about fizzy drinks and brain development and I wasn't sure if I was rambling on without making any real points or drawing any conclusions, and my audience weren't giving me any clues; they just nodded and smiled and picked bits of rocket from between their teeth.

'That is fascinating!' I said every so often, when I couldn't think of anything to say. And I made an inane comment about foie gras. The woman opposite was adamant that it was the liver fat of geese. No, I was the only vegetarian in the room. I was the one who should know. 'It definitely isn't geese. It's goose.'

There was a sudden loud thumping from the playroom above us, causing the lamp over the kitchen table to tremble. I pushed my chair back a few inches, waiting for tears and the yell of *Mummy* but nothing. Then there was a further series of small bangs.

'Oh, don't worry about that,' my aunt said, leaning over me with a platter of crackers and cheese. 'When Jonathan and Florrie were dating, they slept in that room and on Sunday mornings, while we were having breakfast, we'd hear this bang, bang, banging. We couldn't for the life of us work out what it was. Of course it was them all along, going at it like the hammers,' she said, sending a little droplet of spit across the table. Her daughter looked stunned, then embarrassed, then annoyed.

'Now, this is a rennet-free cheese from Ardagh,' she continued, oblivious of her daughter's mortification. She was showing off, giving everyone information about the expensive cheeses she was proffering around the table, dangling her arthritic finger and berry-coloured fingernail above each one as she went.

'And this is a wonderful burgundy brie.'

'What's this one?' I asked, when she reached me, pointing my own grubby-looking finger, which I'd forgotten to paint, at a cheddar type one with red veins running through it. I'd thought I heard her say it was a red Windsor. I wasn't really in the mood for cheese. I was just being polite. Instead of showing off her knowledge as she did in front of all the other guests, she snapped at me as if I were not a guest at all but an irritating teenager.

'Oh, for goodness sake, Eve. I can't remember.'

'I'd go easy on the ice cream,' my cousin said, as I stood over by the sideboard, helping Addie to her second bowl. 'Too much dairy is bad.'

Really, you don't say, I wanted to respond. Oh, but I was told to give her plenty of it, too little calcium will make her bones brittle. And she's on the lower percentile of growth for her age to begin with. But then you're a short arse too, aren't you? What height is your husband? Oh no, that's right, I forgot. He's not your husband. Never was. And now he's gone. Such a shame. Very damaging for the child, very damaging indeed. What she needs is some stability in her life. What that child needs is a firm hand, it's for her own good. For her own happiness. She's far too soft on that little girl. And she needs more clothes on. Shorts in October, I mean what was she thinking? And do you know what I saw her do the other day, she let that child drag her sucky blanket through the grass in the playground, I mean dogs do their business there! Not safe at all. Reckless, I'd say. Well I'm not saying anything, I'm not one to judge but if it were my child I wouldn't let her sleep like that. She'll get a crick in her neck. Raisins? Absolutely not, they rot their teeth, you know. Now be sure to remind her to go to the loo, every twenty minutes. Whatever you do don't ask her if she needs to go, she needs to tell you herself. Ah don't make her say thank you, that puts pressure on her, she doesn't have to if she doesn't want to. Well, I don't know how she is bringing up that child, no manners at all. Too much attention, that's the problem with that child. Spoilt rotten, so she is.

'How are we all doing?' This was my mother, popping her head around the door to check on the young people. The adults were restless a little earlier than usual this year, perhaps it was more fun to be in the kitchen with us because there were so few of them left in the dining room. Mum often didn't notice me on social occasions. I was too familiar to be fussed over, gushed about, and she was too busy being social and helpful, but this Christmas Eve, she seemed slower, quieter, more clear-headed and watchful than usual. She came over and sat down beside me.

'You're looking lovely,' she said, touching my shoulder. 'Are you enjoying yourself?'

I nodded and smiled. 'Not particularly.'

'Where's Addie?' We did this all the time in our family, kept a constant tally of who at any moment was where.

'Under the table, biting my leg. It hasn't been a good day in our four-year relationship.'

'You little rascal,' Mum said, scissoring her legs about, then lifting the table cloth and lowering her head to look under at my beaming child.

'And how are you, little monkey?'

'I'll be cross in a few minutes but right now I'm happy.'

She sat up again, somewhat flushed, and looked back at me.

I told her about the gift and Ben. She didn't want to know.

'Oh, pet, your life will always be full of drama,' she said in a detached, weary sort of way, as if she no longer had the energy or the duty to fix it.

She gazed for a long time at the candlelight. She seemed uncharacteristically pensive. She picked at some wax that was about to drop onto the mahogany table. Then she turned to face me again.

'So, we've said brunch at eleven tomorrow, presents after that and then I'll be going to the Kennedys' up the road if you want to come and we'll eat around five – I have a vegetarian thing for you from M&S – it just needs to be defrosted.'

'OK, Mum. And I'll see you at Midnight Mass.'

'Of course you will, I'd forgotten that,' she said, yawning at the prospect of having to stay awake for another eight hours. 'Oh now, listen, sweetheart, are you going on the McDermott's walk this year? I've promised to let them know how many for numbers.' This was an annual five-mile walk over the Wicklow mountains to a sleepy old man's pub.

'I will, if you do?'

'I'll be in the Galapagos by then,' she said, with some glee.

I'd forgotten all about that trip. 'I can't keep up with you. Will I see you before I go?'

'Of course, if you want to, though you don't really need to and I'm having my old school pal, Bunty, to stay all next week, so I'll be pretty busy, do you remember her at all? Bunty's great, she's big and bouncy.'

All I remembered about this faceless friend were those three adjectives; the ones Mum always used to describe her.

'I'll send you a postcard, love, though it will probably never arrive.'

She pulled me towards her, gave me a kiss on the forehead, got up and left the room.

The first guests were leaving – something to do with picking up or delivering a child – before the adults had even finished their mince pies.

My uncle was telling everyone to 'shush!' in quite an abrupt way while he tried to organise taxis, further addled by people interrupting him in the background with times and locations and routes.

'Oh, for pity's sake, Bruce. Why don't you take the ruddy thing into the hall?' his wife said, pushing past him with a tray of empties.

The front door brought in a rush of icy air; there was confusion over coats and belongings and wiped clean bowls, which unsettled everyone else and soon others were looking at their watches and feeling for their phones.

One of the old women's bowls was missing. She had used it to carry the Caesar salad and now it was gone.

'It's a square, Waterford Crystal one, with a nice pineapple design on it,' she said, describing it half a dozen times to anyone who would listen.

'I don't see why she's so keen on that square bowl,' one muttered to another, while making a half-hearted attempt to locate the missing bowl herself, by scanning her eyes around the room. 'I'm perfectly happy with my round one.'

Mum was too busy reassuring her sister to help with the search for the bowl.

She had given Mum her Christmas present. Always quite mean about her own clothes, she wasn't confident about her ability to buy gifts for others either and even as she handed it over she began making excuses about it. 'It's very plain. It's nothing really. It's a bit creased. But it's quite a good colour, I suppose. And didn't cost much. I hope you like it. You mightn't like the colour and it might be the wrong size. It's just a plain round-neck sweater from M&S, nothing too exciting. You can change it if you like. It mightn't fit.'

And then I made a little girl cry. She had taken Addie's place at the table and was happily dribbling Addie's chocolate ice cream over her pink satin dress. Addie started whimpering and pulling off me and I just didn't have the stamina for another row. All I said was that she was sitting in my child's place and could she please move. She slid off the seat, looking horrified – how dare an adult give her an order – and sought out her mother, a larger, fish-mouthed version of her child with the same horrible ringlety hair. She buried herself in her mother's arms telling her about the cruel and evil thing I'd done. The mother seemed quite unimpressed with my excuses and explanations and her little brat was still shooting me filthy glances. Ten minutes later, both miserable, they left the party and went home.

An hour after beginning my goodbyes, I was out in the open air of Herbert Park.

The moustached boy helped by carrying Addie and strapping her into her seat, before giving me an alarming kiss on the mouth goodbye. In the refuge of my car, I wriggled my Spanx down to below my stomach and breathed out for the first time that day. I kicked off my heels, shoved on my Rocket Dogs. The noise of the party was still ringing in my ears, I was light-headed from all the chatter and gushing.

The windows were frosted up; I rolled them down and breathed in the beautiful crisp winter air. I looked at the road in front of me, at the arch of evergreens as far as the eye could see, and at the frost-covered grass of the park. The old band stand, the Victorian railings, the solid red-brick homes around me all seemed perfectly unreal that evening, like something out of *Mary Poppins*. The day, the party, the weather was making me nostalgic and weepy. This traditional party would one day end, after my mother and the rest of her generation had gone and all of those characters would become mere memories of people, that would in time dissipate and fade. I would talk about my parents to Addie, the way my parents spoke to me about theirs and she might not listen, might not be all that interested in these vague, distant people who she never knew, who were so vivid and animated now but would one day be summed up in several adjectives.

'When the snow's here, can I be an ice-skater?' Addie said, jolting me back to the present.

'OK, sweetie.' I said, turning the keys in the ignition and pulling out.

'Maybe I'll be a good ice-skater. Maybe I'll be bad.'

'Maybe, sweetie,' I said, distracted, looking in the overhead mirror.

'What's your favourite colour?'

'You know what it is. You ask me every day. Blue.'

'Dark blue or light blue?'

'Christ, Addie. I don't know. Just blue, OK. I'm trying to concentrate!'

'Dus tell me! Dark blue or light blue?'

'Light blue.'

'I'm going to make you a surprise card.'

I chose the coast road home because I wanted to see the sea. I needed some air and some space. By Sandycove, Addie was gone and I couldn't reach the toy she'd been given from her godmother to turn it off:

The Pelican's beak holds more than its belly can.
The Pelican's beak holds more than its belly can.
The Pelican's beak holds more than its belly can.
Nothing's quite as big as the beak of a Pelican.

I fell into a sort of nonchalant daze. In hold-ups or at lights I glanced at the tired, preoccupied drivers around me who just wanted to be home and felt happy to be sitting, idling and out of danger for another few seconds. I had a dangerous problem. My left indicator was broken so whenever I was approaching a turn, I had to accelerate to create space between me and the car behind, then swerve at speed around the corner.

I slowed down. The sea by the Forty Foot was milky still under the moonlight. The road through Dalkey village was quiet, fairytale-like with its white lights linked above all the shop fronts and the yellowy glow coming from the steamed-up windows of Finnegan's. People were spilling out onto the streets, leaving Christmas presents in bags beneath tables just waiting to be knocked into – full pints, packets of crisps – as they huddled in messy groups in the cold night air for a smoke. I saw a man who looked like Lars, the gentle alcoholic, who used to drink in the park. He hadn't been around for months. What had happened to him? How come no one mentioned him? How lonely to disappear from a community and for no one to even notice.

I drove on through dark, quiet neighbourhoods, past the graveyard where my father was buried and Addie liked to play, wheeling her baby and buggy between the plots, not understanding why she couldn't have the tiny teddy bear sitting on one of them, or the windmill in a jar.

'You don't need to explain graveyards to her just yet,' Joe used to say.

Bray High Street was a riot of lights: a flashing kaleidoscope of lanterns and reindeers and polar bears and Santa Clauses racing through the sky. I wished my little angel could see them. At the traffic lights at the top of the road, I turned and watched neon shapes pour across her sleeping face. I looked at her soft lips and fluttering eyelashes, her mouth covered in chocolate, her little pigtails askew.

Chapter Twenty-four

Dylan and Juliette were curled up on the sofa; Addie was sitting cross-legged beside them and Juliette was painting her fingernails. They unfurled when I came in, Juliette stood up, tugged her jumper over her bum and blew her fringe out of her eyes. She turned towards Dylan, exposing a large purple love bite on her neck. I didn't think they existed any more. The sight of it made me nostalgic. It was the sort of thing you used to see on cross-water ferries, on the necks of the female staff serving fried eggs in the morning, after a night of grubby sex, putting you off your breakfast.

'Look, Mama, orange and sparkly.'

'Lovely. Now, pyjamas on this minute. Let's go! Santa Claus won't come unless you're asleep.'

'I'd love to help you, Mama, but I've just had my nails done,' Addie said, spreading out her tiny wrinkled fingers as I pulled her tights off and put her pyjama bottoms on.

Dylan hopped up and stretched. 'May I use your loo please?'

'Of course, let me just check that there's toilet roll.'

He followed me down the corridor towards the frosted door of the bathroom.

'You're looking pretty foxy,' he said to my back in the darkness.

'Oh, thank you,' I said, both delighted and disgusted.

'You shine like a jewel compared to all the other mums around here. You're the best looking by far,' he said, standing too close to me, pupils dilated.

'I'm sure that's not true, but thank you,' I said, flattered, flustered, appalled, moving to get myself free. I shouted goodbye to Juliette, told her to call me if there were any problems or to drop down to Irenka, forgetting that she had gone home to Poland to spend Christmas with her family.

The church was fuller than it had been all year, the chatter louder, its ageing congregation up late in silk scarves, fur stoles and camel coats. Even the monsignor in his gold robes had a spring in his step as he took his place behind the ivy-and-poinsettia arrangement at the pulpit to welcome his parishioners to Midnight Mass. Drunk teenagers tried to hold it together in the presence of their parents as the choir sang 'Silent Night'.

'There's Kevin Gallagher,' Mum whispered, on her knees beside me in our pew, peeping up from cupped hands to see whom she recognised amongst the queue of bowed heads taking their seats. 'Oh and that's poor old Stephanie Smith's mother; she's had a terribly tough time.' She tried to remain penitent but found it impossible, being both naturally social and nosey. She was well in with the church, doing readings at the ten o'clock service once monthly and helping to arrange flowers before funerals; she felt on home ground and therefore somewhat entitled to keep an eye on proceedings.

Bella was sitting on the other side of me on the bunched up end of her best coat, with her bag, a missalette and her mobile phone in a tumbling pile on her knee. She seemed to have surrendered to a life of discomfort since having a husband and children. Her own needs were at the very bottom of her priorities. She smelt of 'Paris', a perfume she used to wear as a teenager and which her husband still bought her for every birthday and anniversary, though she now found it a bit cloying.

All three of us were flush-faced from an afternoon of socialising; bloated from too much food and mulled wine, made up again over old makeup, perfumed over perfume. There was a long, curly blonde hair on the back of Bella's top that couldn't belong to her. Mum's neck was mottled red beneath her pearls. Nuala McMenamin was leaning over our pew, her knuckles whitening as she gripped the bench. She was a skinny drip of a woman – sharp nose, warm onion breath – always energised by incidents, accidents, emergencies, dramas of any sort, always happy to be the first with bad news. Someone had had a very nasty fall, the O'Sheas were burgled the night before last, Joe Lawlor had lost his mind. Mum was nodding too much and looking towards the altar, in that slightly cross-eyed way that she had, willing this woman to stop talking, to go away, not wanting to hear any more. 'Yop, yop' Mum said, tutting and shaking her head as Nuala indulged in the details.

Mum reeled off the Gloria, the introduction to the Gospel, running her thumb from forehead to lip, down to chest, and then the Creed, as if demonstrating to me how it should be done. She'd been saying the same prayers for fifty years and her voice had taken on a sort of weary familiarity, sounding loud at the beginning of each new sentence, then trailing away into something tiny and thin.

With a cacophony of nose-blowing and throat–clearing, the congregation sat. An altar boy rang a bell, his frayed jeans and tennis shoes visible from where he knelt. Then everyone else knelt, lowering their eyes in the solemnity of prayer and covering their faces with their hands. Mum sat forward instead of getting to her knees, she was tired and uncomfortable in her heels. She wanted to be at home, wanted to be up in bed, with her mug of hot milk and her new P. D. James. She fell asleep beside me during the sermon, gently snoring and woke startled at communion, determined to appear as though she hadn't missed a thing.

Everyone stood for 'Adeste Fideles', murmurs, creased coat tails, more coughs. And we boomed it out like Protestants, showing off our Latin, the women all upright, puffing out their chests, their husbands beside them giving it everything, the bald patches on their heads reddening with each note. On the final verse, we started softly like professionals and grew louder as we sang on, the sopranos in the gallery in perfect harmony. *Venite adoremus, Venite adoremus, VENITE ADOREMUS! Dominum.* We were communally moved by how good we sounded, by our unexpected tunefulness and energy.

I saw the ambulance first, and as I got nearer, the police car half up on the kerb. There were people in white overalls in our front garden and yellow tape stretched across the front door. Juliette was sitting on the roadside, hugging her knees, chewing on the cuff of her hoodie, wiping her nose with her sleeve.

I pulled in, ran to her, my heart whacking against my ribs.

'What's happened? Is it Addie?' Juliette was red-eyed, trembling.

'No, it's Dylan. Oh Eve, Billy and him had the worst fight. I tried to stop them but I couldn't.' She sank to the kerb; I knelt down beside her and put my arm around her shoulder.

'He's dead, Eve,' she said, looking up at me with bloodshot, mascara-stained eyes. 'He's over in the playground. He killed him, Eve. Billy killed Dylan.'

There, in the foggy early Christmas morning light, framed by the fairy lights trailed around the railings of the park was Dylan's body, beside the see-saw, covered in white tarpaulin. There were three policemen around him, one crouched by his side.

Chapter Twenty-five

Half a pound of twopenny rice,
Half a pound of treacle,
That's the way the money goes,
Pop! Goes the weasel,
Do do do do do do do do do do do do do,
That's the way the money goes,
Pop! Goes the weasel.

Mum was sitting on Addie's bed. She had taken off her shoes and her legs were crossed at the ankle. Her toes were wriggling about in pop socks that looked too tight for her feet. Her handbag with everything that she needed for the evening – reading glasses, *Rough Guide to the Galapagos*, diary, mobile phone – was just below her, on the floor. Addie was snuggled up beside her in her new brushed-cotton pyjamas, the ones we couldn't afford from Avoca, pink with little kittens chasing balls of wool. Mum's arms enveloped her grandchild and their fingers were intertwined. Her cheek was resting lightly on Addie's head and as she sang her little song out of tune, the two of them swayed from side to side. Addie's eyes were squeezed shut; on her face a sleepy smile. The room was warm and clean, the air filled with Mum's favourite perfume, the lamplight, buttery-coloured and soft.

Neither of them had noticed that I was watching. This was how they always sat before a bedtime story but tonight something told me to notice, told me to be grateful. Told me to always remember.

'Go on now, pet. You'll be fine. Just support her. The poor woman. Now off you go. Oh no, wait, let me give you that card.'

Although she had never met her, Mum had heard enough about Belinda and Billy from me and had read enough about the tragedy, to feel it appropriate that she write to her. She bent over from where she was lying to fish the card from her handbag. There was a hole under the arm of her M&S cashmere cardigan.

I put the card in my coat pocket and promised her I wouldn't be late; she was catching a flight to Lima at noon the following day.

'Kiss and a hug.' I embraced my little girl.

And then her mantra whenever I was going anywhere.

'Love you, you're my best friend, have brilliant fun!'

The wind was wild that night, buffeting against the windows, whirling down the chimney, sending icy draughts through the flat. Dylan Freeney, beautiful Dylan, was smiling, in his school uniform, on the front page of the *Wicklow Times* on the hall table. Beside him was a grainy shot of Billy Flynn and a smaller photo beneath of Juliette Larson, looking much younger than she was. Dylan had been stabbed in the heart and had died immediately. Billy Flynn was uninjured and in custody for murder. There was another photograph below their faces, of the park. Yellow police tape surrounded the cordoned-off playground.

I took the tray of cyclamen, now brilliant pink and blooming, from the table and closed the front door behind me, pulled up my hood, and set off across the square.

Street lights came on around the neighbourhood. It was getting dark, people were going indoors. A black sweep of starlings searched for somewhere to perch for the night. I gave a wave to Mr Norman who was out on his front porch, reinstating a toppled bay tree, his comb-over perpendicular in the wind. He raised one hand in a salute, turned and went back indoors.

There had been some changes to the square since Dylan's death: Irenka moved out just after New Year's. Donal had been offered a new, permanent position in London. They had had a yard sale and a small going away party, both of which we'd missed. All Irenka had left me was a list of local emergency numbers and some books on childcare.

Nathan's house had been finished and stood proud, its name, 'Little Wave', wedged in the new lawn; a bright and shining thing in an old neighbourhood. It would take a hundred years to blend in; a youngster surrounded by Victorian grandeur. I supposed I would meet his family soon, now that the house was ready to receive them. Poor old Pamela had passed away, before getting her tattoo, leaving just Edie in the big house. And Arthur from the Cherry Glade had given up going outdoors. He'd abandoned his cart – 'too risky out there', he said. He'd bought a portable TV for his room, his eyes too tired to read Westerns, and now he was bedridden in his own small, and ever-contracting, world. The few visitors he had knew to bring him Guinness.

A bald man I didn't recognise was standing outside Belinda's house: huge belly, Manchester United polo shirt, faded denim jeans. He was smoking, looking around him, shifting from one foot to the other to keep warm.

'Are you after Belinda?' he asked, stubbing his cigarette under his shoe.

'Yes. I'm a friend of hers.'

'Give us a second,' he said, stepping inside, pulling the door closed.

'Will you tell her it's Eve?' I called after him. 'Addie's mum. From the library.'

I handed her the tray of pink cyclamen. 'I wanted to give you back these.'

'Ah, Eve. You're very good.'

I went inside and we hugged in the hall. She was trembling. I could feel her ribs beneath her skin. She wouldn't let me go. I rubbed her back, my nose buried in her sweater.

'It's just such a mess.' She pulled away from me, pressed her fingers against her eyes, squeezing them tight. She couldn't meet mine. She invited me in.

The bald man pressed himself against the wall, holding his hands on his chest to let us pass.

'This is Derek, by the way. The other half.'

We smiled at each other. He offered his hand as I went to embrace him. We ended up doing neither and both.

'I'll give you guys a minute. Tea?'

I nodded. 'Thanks, love,' Belinda said.

'He's been brilliant,' she whispered, as if not to jinx it, pushing the door closed behind her and settling into her seat.

'Don't know if you've heard but Billy's on remand at a detention centre at Wheatfield Prison. It's over in Clondalkin. We're selling up and moving to the North Side. We need to be closer to him.'

I could hear Derek's voice coming from the kitchen. He was speaking to someone on the phone, repeating the same information about Billy that Belinda was telling me, only a few seconds behind her, like an echo. How many times had they had to have these conversations in the last two weeks?

'We?' I asked and gave her a small smile.

'You'd never think this sort of crap would bring people together but somehow it has. He's the only one who understands what I'm going through. For the rest of my life it will be like that. And sure we can't stay around here; it's not fair on Mimi or on poor Juliette.'

'Juliette's doing much better now, isn't she?'

'Thank Christ. Frank's been amazing with her. And God only knows what hell he's going through himself. I saw Mr Larson up in Tesco this morning. Didn't he turn around and go straight back up the aisle as if he hadn't seen me? I'm having people cross roads to avoid me. Can you imagine the carry-on there'd be in the library if I stayed? All those kids, they're broken-hearted, though not about Billy I know. He was always an outsider, never part of any gang or group. It used to break my heart at school when they were told to pick a partner and no one ever wanted to be his. And when he'd come home with a bloody nose or a torn shirt because he'd been set upon and had fought back. At the playground he was always the wrong age. Always too young for the other kids or too old. But sure, you and I were always outsiders here too, weren't we?'

Derek came in at that moment with the tea and a plate of Jaffa cakes.

'I'll leave yous to it,' he said. He squeezed Belinda on the shoulder, told her he was going for a lie down.

'Eve, he stabbed that poor lad three times in the chest.' She tucked her hands into the sleeves of her sweater, shuddered, began to cry.

Juliette had told me it all, curled up on the sofa in our sitting room, chewing the sleeve of her hoodie, trembling and hyperventilating like a child, mascara staining her cheeks. She'd said Billy had called over to see me that evening. He hadn't expected her to be there. Dylan had told him to clear off and Billy'd lost it after that. He'd head-butted him, spat at him, she'd tried to get between them, to separate them. That's when Dylan had run to the park. Juliette had seen Billy run after him, climb onto the railings, yank at the loose spike and jump down into the playground, but she hadn't seen anything after that; she'd run home and back to her dad to get help.

'God, it's so hard.' It was all I could say, the best I could come up with. I leant over, rubbed my hand on her sleeve.

'I'm all right. I'll have a smoke in a few minutes. I just keep thinking what was it he felt? What was in his head to make him do such a thing? I suppose I'll never understand. You know he was very loving, very funny when he was a kid. I remember summers down in Kerry, up to his neck in sand. He was a very generous, kind child. And he was so protective of me when Derek and I split and then even more so with my illness. My only child. My funny, unique little boy.'

She broke down. I hugged her. She couldn't speak for several minutes.

'Three detectives called to the door on Christmas morning. You know the way everyone says they just knew? Well, I didn't. I mean they've been here so often to do with Billy. I know them all by name, for fuck's sake. Garrett, Donal, the little blondie one. Anyway, so I just thought it was the usual messing. Thought they'd give him a warning. He'd been very agitated that day, couldn't stay in one place. He was so jittery. He couldn't sit still. He went upstairs and had a rest and then was down again a minute later. I was so stupid! I thought he was hungry. I brought him out for lunch.'

Neither one of us had the courage to say what we had both suspected – that Billy had come to our flat on Christmas Eve to see me, to hurt me or perhaps even to hurt Addie. He knew that I knew the truth about what had happened on the night of Addie's birthday.

He had never been a hero before in anyone's eyes. He had been loving it and so had his mother and I could have ruined all of that.

We moved outside, I rooted in my bag for the card from Mum. I don't know what it said but her words or the sentiment made Belinda weep. 'Much appreciated. Will you tell her thanks?'

I promised I would. I hugged her again and got ready to go.

'It's just so awful seeing him in there, Eve. He's so fractious with me. There's nothing we can talk about. I can't talk about the sea, the mountains around here, nature, any of that – all the things he loved about home, about Bray. I can't talk about the outside world at all, it would just be too mean, too cruel when he can't see it for himself. And we don't want to talk about the case. So what does that leave us with? Not much. Nothing really. Not a thing.'

Chapter Twenty-six

Five forty-five a.m. I couldn't sleep. I got up, sat in the sitting room, logged onto Facebook. Sophie had changed her relationship status from married to single. Everyone had responded with question marks or concerned comments or kisses. I looked across the square at her house in the darkness, wondering if Mark were still there, if Sophie were OK, or if she were sitting awake, staring out the window, as I was. There was a rattle of wheels on the street below; a lone figure was striding along the middle of the road, pulling a suitcase behind him, on his way to the catch the Aircoach. And walking in the opposite direction, Sumita, head down, runners on, rucksack on her back, coming home from a late night of babysitting. I knew from Belinda that she had made her decision, that she had sent her little girl back to India, so that she could give her a better future.

Teddy bears, Bray Wanderers scarves and Bauhaus T-shirts were still tied to the park railings alongside cards with smudged messages and dead flowers in rain-spattered plastic. Someone had lodged a single child's glove on one of the spikes. A leaflet had been dropped through the letterbox yesterday, suggesting that the playground be renamed Dylan's Park.

I sat on the edge of my bed. When she saw that I'd been crying earlier, Addie had taken me by the hand and had led me to her bedroom, like a little adult. She'd said we should make a card for

Dylan. A green one. 'That's why because green was his favourite colour,' she'd said, and she'd drawn him as she remembered him: a head with spiky 'up' hair, no body but long, long legs and huge, outstretched hands. One of his feet was turned in and she did a straight line for his mouth, instead of the smiles she normally gave her stick figures on birthday cards. She'd drawn so many flowers on the inside that there'd been no room left for words. 'When you look at this card it will make you happy every day, OK?' she'd explained, using little hand gestures as she'd placed it on my bedside table.

I stripped the bed, pulled on jeans and a sweater, grabbed the holdall from the top of the wardrobe, shaking off its layer of dust. I emptied the drawers, stuffed everything in, put the card for Dylan in my back pocket and closed the bedroom door behind me.

Then on to the kitchen. Mum had already done the washing up, as she always did when she babysat. The scent of her perfume still lingered in the air.

I stood on the kitchen table, yanked down the Happy Birthday banner that had hung there since Addie's birthday, since the night of the accident.

I took the origami swans Addie had made with Joy from the mantelpiece in the sitting room, and filled my pockets with all those tiny things that there is never a particular place for: a hairclip, a box of matches, a Sylvanian mole in a waistcoat.

I thumped our bags downstairs, loaded up the car, slammed the boot. Then back inside and up the stairs again. I was running on adrenalin now. I lifted Addie out of her bed and carried her, still asleep in my arms, my hands cradling her head, out to the car. She grizzled for a few moments when I struggled with the straps of her car seat, but she worked on her sucky blanket and settled back to sleep.

I went inside one last time to grab the Happy New Year's card I'd written for Nathan, re-read its coded, flirtatious message, tore it up, stuffed the keys for the flat in its envelope along with a cheque for last month's rent. Addie's scooter was propped up against the wall, we couldn't forget that. I made room for it in the boot.

Then I crossed the road to leave Addie's card for Dylan on the railings of the park along with all the others. I saw his beautiful face, Billy up in the cherry tree, little Ben surrounded by flames, Belinda sitting in her armchair, broken.

I ran from there to Nathan's, dropped the keys through the letterbox, heard them chime as they landed on the marble hall floor he'd fitted for his family, turned and left without looking back.

I got into the car. As I slipped the key into the ignition, a clang of bells rolled down the hill from the Protestant church. Addie stirred awake in her booster seat.

'Where are we going?' she said, still in half-sleep. 'Are we meeting Sophie for a picnic?'

'No, sweetheart,' I said, as the square receded behind us. We passed quickly along the deserted high street.

'Why don't you like Sophie any more?' she asked, coming round.

'It's not that I don't like her any more, we're just not going to be friends.'

She was quiet for a moment. 'Like you and Dada, you mean?' I glanced at her face in the overhead mirror.

'A bit like that.'

She sat forward in her seat. 'So you and me are the whole family now?'

'Yes, we're the whole family now. You, me and Alfie.'

'But Alfie's gone away.'

'That's where we're going now. We're going to get Alfie.'

'Oh, Mama! I'm just going to hug him and hug him!' she said, hugging herself and beaming.

'And then where are we going with Alfie?'

'We're going on a big adventure.'

We turned onto the southbound dual carriageway, accelerated into the flow of traffic heading away from the city. I rolled down my window and the car filled with the rush of motorway air.

Acknowledgements

Sincere thanks to Marianne Gunn O'Connor, my agent and friend, who inspired and supported me through every stage of producing this novel. To Aine Hyland for her enormous generosity, encouragement and hospitality, to Nick Kelly for all his brilliant advice and the days he devoted to reading and re-reading drafts, never appearing bored. And to Judy Kelly for believing in and encouraging my scribbling since my earliest attempts.

I'm enormously grateful also to Annabelle Comyn, Niamh Hyland, Jeanne Moore, Cara Augustenborg and Alison Walsh, for reading through early drafts and for offering invaluable feedback and advice.

To everyone at Quercus, for their patience and belief and for being so lovely to work with: Jon Riley, Charlotte Van Wijk, Jo Dickinson and in particular, Rose Tomaszewska, who helped me so skilfully over the final hurdles.

For their excellent research advice: Suzanne Kavanagh, Ballymun Job Centre, Glynis Peel, the Burns Unit at Crumlin Hospital, Aidan Kiernan and Kiernan Homes. Also Alison Tully, Zuzana Tilson and Alison O'Neil.

To Craig Brunker, Chris and all the exceptionally friendly staff at Mugs café Dalkey, for putting me up for all those months and for putting up with me. And to all the staff at the beautiful Greystones library for making me feel so welcome and at home.

For helping me in every way through the four rocky years it took to get this book written: Alexia Kelly, Carrie Nathan, Naomi Bates, Ray Beggan, Ciaran Fallon, Chiara Milzani, David Matthews, Caroline Osborne, Aisling Walsh, Gillian Comyn, Jennifer O'Reilly, Alex Diana, Reggie Manuel, Marc Coleman, Keith Parker, Amanda Brady, Sam Gibson, Sinead Corr, Nicky Flavin, Joey Limin Bai and my wonderful godmother, Rosemary Comyn.

And thanks especially to Charlie for his enduring company and love, to my beloved family for pretty much everything, and to my little lady, Ruby Mae, for being my endless source of joy.